THE SANGRITA CLUB

Amanda Adams

THE
SANGRITA
CLUB

Amanda Adams

220 Publishing

Chicago, Illinois
220 Publishing
(A Division of 220 Communications)

The Sangrita Club
Copyright © 2016 by Amanda Adams
All Rights Reserved.

Published by 220 Publishing
December 2016
(A Division of 220 Communications)

PO Box 8186
Chicago, IL 60680-8186

www.220communications.com
www.twitter.com/220Comm

Cover Design by: Kelly Webb
Cover Image by: blinkblink/shutterstock.com
Cover Image by: Debby Wong/shutterstock.com
Back Cover Photo by: Ron Wu/ronwuphoto.com

ISBN: 978-1-68419-779-8
Printed in the United States of America

Dedication

For all of the women who have ever been told
any of the following:

"You can't do that!
You'll never be anything but a...
You ain't nothing without me!
You ought to be glad I'm with you.
You can't do it alone.
If you leave me, I'll kill you!
You'll never be anything except what you
are right now."

For all of the women, who after reading this
book, can say to themselves any of the following:

"If I stay, I will never get the chance to live.
I can do whatever it is that I desire.
I can be whatever it is that I want to be.
I am whole.
I am worthy.
As long as God is with me, I'm never alone.
What I do and who I am right now is
just the beginning!"

Acknowledgements

I truly appreciate my mother, Mary Jacobs, for instilling in me the importance of getting an education, traveling the world, preparing for the inevitable, and being spiritually grounded.

Special thanks to my husband, Robert Gay, for your loving support and being the ever-present wind beneath my wings.

Hugs and kisses to my daughter, Moorea, my sweet, beautiful cherub, constant source of joy, and deep well of patience.

To my *Don't Hold Your Breath* Divas: Thanks for always being fabulous role models of intelligence, grace, strength and beauty.

Gratitude and appreciation to Glenn Murray, Founder of 220 Publishing, for taking a leap of faith with me when 48 agents and 15 publishers were not brave enough to jump.

Special thanks to all those who were persistent with their inquiries, encouraged me throughout the years, and wouldn't allow me to give up on my dream.

I am truly thankful to everyone who assisted me throughout the process of developing this work. It passed through many hands that shaped it along the way to become a gift.

Most of all, I thank God for sparing my life, giving me the gift of stories to tell, and preparing me for this journey.

Table of Contents

Prologue

Dear Diary,

> *Today my prayers have been answered! He's dead. He's really dead. He got what was coming to him and my mother got what was coming to her. Now I don't have a reason to cry anymore.*

"What's wrong with you?" she whispered as the orchestra played on around them.

"We're not supposed to be talking."

"And you're not supposed to be playing bad notes, so I know something is wrong."

"I just can't concentrate today."

"That's obvious. Why not?"

They instantly lifted their violins and bows to join in for a lengthy refrain.

"That sounded horrible."

"Oh, shut up!"

"What is going on with you?"

"Well, if you must know, my father is flying to New York."

"So, what's the big deal?"

"I hope his damn plane crashes!"

The room was immaculate, not at all like it was on a typical day. The bed was made, the air was clear and free of cigarette smoke, and there were no liquor or pill bottles on the nightstand. She stood there in silence trying to absorb the reality of the moment.

"Well, serves her right! It's her own fault. She drank her way to an early grave."

"She did have liver disease; however, it was the breast cancer that ultimately took her."

"Breast Cancer? I didn't know she had cancer! Why didn't she tell me?"

"She wanted you to live a full, vibrant life without having to share in her pain and misery."

"Why was she trying to protect me? She didn't love me. She wasn't even a mother to me anymore."

"She never stopped loving you. She just couldn't love herself anymore."

"Run. Run into the bathroom!"

"Lock the door!"

"Get in the tub.   Hurry up!"

"Close the shower curtain!

"Shhhh, be quiet!   Stop crying!   Come here, I'll hold you. It's gonna be alright. I promise."

CHAPTER

1

Squatting over a toilet in high-heeled shoes was like getting in a quick workout several times a day. As Vanessa hiked up her skirt, she was thankful she had developed strong thighs and calves as a track and field athlete in high school and college.

After finishing her business, she grabbed her black, calfskin, Ralph Lauren Ricky bag from the hook on the back of the stall door and made her way to the sink. As she washed her hands, the door to the restroom swung open. Vanessa looked up at the reflection in the mirror of the woman that entered. She recalled seeing her from across the room during the board meeting that had just adjourned for lunch. They exchanged polite smiles as their eyes met.

"Is this meeting boring or what?" said the woman as she entered the first stall directly behind Vanessa.

Not knowing who this woman was or who else might be listening, Vanessa replied tactfully, "Well, it is moving a little slower than I anticipated." As Vanessa dried her hands and applied some lotion, the woman continued to carry on the conversation through the stall door.

"Oh, you don't have to be guarded and politically correct with me. I say what I mean, and I mean what I say. And tell anyone who doesn't like it to kiss my..." the sound of the toilet flushing reverberated off the tiled walls, muffling the rest of her response.

Vanessa's eyes grew as big as half-dollars as her mouth transitioned from shock to a broad, chuckling smile. The woman exited the stall and placed her bag on the ledge above the sink as she turned the water on to wash her hands. It was a black, crocodile-finish, Ralph Lauren Ricky. "I see you have great taste too," Vanessa said pointing to her own bag.

"Ah, yes we do!"

"Hi, I'm Vanessa Baldwin."

"I'm Anne Wu. Pleased to meet you," she said with a slight nod of her head as she dried her hands on a paper towel.

"I don't recall seeing you before. Are you visiting from one of our off-shore offices?" Vanessa inquired.

"No, I just relocated here from L.A. Do you work here in the Manhattan office?"

"Yes, I do."

"So, how long have you lived in New York?" Anne asked as she spied Vanessa's empty ring finger.

"Hummm, I've been here for almost thirteen years now. I'm originally from the D.C. area," Vanessa replied.

"Well, I transferred here to help orchestrate this merger. That's what brought me to this God-forsaken, cold-ass, gray city. But anyway, enough of my negativity," Anne offered with a phony smile. "So, what do single professionals do, and where do they go for entertainment in this city, where they won't get mugged, raped, or sodomized?" Anne said with a sarcastic tone as she applied hand lotion.

"Oh, come on. New York is a great city! There are so many things to do and so many safe places to go. There are concerts, clubs, art galleries, museums, the best restaurants, and Broadway! Oh, and don't forget the shopping; it's fabulous! There is no better place in the world to shop than right here!"

"Yeah, I lived here for several years when I was a child and traveled here many times on business, but just never took the time to do the tourist thing or check out the night life," Anne replied with a melancholy tone of reminiscence.

Vanessa could tell that under Anne's brash exterior there was a great sense of humor. She had just the right cure for Anne's negative attitude. "Hey, why don't we get together sometime and I'll give you a tour, you know, show you the ropes of NYC. I'll bet I can improve your attitude." Vanessa said with a mischievous tone.

Anne smiled, "Hummm, I don't know if anyone is capable of adjusting my attitude. But sure! Why not? I'm getting a little tired of sitting in my apartment looking at the mountains of boxes that I need to unpack." They both laughed as they made their way out into the hallway and towards the elevators.

"If you don't mind me asking, where are you living?" Vanessa inquired.

"At the San Remo on Central Park West between seventy-fourth and seventy-fifth," Anne replied.

"We're practically neighbors. I'm two blocks down at the Langham. You know, we have about forty-five minutes left before the board meeting resumes. Would you like to grab some lunch and devise our plan to paint the town?"

"Sure, why not? Let's go!"

Anne and Vanessa enjoyed a nice chat during lunch and seemed to click. They talked about office politics, as well as their struggles to climb the corporate ladder and succeed as women, while being surrounded by the good-ole-boy network.

"My head has hit the glass ceiling so many times, I've developed a chronic concussion," Anne revealed. "The world of corporate law is still dominated by males who think that a women's place is to be a paralegal. I've worked for several firms during my career. Needless to say, whenever my head hits the ceiling, I hit the door. I must admit though, I haven't run into any issues since I started working here, at least not yet. It's only been a couple of weeks – time will tell!"

"Well, I've worked for the firm more than 10 years and I've been able to take advantage of some really good opportunities. Initially though, I did run into a few men who were reluctant to give me a chance, but as soon as they realized that my ideas were translating into tangible increases in our sales figures, they gave me all the respect I deserved. It's unfortunate though that, as women, we have to prove ourselves to get respect, versus men who are given respect right off the bat without having to earn it. But, we do have one advantage. . ."

"We do? What?"

"There are only a few of us around here, so we never have to wait in line to use the restroom." They both chuckled as they devoured their salads.

As their discussion continued, they lost track of time and returned to the boardroom fifteen minutes late, slipped into two seats in the back, and spent the remaining three-and-a-half hours listening to multiple presentations on the merger. To beat the boredom, they began whispering and passing notes like two adolescent schoolgirls. They continued to form their newly found friendship into the evening by going to Sangritas, a little Spanish/Mexican fusion restaurant in the Wall Street district, right around the corner from work.

"This looks like a really nice place," Anne observed as they were being seated. The restaurant was tastefully decorated with rich, jewel tone wall colors, flowing draperies, and murals depicting iconic Spanish and Mexican cultural scenes.

"Yes, it is nice! I come here quite frequently. This place is the product of a marriage between two chefs: A Spanish woman and a Mexican man, who are the owners. The name Sangrita is a combination of Sangria and Margarita, which also happens to be the name of the restaurant's signature cocktail. It is absolutely fabulous! You've got to try one! I guarantee that once you try this drink, you'll be hooked."

"Mmmm, sounds tempting," Anne replied with intrigue in her voice.

"Oh it is, believe me! The owners are really nice people; however, you never see both of them here at the same time. They have twin girls, so they tag team their duties; that way one of them is with the girls at all times."

"It's nice that they've worked out an arrangement so that their kids have exposure to both parents." Anne said with a slightly distant, sad tone. A server approached and presented them with a pitcher of Sangritas. He poured their drinks into Margarita glasses rimmed with a mixture of red sugar and salt, and took their dinner orders.

"So, what shall we toast to?" Vanessa asked.

"Hummm, let's see. To new friends and new libations," Anne suggested.

"Perfect!" Vanessa said as they clinked glasses.

Anne lifted the ruby colored potion to her lips and took a sip. "Mmmm, this is soooooo incredible."

"I told you it was awesome!"

"This is better than awesome! This is I-might-dance-the-Flamenco-by-the-end-of-the-night, awesome!"

They laughed, chatted, and finalized their plans to take in the sights, sounds, and attractions of New York City as they sipped another round of Sangritas.

"Well, hello, Vanessa!"

"Oh, hi, Eva!"

Vanessa turned to Anne and said, "This is one of the owners of Sangritas I was telling you about! Eva, I'd like to introduce you to my new colleague, Anne Wu."

"Hello Ms. Wu, pleased to meet you," Eva responded while shaking Anne's hand.

"Oh, believe me the pleasure is all mine. And please call me Anne.   Your signature cocktail is absolutely fabulous! How did you come up with the idea for the Sangrita?"

"Well, my husband, Rico, and I were at home with a few of our close friends celebrating the approval of the loan to start this restaurant. I wanted to serve a fruity Sangria, but Rico wanted to make a pitcher of Margaritas. Our two little girls heard our heated discussion and suggested that we mix the two drinks together. And the rest is history!"

"Success, out of the mouths of babes," announced Vanessa.

"What a great story! I'm so glad Vanessa turned me on to your restaurant."

"And I am too!" said Eva with an appreciative grin. "Well, ladies, please enjoy the rest of your evening. Anne, I hope to see you again soon."

"Oh, trust me, you will!"

As they munched on crunchy tortilla chips and a delicious, spicy salsa, the conversation began to shift from sight-seeing plans to the personal topic that is at the forefront of every single woman's mind: men!

"Girrrrrl," Vanessa said with a slight Sangrita-induced slur in her voice, "I gave my man a pink slip last night. My ovaries are thirty-six years old, on their last legs, and I don't have time to wait for his tired behind to make up his mind to marry me. I had opportunities to date other men, but refused to because I wanted to be Mrs. Vanessa Baldwin Black. But for now, and probably the rest of my life, I guess I am destined to be Miss Baldwin."

"Ahhhh, cheer-up. Hey, at least you have... excuse me, I'm sorry. At least you had a man. I can't even get a guy to give me the time of day once they find out I don't give massages or do manicures. No one wants to have a serious relationship with a professional Chinese woman. Not even Chinese men, because they want some little, docile, stay-at-home, never-open-her-mouth type. And if you hadn't noticed, I don't exactly fit that profile. Besides, I wouldn't date a Chinese man anyway, because they are cold, little prick, son-of-a-bitches."

"Well, let me tell you, African-American professional men, who are single, no kids, and not swinging the other way, or both ways, are a rare breed. So, needless to say, I don't have a mob beating down my door either."

"Now, I have to admit, I do have a surrogate man on-call, but he's battery operated!" volunteered Anne. They both laughed uncontrollably.

"Girl, I know that's right!" Vanessa cosigned as their entrées arrived.

They plunged into their delicious meals of Paella Valencia with shrimp, mussels, clams, chorizo sausage, and chicken with rice. As they continued to dine, their bond was solidified and their friendship was forged.

CHAPTER

2

"Up, Mommy, up!" Sleepily, Monica turned over to meet the up-stretched arms of her little, curly-haired blonde cherub, Lizzy. All of a sudden, a feeling of horror overcame her as she carefully slid out of bed and whisked her daughter up into her arms, away from the sight of the unconscious man in her bed camouflaged by a down comforter.

"Good morning, Sweetie! Are you ready for breakfast? Let's eat some Cheerios this morning," she said while placing Lizzy into her highchair. She hurriedly poured the milk and cereal in a bowl simultaneously while looking over her shoulder, praying that the sleeping giant wouldn't awake before she had the opportunity to return and sneak him out the front door.

"All right Sweetie, be a good girl for Mommy, eat your breakfast, and please keep your bowl on the tray, okay?" Monica pleaded while buckling Lizzy's safety straps.

"Okay, Mommy!" Lizzy replied happily, as she stuffed her mouth with cereal.

Monica mumbled under her breath, "I know I might as well say, 'Throw it on the floor,'" as she left the kitchen.

She quickly made her way back to the bedroom and partially closed the door behind her. She quickly put on her robe, poked the mound on her bed and it began to stir. Monica ripped the covers off while holding an extended index finger over her lips, whispering, "Shhhh, Lizzy's awake! It's a quarter to six! I accidentally fell asleep last night; I didn't intend for you to stay over! Why didn't you . . . Oh, never mind? Just hurry up and get dressed," she said as she threw his clothes at him. "I've got to get you out of here without her seeing you!"

He sat up on the side of the bed, grumbled something under his breath, and shook the sleep from his head as he put on a pair of well-worn jeans and a turtle neck sweater. Monica stood peeking through her bedroom door down the hallway to the kitchen. Luckily, Lizzy was still occupied with her cereal. With his boots in hand, they tiptoed single file down the hallway with Steve crouching low behind Monica, as if her little body could really hide his six-foot-four frame.

They made it all the way to the living room without being spotted. Monica grabbed Steve's jacket from the hall closet in the foyer and they stepped out into the hallway. She laughed as he put his boots on because he had put his sweater on wrong-side-out. Her chuckle faded though when she heard nosey Mrs. Florence from next door making a snide remark under her breath as she retrieved her morning newspaper from the doormat. Monica pretended to ignore her, but was fully aware she had been busted and would hear about it later. Mrs. Florence disappeared with a loud slam of her apartment door.

"Steve, thank you for last night," she said as she self-conscientiously adjusted her black, satin robe to cover her partially exposed cleavage peeking from her leopard-print chemise.

"The pleasure was all mine, Monica," Steve relayed with his deep baritone voice.

"Hummm, not quite," Monica said with a wink.

"I'll call you later. Bye," he said as he planted a kiss on her forehead.

"Okay, bye-bye," she responded softly, knowing full well that they would not talk again until one of them was at the breaking-point. They had a mutual understanding that they were using each other as a way to forget the chilling reality of their pasts, the loss of their spouses – hers in an accident as she looked on and his in Tower Two as he rushed to her rescue.

Monica, entranced, smiled as she watched Steve walk towards the elevator, but was startled back to her mommy role when she heard her daughter's cereal bowl hit the ceramic tile floor. Lifting up her eyes, she secretly asked for strength to make it through another day and ran to answer Lizzy's distress call.

"Good morning! It is six o'clock on this brisk, autumn Saturday morning in the Big Apple," announced the smooth, bass voice from the radio. Anne had been up for some time and had already done forty-five minutes of cardio on the elliptical, showered, shampooed, and viewed the day's top headlines on cable news. She rarely got more than four hours of sleep at night, plagued with bouts of insomnia that contributed to her always less than bubbly attitude. Now, she was in her home office wrapped in a white cashmere robe, checking Friday's closing stock prices. Normally, she would have checked before she went to bed, but her evening out with Vanessa combined with the tequila and vermouth had made her unusually tired.

Since the news broke two days earlier about the finalized merger, the stock price had jumped thirteen percent. Her 401K was looking better than ever now and she knew a nice fat year-end bonus was in store. Being a corporate attorney, Anne managed the due diligence and contract development for the merger. She knew it would have a positive impact on the stock price, but this was more lucrative than she had anticipated. She sat smiling at the results of her handiwork while nibbling on her naked, 100% whole wheat, whole grain toast.

Anne made her way into the living room through aisles formed by towers of boxes that were stacked high above her head, waiting to be unpacked. While sipping on a cup of green tea, she took in a pleasant view of the sky beginning its morning transformation flanked by the twinkling lights of skyscrapers from her 29th floor penthouse apartment. Her only solace was her work, which kept her occupied most of her waking hours. Her evening out with Vanessa had been the first time since moving to New York that she'd left the office before 8:00 p.m. She couldn't even recall the last time she'd cooked a meal. Her pots and pans were still packed away in boxes, somewhere.

Anne wandered into her closet that looked like the inside of a high-fashion, designer boutique. She had it all: money, jewels, couture clothing, and cars, yet she felt miserable, lonely, and empty. As she wrapped one of her fur coats around her shoulders and sat down on a cashmere-upholstered ottoman, she thought about how desperately she wanted to have someone with whom to share her life and love. However, she knew that at the age of 39, this was a fairytale. Her chances of winning the lottery or being struck by lightning were far better than her odds of finding Mr. Right.

As usual, the alarm clock went off at 6:30 a.m. Vanessa dragged herself out of bed and tripped over the latest issue of *O* magazine as she made her way to the bathroom. The radio blared out a Peter White instrumental as she brushed her teeth with one hand and covered her eyes with the other to shield them from the bright bathroom lights. She made a mental note to have a dimmer installed on the light switch. The radio announcer ran through the weather forecast, and then Vanessa froze as she heard him say, "Have a great Saturday!" She looked up, stared in the mirror at the shocked look on her face and said, "I had too many Sangritas last night." She spat in the sink, rinsed her mouth out, ran back to her bed, and pulled the covers over her head. Her arm emerged from underneath the covers to hit the off button on her clock radio, and then disappeared again.

Maria walked into the room that her two daughters shared and pulled back the curtains on the windows to let the morning sunshine in.

"Okay sleepyheads, it's time to get up!"

Her youngest, Christina, began to stir, stretch, and rub the sleep from her eyes. Maria just smiled at the precious sight. She looked over at her eldest daughter's bed and a look of concern came over her face. The bed was empty. She walked over to it calling her name and threw back the covers. The bed was soaked with urine. Maria looked around the room and saw that the closet door was ajar. She pulled it open and there she found Elizabeth, sound asleep on the floor with her thumb in her mouth.

Maria knelt down and called her daughter's name once again in a concerned whisper. Elizabeth began to stir, then sat up and immediately began to cry.

Maria wrapped her arms around her and noticed that she was only wearing a robe. Her urine-soaked nightgown and panties were lying on the floor next to the hamper.

"It's okay, Sweetie. Did you have an accident? You should have woken mommy up. I would have changed your bed and got you all cleaned up," Maria said as she rocked her. She was worried; this was the second time her daughter had wet the bed in a week. She hadn't done that or sucked her thumb in well over three years. She made a mental note to mention it to her pediatrician on their next visit.

"Come on, let's get this day started right. How about showers?"

The girls squealed with joy because they always had to take baths. A shower was a luxurious privilege.

Suddenly, the phone rang. The covers flew back as Vanessa scrambled to find it. She could hear it ringing from somewhere underneath the mound of bedding. She tore through the sheets, blanket, comforter, and quilt until she found it. When she finally answered the phone, she sounded like she had been running a 100-meter sprint with hurdles.

"Hello?"

"Well, hello!"

Vanessa fell backwards on the bed with a sigh.

"Oh, hi Mama. What time is it?"

"It's 7:30, Baby. I know you're not still in bed! Girrrrl, you gonna sleep your life away."

"I'm up now, Mama. Saturday is my only day to sleep in." Vanessa said, trying not to sound too irritated. "What's going on?"

"Nothing. Can't a mother call her daughter if she wants too? I tell you, children these days are so ungrateful. When I'm dead and gone, you gonna wish you had talked to your mother more often."

Vanessa sat up and held her head in her free hand, realizing that she had a splitting headache. She struggled to hold a conversation and regretted that she didn't let her voicemail pick up the call. Her mother had one of those voices that did not go well with a hangover.

Anne's phone rang, which was a rare occurrence for a Saturday morning. She checked the time. It was 8:00 a.m. Then, she checked the caller ID to see who it was.

"'Unknown caller.' Hummm, probably a wrong number, but I'd better answer it. It might be Vanessa calling to check on me."

"Hello?"

"Hi Anne. It's Vanessa."

"Oh, hi!"

"I hope I didn't wake you."

"No, I've been up for hours. I'm an early riser."

"Good! I couldn't sleep, or should I say, my mother wouldn't let me sleep, so I decided to give you a call about our plans for today."

"Oh, do you need to reschedule?" Anne asked in a disappointed voice.

"Absolutely not! Your official NYC tour starts at 9:00 a.m. today!"

"Sounds great!" Anne was so relieved. "And Vanessa, thank you so much for last night. I really had a great time, I needed a positive diversion."

"I had a great time too! I enjoyed your company and it's been a long time since I've had a good laugh. Thanks for hanging out with me."

"Anytime!"

"Look, I'll come by your building and pick you up. Then we'll be on our way to the first destination on your whirlwind New York City tour!"

"Okay, I'll be waiting for you in the lobby!"

"Great! See you in a bit."

"Bye!"

Anne was excited about her newfound friend and the day of sightseeing that lay ahead. For the first time in a long time, she felt a sense of belonging. She looked at the boxes surrounding her and walked toward one that she had been purposefully avoiding. Anne pulled back the tape, opened the top, and dug down into the sea of foam peanuts. She pulled out a beautiful, monogrammed, black leather case and wrapped her arms around it as she pressed it gently to her chest. New York was finally starting to feel like home.

Vanessa began her daily ensemble search by standing naked in front of the full-length mirror located in her palatial walk-in closet. She examined herself to determine if anything new was sagging or dragging, but her attention was diverted to the gray hairs from her new-growth that were screaming to be dyed. Normally, she wore bangs, which covered them up. But since she neglected to tie her hair down with a silk scarf the night before, her bangs were standing straight up, exposing her ugly, little secret. She made a mental note to call her hairstylist to make an appointment. For the moment, her attention was drawn from what clothes to wear, to searching for a hat on the top shelf of her closet. She found a few suitable options, but chose a bright, red one and began the process of finding a stylish outfit to go with it.

Vanessa and Anne spent the day touring the town. They visited the usual spots: The Empire State Building, Times Square, and of course, China Town. As they rode around the city in the black, Lincoln

Town Car she reserved for the day, Vanessa pointed out various points-of-interest such as art galleries, museums, nightclubs, theaters on and off Broadway, and popular restaurants. After a late lunch at Tavern on the Green, the tour continued with a stop at Ground Zero. They paid their respects and reflected on where they were when they'd heard the news. They shared stories with one another about their friends and business associates who had been snatched away on that day. After hugs were exchanged and tears dried, they headed for Fifth Avenue to do some serious damage to their credit cards. Shopping always seemed to chase away the blues.

For some, Sunday is a day like any Saturday, to run errands, do chores and spend quality time with family and friends. For others, it is a day set aside for worship and reflection. Some utilize it as a combination of both.

Vanessa spent the day as she always had since she was a child. She went to Sunday school, worship service, and slaved over a hot stove preparing a delicious, home cooked meal. Usually, she made traditional southern dishes such as crispy fried chicken, baked macaroni and cheese, candied yams, collard greens and cornbread muffins. Normally, Damon joined her for dinner on Sundays, but not today or ever again, for that matter; however, she decided to cook anyway to keep her mind off the break-up. At least she would have leftovers to put in the freezer. She enjoyed eating out regularly, but there were times when she just wanted to curl up in front of the fireplace with a good book and a bowl of homemade peach cobbler with vanilla ice cream. Food was comforting and good company. It didn't argue, disappoint, or make demands. It felt so good caressing her insides as it made its way down. She cooked to keep her hands occupied and her mind off her desire for Damon. Vanessa's mother always said, '*An idle mind is the devil's workshop.*' Vanessa was determined not to let Damon back into her heart ever again. At least, that was her intent.

Anne spent her Sundays in the usual fashion: relaxing and reflecting. She would start with her daily workout routine, bathe, and sip herbal tea while still in her bathrobe. Then she would recline on her chaise lounge with the *New York Times*, *Business Week*, and her laptop as she researched various companies she considered investing in. Her focus was on the performance of the stock market in the previous month and market analysts' future recommendations, which helped her to plan tactical trades for the week ahead. Anne loved the stock market; she got such a rush from it. She was a very savvy investor and had made hundreds of thousands of dollars doing so. She didn't need the money; she did it for the thrill of the game. Is there a better way to gamble legally than from the comfort of your own home? No smoke-filled rooms or drunken men.

Monica spent the day with Lizzy doing what they always did on Sundays; exploring the city. They would go to museums, plays, the Bronx or Central Park Zoo, take horse-drawn carriage rides, or take in a movie. They would also go to Coney Island for a Nathan's hot dog or the Statue of Liberty just for the boat ride and a spectacular view of the city. Needless to say, they enjoyed shopping too, with F.A.O. Schwartz being at the top of Lizzy's list of favorite stores. Although Lizzy was a bit young for some of the activities, Monica wanted to expose her to as much of New York's culture, history, and fun as possible. She didn't want Lizzy to grow up as she had, a sheltered suburban child with no real idea of what the city had to offer.

Sundays for the Cabrera household were filled with a flurry of family activity. Maria helped the girls into their lace dresses, white tights, and patent leather shoes in preparation for Sunday mass. They always sat in the same pew each week, third row left from the front, with the girls sandwiched between José and Maria. After leaving the parish, they would go to visit Maria's in-laws. Maria really didinn't care to eat lunch with them every Sunday, but her husband insisted. Maria yearned for the days when she was single. She missed going to her mother's house for lunch every Sunday afternoon. They would cook, talk, argue, make-up, and eat together as she spent time with her siblings and their families. Since getting married, Maria seldom saw her family except on major holidays. José thought he had driven a wedge between

Maria and her mother by always starting an argument with her or the girls when she was on the phone with her mother. However, Maria always kept the lines of communication open by calling her mother from work every day. José tried to control everyone and everything around him. He had been that way from the day they met when she was a graduate student and he was an up-and-coming professional middleweight boxer. But little did José know, his tactics to isolate Maria from her family drove her to cling even closer to them than ever before.

CHAPTER

3

On Monday morning, Monica sat in her office going over the last few details of her impending presentation. The phone on her desk rang, startling her; Maria's home number came up on the caller I.D.

"Maria, it's seven-thirty! Why the hell aren't you here yet? You know we're scheduled to present at eight o'clock!" Monica said with desperation in her voice.

"I'm sorry. I'm not going to be able to make it," Maria said softly as she winced with pain.

"What!"

"I was in a car accident late last night."

"Oh my God, Maria! Are you all right? Did you get hurt?"

"I'm fine. Just two black eyes from the air bag and some bruising on my neck and chest from the seat belt."

"What happened?"

"I was rear ended by some guy talking on his phone."

"What a dumb…" Suddenly, Monica remembered she was at work, so she lowered her voice and skipped the second part of the compound word. "Everyone knows that men can't multitask like women; they can't do more than one damn thing at a time. They should make it illegal for all men to talk on the phone while driving, even with hands-free technology!"

Maria's pain intensified as she chuckled at Monica's comments.

"Well, I hope you got his information so you can sue his insurance company. Thank goodness you were wearing your seat belt. Are the girls okay?"

"They're fine. They weren't with me."

"Oh, thank goodness! Oh, no. What am I going to do about your part of the presentation?"

"Monica, just wing it!"

"Wing it? I'm going to need a wing, and a prayer!"

"Just give a brief overview of the proposal, go over the three phases of the project, and highlight the long-term benefits. You're the COO; they'll believe anything you say. Besides, they don't know what we were going to say in the first place. I'm sure you'll do fine."

"I hope you're right, otherwise they're going to eat me alive!"

"Break a leg, and thanks. I owe you one."

"You owe me more than one for this! I'll take two Sangritas as compensation." They both laughed.

"Take care, Honey. Heal quickly! If you need anything, call me on my cell."

"Okay, thanks, Monica. Bye-bye."

Maria emerged from the bathroom, silent tears flowing from her two blackened eyes. She tiptoed into her bedroom to return the cordless telephone to its base on her bedside table and looked down at José who was sound asleep. He was still such a handsome man with thick, dark, wavy hair, a meticulously groomed mustache that sat sensually atop full lips, and big shoulders and arms that reflected the chiseled, muscular build from his boxing days. José looked so calm and serene as he lay there. It was a stark contrast to the man he had been the night before when he stumbled in drunk from a night out with his boys. She replayed the events in her mind as she stood over him.

"Hey Chica, wake up!"

"Shhhh, you'll wake the girls," Maria whispered sleepily.

"Oh, you'll be waking them up with your screams of ecstasy by the time we get through, Chica," José slurred in a thick Spanish accent as he climbed onto the bed."

"Don't even think about it, José! You're drunk and you smell like a brewery. Go take a shower!" Maria said trying to push him away.

"Who the hell do you think you're talking to? I'm gonna get some tonight!" José switched over to full-on Spanish. Maria's alarm bells went off in her head; she knew she was in trouble.

"José, come on. It's late, I'm tired, and I have a presentation in the morning," she said in a soothing voice.

"Do I look like I care about your damn presentation?" He grabbed Maria around the neck. "Here, show 'em this at your presentation," José said through gritted teeth as he punched Maria in the left eye. Maria screamed with her mouth closed, deathly afraid of waking the girls. "Oh, and don't forget to take this one with you too!" He punched her in the right eye. She screamed another muffled cry. José pinned her down on the bed with his hand wrapped around her throat as she gasped for air and struggled to get away. Her efforts were in vain as he snatched the front of her gown and ripped it open; buttons flew everywhere. Next, he ripped off her panties.

"Now, I dare you to move. If you do, I'll kill you!" He let go of her throat for a brief moment to stagger to a standing position and unfasten his jeans; they dropped heavily to the floor due to the weight of his keys in the right front pocket. Maria trembled with fear as she gagged and coughed for air. José stepped out of his shorts, climbed back up on the bed, pushed her knees apart, and positioned himself between her legs. He wrapped his hand around her throat again, while angrily forcing himself inside her.

"No, no, please don't…" Her words were cut-off by his tightening grip around her throat. Maria bit her lip and her body flinched as he ripped through her. She covered her mouth with both hands to mute the cries that coincided with each of his thrusts. She didn't want her girls to witness the abuse that their father inflicted on her; that was her greatest fear.

31

After he huffed, puffed and tried, but failed to climax, José rolled off Maria and said "You'd better be glad I'm too tired to give it to you the way I wanted to." Maria began to sob uncontrollably and ran into the bathroom where she took up residence for the night. Once again, like many nights before, she locked the door, recited the prayer to St. Michael for personal protection, stepped into the tub, crouched down, pulled the shower curtain closed, and rocked herself to the rhythm of José's snoring. The tub was her safe haven; a place she was all too familiar with. She sat there shaking, remembering the countless occasions when she, along with her brothers and sisters had sought refuge behind the curtain. She recalled hearing the screaming, the sound of breaking glass, and the jolt of something heavy hitting the wall. They huddled together, clinging onto one another, whispering reassuring words, waiting for silence, and the all too familiar secret code knock from their mother. When they received the all-clear sign, they would rip back the shower curtain, clamber out of the tub, unlock the door and run into the arms of their battered and bruised mother.

Monica finally finished going over her presentation notes, which now included Maria's portion. She stepped into the outer office and told her administrative assistant about Maria's accident.

"Please send her a get-well bouquet from me and Vanessa. Oh, and thanks for coming in early to help me prepare for this meeting."

"No problem, Boss, anything for you," Julie said.

"And don't you forget it," Monica said with a wink, knowing full well that, without Julie, she wouldn't be able to manage her responsibilities effectively. Julie was invaluable to Monica and she rewarded her well in return.

Maria wiped off the kitchen counter tops as her two daughters, Christina and Elizabeth, finished up their pancakes while watching *Cinderella*. José stumbled into the kitchen, squinting from the bright lights. He began to complain about the noise from the television, but stopped in the middle of his sentence when he looked at Maria and saw her black eyes.

"Chica, what happened to you?" he said as he reached over to gently touch her face. She quickly turned away toward the sink and began to rinse the breakfast dishes and load the dishwasher.

"Remember Papi you and Mami were in a car accident last night," Elizabeth said. Maria wiped a tear from her face and turned the TV off.

"Girls, it's time to get your things together. You don't want to be late for school." The girls scampered off to their room as Maria cleared their plates. José slumped into his chair at the head of the kitchen table and put his head in his hands.

"Maria, I, I'm so sorry. I don't remember," he whispered as he raised his head with tears in his eyes. "Maria, please forgive me. I promise it won't happen again. I, I'll get help again, but this time I'll stick with it," he pleaded as he got up and stumbled toward her.

Maria slammed the dishwasher closed and backed away while she dried her hands on a kitchen towel. She folded it neatly, hung it over the handle on the oven door, and said with an indifferent voice, "Your breakfast is in the microwave," as she walked out of the kitchen.

As Chief Marketing Officer, Vanessa was up to her elbows in preliminary reports of quarter-end sales when a knock came at her office door. She looked up and saw Monica leaning against the door jamb with her arms and legs crossed.

"Hi, Monica! Come in and have a seat. How did the presentation go to our international counterparts?"

"Well, I hit a bit of a snag."

"Yeah? What happened?"

"Well, first of all, we got approval to move forward from the CEOs of our Asian, European, and Latin American groups."

"Great! That's what you wanted, right?"

"Yes, but I had to do the presentation alone."

"Alone? Where was Maria?"

"She was in a car accident last night."

Vanessa gasped, dropped her pen, and crossed her hands over her heart. "What! Is she okay?" What happened?

"She said she's okay, just two black eyes from the damn airbag and some bruises from the seatbelt. Some jerk talking on his phone rear ended her."

"Figures. What about her husband and the girls?"

"The girls weren't with her. Hmmm, come to think of it, she didn't mention José. I assume he wasn't with her, otherwise I think she would have said something."

"Well, I'm glad she's all right."

"I had Julie send her some flowers from us."

"Oh, okay, thanks!"

"My guess is she will be back to work within a few days. I'll try to get Maria to let us come over and cook them a nice dinner. You know José can't boil water, but I'm sure her mother is taking good care of her."

"Yeah, she is really close to her mother," Vanessa said with longing in her voice. "Hey, why don't we get together for drinks when Maria returns to work? I've got someone I want you both to meet."

"Okay. . . who is it? Don't tell me you've been seeing someone behind Damon's back."

"No, not quite. I've befriended the new Chief Corporate Legal Counsel; she helped with the orchestration of the merger. Her name is Anne Wu and I think she'd be a great addition to The Sangrita Club. Her office is up on thirty-four."

"Okay, sounds great!"

"Oh, and by the way," Vanessa said as she got up to close her office door. "It's over between me and Damon."

"What!"

"I broke up with him Thursday night."

"I thought you said he was going to finally pop the question?"

"Well, I guess it was just wishful thinking on my part."

"Vanessa, you are crazy! That man is gorgeous, smart, and has a career with great fringe benefits. He has a corporate jet at his disposal for God's sake!"

"I know, but I can't keep limiting myself to seeing only him. He may never want to commit to marriage. It's been three years!"

"I know, but you have to take into account that he is four years younger than you are. You can't expect him to make decisions about his life based on your biological clock."

"Yeah, I realize the age gap creates different priorities for both of us, but I'm at a point now where I need to start doing what's best for me."

"Look, it's not too late. Don't break it off all together. Just tell him you need some breathing room and that you want to date other guys. Suggest that he date other women too. That should make him jealous, piss him off, and perhaps get him to commit and pop the question!"

"Hummm, I don't know.   But, maybe you're right. I'll give it some thought."

"You know I'm always right!" Monica said with a sarcastic grin as she rose to leave the office.

Vanessa playfully threw a paper clip at her as she exited through the door.

Maria donned big, "Jackie-O" sunglasses and a scarf wrapped around her head to hide her battered state. This was not a new look for her; she had worn it many times before. She walked her girls to school and watched them go in from across the street. She didn't want to get too close. One of the other parents might see her and try to strike up a conversation.

As she made her way back to her apartment, she saw a young couple walking in front of her, hand in hand. They reminded her of when she and José were dating. When the couple reached the corner, they embraced, kissed passionately, and reluctantly went their separate ways.   At that moment, a large knot formed in the pit of Maria's stomach and tears began to well up in her eyes. She hurried towards home, but when it was in sight, she began to slow her pace. Her stride became measured and her posture became confident. She realized what had to be done and how she was going to accomplish it.

"Forgive me, Father, for I have sinned. It has been six months since my last confession."

"Tell me, what is upon your heart, my son?" a voice said from the other side of the confessional grill.

"It's happened, again," José said in a remorseful Spanish whisper.

"What, my son?"

"I hit her. I hit my wife again."

"Why? What caused you to commit such a violent act?"

"I, I don't know. I, I can't remember! I was drunk, Father, and I must have lost control."

"Violence is a way to gain control. Why do you feel the need to control her?" the voice asked. José fell silent. "Drinking is a way to cover your pain, to medicate yourself. Why are you hurting? What happened to you to cause you to seek solace in the bottle?"

"Father please, can you offer me penance? I'll do whatever you ask."

"Have you asked for forgiveness from your wife?"

"Yes Father, but I don't think she will forgive me this time."

"That does not matter my son. What matters is that you've asked. I suggest that you seriously consider the questions I presented to you about your need to control and why you are in pain. In addition, pray the Rosary including the Fatima prayer."

"Thank you, Father!" José said with relief. "I will do all that you ask of me."

Vanessa thought about Monica's advice. Maybe she had been too hasty in breaking up with Damon. Her mind began to drift away from her overloaded email inbox back to the night she broke up with Damon . . .

His back glistened with sweat and heat radiated from his body as she held onto him as if for dear life. With each thrust, her sound effects became louder and louder, drowning out Luther Vandross' smooth, silky baritone voice resonating from her Bose sound system. She kissed him hungrily and sucked his tongue passionately as she arched her back and pushed her hips upward to meet his every downward stroke. Then, just as she began to gasp for breath from the weight of his muscular chest pressing down on the erect nipples of her breasts, he stopped and pulled-out abruptly, without warning.

Vanessa felt as if she had been turned inside out. She started to protest, but before she could utter a syllable, he flipped her over and plunged in again. Out of her mouth came a moan of pleasure so intense that the expletive she was going to use to vent her frustration was immediately forgotten. The sound of their bodies slapping together was in double-time to the music as Damon gripped her hips and Vanessa braced her hands against the headboard. The motion of their bodies sped up as they worked their way toward the summit. When she had almost reached her peak, Damon emitted a quiet sigh and stopped again. There on his hands and knees, dripping sweat down her back, and still firmly tucked inside her, his chest heaved in and out as he attempted to catch his breath.

Vanessa wore an expression of rage as she flipped her head up. However, before she could respond, he pulled out again with no warning, flipped her over on her back, and plunged his hot tongue deep down inside her. He sucked with intensity, and then licked with gentle strokes that made her moment of anger melt away as her screams of supreme ecstasy pierced the air.

When their heavy breathing subsided, Damon slid out of bed and went into the bathroom. Vanessa lay on her back unable to move, paralyzed with pleasure and glowing in the moment. When she was finally able to lift her head, she rolled over on her side in an attempt to sit up, but felt so dizzy that she settled for the fetal position. Vanessa heard Damon turn on the shower, so she grabbed her quilt from the foot of the bed and pulled it up over her as she waited. After a few minutes the bathroom door opened and the harsh, bright lights from within blinded her as she quickly pulled the quilt over her head.

"Could you please turn the lights off?"

"Oh, sorry." Damon flipped off the switch.

Vanessa emerged from under the covers and reached up to hug him as he made his way toward the bed. She realized with deep disappointment that he was fully dressed when her hands felt the smoothness of the heavily starched dress shirt.

"It's only eight-thirty. Are you leaving so soon?" Vanessa said as she sat up and rewrapped herself in the quilt.

"Yeah, I'd better head out. I've got an early meeting, so I need to get some rest tonight," Damon said as he sat down on the bed beside her.

"Oh, stay here with me. I promise, I'll let you rest," Vanessa whispered with a mischievous voice as she stuck her tongue in his ear.

"I can't, really," he said as he gently pushed her away. Vanessa began to feel the warmth of her insecurities rise up within her.

"But, but I want to talk to you about something," she said with a hint of desperation.

"What is it?"

"You know, about us, our future," Vanessa said playfully while tracing her finger around the edges of his breast pocket.

"Vanessa, you know how I feel about that subject," Damon said sternly.

"But Damon, after that performance, surely you must have some thoughts and feelings to share with me about our future together." She drew a path with her finger from his knee up his thigh.

41

"That's not something I'm ready to discuss," Damon said as he pushed her hand away before her finger made its way to his zipper.

Vanessa's insecurities took a back seat as her anger grabbed the steering wheel. "Not ready!" she shouted as she jumped to her feet, grabbed the remote from the nightstand, and hit the pause button for the sound system. The quilt dropped to the floor, her hands flew to her hips, and the black woman's neck roll began. "I am so sick and tired of hearing you tell me, 'I'm not ready'," Vanessa said as she formed quote marks with her fingers. "What the hell is it gonna take for you to get your ass ready? Huh? What more can I possible do to you, or for you, to prove that I am the one."

"Vanessaaaaaaaaaaa," Damon said calmly as he rose to softly stroke her shoulders. "You're wonderful, you know that. It's just me. Look, I'm just not ready to make a long-term commitment."

Vanessa pushed his hands away. "You make it sound like a contract or something. It's not a merger! It's a relationship between two people who, who, who care deeply for one another." She stuttered because he had not told her that he loved her yet, but she had professed her love to him over, and over again.

"Vanessa, I don't respond well to pressure," Damon said as he looked down at her with an intimidating stare.

Vanessa's anger pushed the pedal to the metal and became rage. "Pressure? Nigga please! You don't know what pressure is," Vanessa said as she poked her finger in his chest.

"Look, Honey…"

"Honey? You damn right! I am sweet as honey and you ain't gettin' no more. Get the hell out my house." Vanessa pointed toward the bedroom door.

Damon dropped his head and quietly walked out of the room and down the hall. Vanessa followed, completely naked, waving her arms as if directing traffic.

"Oh, I been waiting a long time to say this! Damon Black, git yo black ass out my damn house and don't call me no mo. It is over. Fo' real!"

Damon paused at the door to grab his suit jacket from the coat rack and turned around to meet Vanessa's piercing eyes as she stood there tapping her foot with her arms folded across her bare, heaving breasts.

"Baby, I hope you'll reconsider…"

"Baby? Oh, I ain't no baby. I am a grown-ass woman," Vanessa shouted as she rolled her neck again and opened the door. "Get the hell out!"

Damon walked through the door and turned to plead his case one more time, but Vanessa slammed the door in his face before he had the chance to say a word. She stood with her backside up against the door, as her chest heaved up and down. Tears began to silently flow down her cheeks.

"No, no, I'm not going to do this again," she vowed as she flicked the tears from her face. She stomped her way back to the bedroom, ripped the sheets from her bed, and threw them in the hamper. As Vanessa pulled fresh sheets from the linen closet, she resolved to make this break-up different from the last one. She'd been dumped before and suffered through a long bout of depression, but this time she promised herself not to let the feelings of "what could have been" get her down. After remaking her bed, she grabbed her rubber gloves and flip flops, and began cleaning the shower with bleach. "I don't want any traces of him left in my house," she enunciated with each stroke of her scrub brush. Vanessa grabbed the hand-held showerhead and rinsed off the marble walls, floors, and shower seat, as well as the glass doors. "There, all fresh, clean and Damon free!" Vanessa smiled as she stood back and admired her hard work. She tossed her rubber gloves under the sink, turned the water on in the tub, and added some luxurious bath salts. "A nice, leisurely, relaxing bubble bath with a good book is all I need."

She had disinfected and deodorized Damon out of her life, or so she thought.

A knock on the office door broke her train of thought. Francine, Vanessa's administrative assistant, opened the door and stepped in with a huge bouquet of two-dozen pink and red roses.

"Where would you like them?" Francine inquired.

"Oh, my goodness! Right here on my desk is fine!"

She handed Vanessa the card, "Somebody must be in the dog house. If my man sent me flowers like this, I would forgive him," Francine said as she closed the door behind her.

Vanessa was stunned and at a loss for words. She took a deep breath and opened the card. It read,

> *My dearest Vanessa, the pink roses represent our friendship and the red roses represent the future of love's possibilities. Truly, Damon.*

Vanessa kissed the card as she dialed his number.

"Damon Black," he answered on the first ring.

"Hi Damon," Vanessa said meekly.

"Vanessaaaaaaaa!"

"I received your flowers and the card. They're beautiful. Thank you," she said as coolly as possible, trying not to reveal her excitement.

"Vanessa, can we get together tonight? I really need to see you."

"Oh, I'm sure you do need to see me," Vanessa said warming up a bit.

"How about my favorite spot, say around seven?"

"Sure, why not."

"Would you be a sweetheart and call to make our reservation?"

"Yes, Damon."

"Until then... Thanks Baby. Bye."

Vanessa sighed as she hung up the phone with thoughts of proposals and diamond engagement rings dancing in her head. She was sure that he had come to his senses and realized that it was time to settle down and marry her. She immediately began scribbling Mrs. Vanessa Black, Ms. Black, and Ms. Baldwin Black on her note pad. Vanessa picked up her phone and sent a voice message. "Monica and Anne, I think this is it! He's going to propose! I'll call both of you tomorrow and give you a blow-by-blow. Bye-bye!"

Maria took a detour as she walked back toward her apartment. It was a sunny, but brisk morning, so she stopped and bought a cup of coffee and a newspaper, anything to delay her return home. She sat down on a bench near a playground to strategize, going over and over again in her mind the things required to execute her plan. After a while, her toes and fingers began to get cold, so she finally decided to head towards home. She would have all day, once her husband left for work, to set the wheels of her plan in motion. As Maria opened the door to her building, she felt a familiar feeling of dread. With each stair she climbed to her third story walk-up, it seemed like her feet got heavier and heavier.

As she opened the front door quietly, she noticed that José's coat was missing from the hook. She breathed a sigh of relief and the tears came flooding down, stinging her blackened, swollen eyes. All of a sudden, something came over her as she removed her sunglasses and scarf, stood up straight, and looked into the hall mirror. What she saw looking back at her was not a battered woman, but a determined woman with a tremendous task ahead of her. She whispered sternly to herself, "You can do this!" She turned on her heels, made a beeline for the kitchen table, opened up her newspaper and laptop, and began scanning through the real estate listings in search of an apartment. She then called a realtor to arrange some showings. Next, she called the bank and transferred money from her and José's joint checking and savings accounts into her own personal account, being careful to move out only the amounts that had been previously direct deposited from her paycheck. She needed to protect her money to ensure that she could get everything that she and the girls needed.

A knock on the door startled Maria as she studied her to-do list. She looked at her watch. Normally, she was at work this time of day.

"Who is it?" Maria asked.

"Floral Delivery," someone shouted from the hall.

Maria looked through the peephole and saw a man in uniform. She opened the door and was greeted by a beautiful autumn bouquet. She tipped the delivery person, brought the flowers in and placed them on the kitchen table where she had been working. José always sent flowers after he beat her. She opened the pantry door and pulled the trashcan over to the table. Just as she was about to lift the flowers from the vase and throw them away, she noticed the card. Against her better judgment, she opened it and was surprised by what it said.

Maria, get well soon!
Love, Monica and Vanessa

As Vanessa entered the restaurant at 6:55, the owner, with whom she was on a first name basis, greeted her.

"Good evening, Vanessa. Welcome! Your table is available if you'll follow me."

"Thanks, Dave. Has Damon arrived yet?"

"No he hasn't. Would you like to wait for him at the bar?"

"No thanks. Just show him to our table when he arrives, which should be soon," she said with an eager smile on her face.

"Very well, Madam," Dave said as he seated her, smiled and walked away. Vanessa sat in the private booth practicing in her head how she would accept Damon's proposal. Ten minutes passed and there was no sign of Damon. Dave stopped by her table.

"Would you like to order a drink while you wait?" Dave asked.

"No, I think I'll wait for Damon."

"Very well."

Another ten minutes passed and there was still no sign of Damon. Vanessa was dialing his cell phone number when Dave stopped by her table again.

"Are you sure I can't get you a cocktail while you wait?"

"Ah, sure, I guess so. I'll have a glass of white wine. Thanks. Oh, and could you put a bottle of your best champagne on ice."

"Sounds like a celebration is in store."

"It will be. Damon's going to propose," Vanessa said with a whisper and a wink. "But don't say anything. I'm supposed to be surprised."

"My lips are sealed," Dave said with a serious look, which then yielded to a broad smile.

Dave returned moments later with Vanessa's glass of wine and Damon in tow. Dave sat the glass down, nodded, and walked away.

"Damon, I was getting a little worried. What happened?"

"Sorry I'm late, baby. I lost track of time. I stopped by the barbershop before coming here and it took longer than I anticipated. I wanted to look nice for you," he said as he leaned over and kissed her on the cheek. "Forgive me?"

"Hmmm, I guess so," she smiled. "Let's order. I'm starving". Vanessa motioned toward a server standing nearby who was waiting for her beckoned call. "I'll have the Chicken Dijon over rice with broccoli, no mushrooms please."

"And I'll have the seafood primavera with fettuccini, and throw the mushrooms she won't be eating on my plate," Damon said with a playful smile. "Also, would you please bring me a Beefeaters and tonic?"

They sipped their drinks, devoured their salads, and talked about work, the weather, and current events. Meanwhile, Vanessa's mind was racing, trying to decide if he was going to pop the question before or after dinner. After the server removed their empty salad plates, Damon turned toward Vanessa and took her hand and kissed it. At that point, Vanessa felt a tingle run all the way up her spine. This was the moment she had been waiting for all of her life. She glanced at her watch, because she wanted to remember the exact moment when she received Damon's marriage proposal.

"Vanessa, we've been together for three years and shared some of the most wonderfully intimate moments," Damon said.

Vanessa thought to herself, "Here it comes," as tears began to well up in her eyes.

"But,"

"But? What do you mean, *but*?" Vanessa said as she wiped a tear shed in joy from her cheek.

"But, I'm not ready for a commitment. I need some time and space."

"Space!" Vanessa practically shouted.

"Calm down. Now, I think we should continue to see each other, but maybe we should also date other people," Damon said in a hushed tone.

"What? I don't believe this!" she said at the top of her lungs just as their server approached with their entrées. Vanessa thought to herself, *Dammit, Monica was right again! I should have beaten him to the punch!*

"Honey, look, let's be real about it. You know I'm a hot commodity out in the dating world. I still want you, but …"

"But? But my ass," Vanessa screamed as she jumped to her feet. They looked at the server who quickly slid their plates on the table and disappeared without a word. At that point, everyone in the restaurant craned their necks to see what was going on in the private booth. Vanessa threw her napkin on the table and grabbed her coat and Ricky bag. By this time, Dave was heading to her table to see what all the commotion was. He met her in the aisle face to face. She looked up at him with tears streaming down. She felt so foolish and humiliated.

Before Dave could say a word, she pushed past him and made her way to the door.

She ran out into the cool misty rain towards home.

Vanessa sat in the darkness of her bedroom and watched the raindrops as they slid down the outside of her window in sync with the tears sliding down her cheeks. She was at the lowest point in her entire life. Vanessa had always been able to excel at whatever she did. She asked herself out loud, "What's wrong with me? Why can't I master this stupid relationship thing?"

Before she could attempt to respond to her own question, her phone rang. She fumbled through the covers, found the phone, and checked the caller ID. It was Anne. She decided to let her voice mail get it. She called to pick up the message a few moments later.

"Congratulations Vanessa! I'm really excited for you and…" Vanessa hung up; she couldn't bear to listen to the rest of the message. She knew the next call would be from Monica. She had no intention of answering that call either.

She slowly walked to the kitchen, took a knife from the butcher block, and held in front of her as thoughts of slitting her wrists clouded her mind. As she studied the knife, a tear slid off her cheek and landed on the blade of the knife. A bright light from the hall that shone through the kitchen reflected off the blade. It startled her and she dropped the knife in the sink and ran back to the safe haven of her bed. She searched through the covers, found the phone and dialed it desperately. After three rings, an all too familiar voice said, "Hello?"

"Hi, Mama," Vanessa whispered,

"Hi Honey, I can barely hear you. Do you have a cold?"

"No, just the *I Ain't Got No Man Blues*."

"Oh, Baby. It's gonna be all right. The Lord is gonna bless you one day if you just trust Him."

"I know Mama; I know. It just hurts so bad right now."

"Vanessa, you know I love you and want the best for you. Sometimes things work themselves out the way they do for a good reason. Maybe Damon just wasn't the best man for you. But you know what? There is someone who is best for you. When you two find each other, there won't be any tears of pain and signs of struggle. Getting to know one another will seem effortless and inevitable. You just need to be patient. Wait, you'll see!"

"Mama, I know you're right. You always know just what to say to make me feel better. I love you."

"I love you too, Baby!"

"I'll call you tomorrow Mama. Bye."

"Good night, Baby."

Vanessa knew that her life was more valuable than any relationship, but she had never felt so humiliated in her life. She just wanted the pain to stop. Damon obviously knew she wasn't serious when she called it off on Thursday night. All Vanessa really wanted was for Damon to tell her that he wanted her back, for keeps. There's an old saying, "Be careful what you ask for, you just might get it." Damon told her he wanted her back all right, but this time he was honest about wanting to have other women in his life also. Vanessa felt foolish and used.

She couldn't believe she had let the charade go on for so long. Vanessa wailed a cry of shame and regret, well into the night.

4

"Hmmm, that's odd. Vanessa isn't answering her cell phone," Monica said as she hung-up to dial another number.

"Vanessa Baldwin's office, Francine speaking."

"Good morning, Francine!"

"Hello, Ms. Kennedy."

"Is Vanessa in?"

"She called in sick."

"Oh, I hope she's okay," Monica said while trying to stifle a laugh.

"She said she should be back in the office tomorrow."

"Okay, thanks, Francine!"

"You're welcome, Ms. Kennedy."

"For the hundredth time, would you please call me Monica," she said with a pleading voice.

"Sure, Ms. Kennedy. Whatever you say," Francine said with a sarcastic tone. They both laughed and Monica hung up.

"Yes!" Monica exclaimed with a fist pump of joy, suspecting Vanessa couldn't get up for work because of the "workout" she put in last night after Damon's proposal. She couldn't wait for noontime because she knew even though Vanessa called in sick, she would still want to get together for lunch and recount each and every delicious detail from "Will you marry me?" to "What would you like for breakfast?" Monica asked Julie to reschedule all of her afternoon meetings, because she knew she would be in no shape to return to work after the Sangritas began flowing in celebration of Vanessa's engagement.

"Well, she didn't answer her phone last night or return my call, so I guess no news is good news. Damon must have come back to her place last night," Anne thought to herself as she sipped her green tea and scanned a legal brief. Anne began to daydream about how elated her mother would be if she were to announce that she had finally found a man and become engaged. Her thoughts were interrupted by a knock at her office door. She looked up to see a tall, dark, handsome man with a boyish grin walk through her doorway.

"Good morning, Ms. Wu" he said in a throaty baritone voice that made her legs cross.

"Y-yes, g-good morning," she stammered. "May I help you?"

"Your administrative assistant told me that I could come right in. She said you were expecting me."

Anne looked at him with a puzzled look.

"I'm Brad Cole. I'll be handling the patent verification process for the merger."

"Oh, yes! Mr. Cole,"

"Please, call me Brad."

"Brad, I do have you on my calendar. Please forgive me. I was a bit distracted. Call me Anne," she said as she stood to shake his hand. His handshake was firm and the palm of his hand was so smooth and buttery soft that Anne almost forgot to let go.

Anne blushed as she offered him a seat. She picked up her pen and raised it to touch her chin as she attempted to listen to him intently, but the sexy aroma of his cologne that transferred to her hand during their handshake made her completely miss what he was saying. Anne thought to herself, 'Damn, he smells sooooo good!' She tried to shake off the trance he had put her in by saying silently to herself, 'Focus, Anne, focus.'

Brad paused in the middle of his sentence and said, "You look a bit confused. Do you have a question?"

"Oh no, no! I had Connie pull all of the patent files that were indicated in your email. Why don't we just roll up our sleeves and do a complete review over there on, I mean at the conference table," Anne said with a nervous laugh. She removed her suit jacket and hung it on the back of her red leather, executive chair. Brad also removed his jacket as they headed for the table. Anne's cheeks began to flush because of Brad's extremely broad, muscular shoulders that were now revealed. She pressed the intercom button on the phone and asked Connie to bring them some chilled bottled water; Anne hoped that the water would lower her body temperature and help to keep her cheeks from appearing too red.

Connie came in moments later and set down an ice bucket on the credenza filled to the brim with ice and bottled water. With a poker face she said, "If you need more ice, just let me know."

Anne knew that Connie was being facetious and that she was going to tease Anne unmercifully after Brad left. Anne responded graciously with a slight smile while gritting her teeth. "Thank you Connie, I think we'll manage with what you've brought us. Please hold my calls."

"Ow, Ow, Ow, Ahhhhhhhh!" A blood-curdling scream came from Vanessa as her body thrashed from side to side. She fell off the couch and awoke from a recurring dream, a dream that had once been a reality some thirty years ago. Instantly, she sought refuge by bolting down the hallway to her bedroom and plunging underneath the quilt that her grandmother had made for her when she was a little girl. It covered her like a shield from the ugly demons that haunted her from the past. Her sobs wet the pillow and her trembling shook the bed as she lay holding her knees to her chest gasping for breath. She had not had that dream in three years, not since she started dating Damon. "Why did it come back? Why?" she exclaimed aloud as she rocked to comfort herself. Although it had been a long time, she knew what she had to do, yet again.

When Vanessa had calmed down, she unwrapped herself from her cocoon and went to the kitchen to find a magnetic business card that was attached to a metal bulletin board next to the refrigerator. She stood there looking at the numerous photos of her and Damon smiling happily on various occasions. One by one she began pulling each photo from under the various magnets that represented different places they had visited around the world. She ripped each picture to shreds, and threw the debris in the garbage. After completing the purging process, she said aloud, "What a waste of my time, my energy, and my life." She took a deep breath, slowly let it out, put her hands on her hips and asked, "Now what did I come in here for?" She stood there for a few seconds and scanned the bulletin board that had been stripped of its memorabilia. Right next to the magnet from Paris was the business card. Seeing it jogged her memory as she picked up the kitchen phone from its cradle and dialed the number.

"Dr. Porter's office. Sara speaking."

"Hi Sara, it's Vanessa, Vanessa Baldwin."

"Oh, hi Vanessa!"

"I know it's been a while, but I need an appointment to see Dr. Porter. Your first available please." Vanessa gnawed on her cuticle while Sara searched for an opening.

"I have a Friday afternoon opening at three o'clock."

"Perfect, I'll take it. Thank you Sara."

"You're welcome. We'll see you on Friday."

"Good-bye."

Vanessa knew that Monica and Anne were expecting a call from her, but she wasn't ready to update them just yet. Shopping always made her feel better. She knew that it wouldn't mend her broken heart, but it sure made the healing time pass with less pain. She needed a diversion, a pick-me-up, especially now that she was officially back in the dating scene. She needed some new dating clothes. Vanessa got dressed, grabbed her emergency credit card from her jewelry box, donned a pair of sunglasses to hide her swollen red eyes, and hit the stores.

Noon came and went without a word from Vanessa. Monica began to worry, so she decided to call Anne. She searched the intranet employee directory and found her number.

"Anne Wu's office. Connie speaking."

"Hello, this is Monica Kennedy. Is Anne available?"

"Is she expecting your call?"

"No, I'm calling regarding Vanessa Baldwin."

"Oh, okay, one moment please." Connie buzzed her boss.

Anne heard the buzzer and immediately got an attitude and an annoyed look on her face to match. She walked over to her desk, picked up the phone, turned her back to Brad, and spoke in a hushed tone.

"Connie, I asked not to be disturbed," she said gritting her teeth once again.

"Sorry, but I thought you might want to take this one. It's Monica Kennedy, regarding Vanessa Baldwin."

"Oh, okay. Thanks." Anne hit the button to pick up Monica's call.

"Anne Wu speaking."

"Hi Anne, this is Vanessa Baldwin's friend, Monica Kennedy."

"Hello!" said Anne cheerfully.

"I know we haven't formally met yet, but I haven't heard from Vanessa today and I was getting a bit concerned. Have you heard from her?"

"No, I haven't. When I called her office this morning, Francine told me she had called in sick. I just assumed she was probably tired from the celebration."

At that moment, both Anne and Monica thought, "What if he didn't propose?" They knew Vanessa would be shattered. Neither Anne nor Monica mentioned their private thought to the other, but both of them knew how much Vanessa had been clinging to the hope of marriage. If Damon didn't propose, they were both afraid of how devastated Vanessa would be.

61

"That must have been some workout last night!" Monica said and they both laughed.

"Yes, I guess they needed some recovery time," Anne tried to say discretely.

They laughed and said good-bye, but not before vowing to call the other if either one of them heard from Vanessa. Anne hung up the phone and turned back to Brad.

"Now, where were we, before we were so rudely interrupted?" Just then a knock came at the office door. Connie appeared with a rolling cart.

"I took the liberty of ordering lunch for the two of you."

"Why thank you Connie, that was so thoughtful of you," Anne said sincerely.

"Oh, and there's another bucket of ice if you need it," pointed Connie as she closed the door behind her and put her hand over her mouth to keep from laughing out loud.

Anne tried to contain her embarrassment, but it was written all over her face. Brad pretended to be oblivious, but he knew Anne was attracted to him. She silently vowed to get Connie back for being so obvious with her jesting.

Anne had received a referral to a therapist in New York City from her doctor in L.A. Today was their first session. Anne hated starting over with someone new again. Every time she moved, which was about every two to three years, she had to start from square one. It felt like she had to relive her painful past over and over again, but her secret was never part of the dialog.

"Hi, Anne Wu. I have a three o'clock appointment," she said to the receptionist.

"Oh yes, I'm Sara. Since this is your first visit with us, I'll need you to fill out these forms, provide me with your co-pay, and I'll need to make a copy of your insurance card." Anne filled out the necessary forms and sat waiting with her legs crossed, nervously twirling her foot until her name was called.

"Here we go again," she said under her breath as she walked into the doctor's office.

Dr. Porter was not at all what Anne expected. Usually, she got someone who was a combination of old, short, fat and bald. Dr. Porter was tall, lean, thirty-something, and had a full head of thick, wavy, blond hair. He looked like a surfer dude in a business suit. Anne wondered what he would look like sprawled across a bed in Calvin Klein underwear on a billboard in Times Square. She shook the fantasy from her head as she reached for his hand. He had a gentle but firm handshake, and honest, sincere hazel eyes. They exchanged professional pleasantries, and then Anne began the arduous task of unfolding her story without revealing too many wrinkles.

"When I was two-years-old, I still had not begun to speak, so my father finally broke down and let my mother take me to a therapist. The therapist worked to develop a rapport with me for two years, yet I still did not utter a word. It was discovered through testing that I was exceptionally gifted, so it was suggested to my Mother that I be put into a special preschool program. My first day in the program, I was introduced to the violin and showed great promise, even though I had never played before. My violin teacher, Mr. Chin constantly praised me and I quickly progressed. By my third week in the program, I began talking to Mr. Chin and my mother, and then to my therapist, but not to my father. Thirty-four years later, I still have not spoken to him.

"I had it all, all that a rich, little, Chinese girl could have ever have hoped for and dreamed of. I had the most beautiful clothes and toys imaginable, and no siblings to have to share them with. I went to the best schools, had lots of friends, yet I would have traded it all for a single kiss on the forehead from my father. I wanted so much to curl up in his lap and feel his eyelashes with my tiny little finger or see his eyes sparkle and beam at me when I won the scholarship to Julliard and graduated at the top of my class. Instead, I experienced the all-to-familiar cold, distant stare that never quite met my eyes, but looked a measure beyond me as though he was imagining how the moment would have played out had I been born a boy. My home environment was very lonely while I was growing up.

Anne wasn't really sure why she kept going to therapy, perhaps out of habit; it was something she had always done throughout her entire life. But, deep down she knew she couldn't stop, at least not until she had the answer to the question that haunted her. Why didn't her father love her? Little did she know, someone knew the answer and had kept it from her all of her life.

Maria knew that José had been to confession. She overheard him in the bathroom whispering in Latin the night before while he thought she was asleep. But, she had been awake counting each and every "Hail Mary", "Our Father" and "Glory Be".

"His penance is pittance in comparison to the price I'm paying to wear these physical and mental scars," Maria said to herself as she heavily applied make-up to her swollen black and blue eyes. "Well, he can hail Mary all he wants to. One day real soon, I'm gonna hail a cab and get the hell out of here!" she continued as she looked in the mirror and pulled her hair back into a ponytail.

While the girls were in school, Maria met with a realtor, saw three apartments, and decided on one. There was no time to waste. She wanted to be moved into her new place before she returned to work. That meant she didn't have much time to pack up the belongings she had accumulated over the past nine years of her marriage. She contacted a mover and called to have the utilities cut off, because they were in her name. She then called an attorney to file for divorce and full custody of the girls. She also filed a restraining order against José. She knew she had to keep her new home location secret because she didn't want José stalking her and begging her to come back. She also knew she had to switch the girls' schools to keep him from trying to kidnap them.

With all that accomplished, she made her way to the bedroom her girls shared and began packing some of their clothes and toys. She began packing her things too and stashing the suitcases and boxes in the back of the girls' closet; her husband would never notice. But, she knew she had to be careful to keep her plans hidden, because José would be sober for the next few days. He always laid off the liquor for a while after he beat her in an attempt to prove he could change and make amends; however, he always fell off the wagon and returned to his abusive ways. He had crossed the line many times before, but this time he went too far. He had raped her and that was the last straw. The camel's back had been broken.

That morning, things had looked pretty bleak, but after a day of shopping, Vanessa had her game-face back on. It had turned into a day of celebration. Not just any old kind of celebration, but a day where she felt compelled to email her sistah-girls and tell them about the miracle she found. She had been on a mission, a mission that all African-American women had been on many, many times in their lives, but were most likely unsuccessful and unsatisfied. This was a mission of epic proportion that was only accomplished by enduring the challenges of grunting, pulling, and pushing, over and over again. That mission was the taming of the booty! She had no allies, only one enemy: the mirror. She slipped in and out, pulled up and down, over and over again, but was always disappointed by the results. She stooped and bent, sat and stretched, as well as jogged in place. Then, as if the clouds rolled back and the angels began to sing, a Cheshire cat smile formed on her face. But, before she got too excited, there was the final test, dancing in the mirror. It was at that point she knew that the hours of drudgery she'd been through were well worth it and she'd hit pay dirt. She bought those jeans in every finish and color available, because she never wanted to go through that awful experience again. Well, at least not until the new fall styles come out the next year. She had accomplished the nearly impossible mission: finding the right pair of jeans to fit her tiny waist, thick thighs, and ample booty, which made her look delicious and made men say, *Damn! She's fine!*

Vanessa sat in the middle of her bed amongst the rumple of covers, clicking away on her laptop. She was composing an email to her sistah-girls with the details of her blue jean find. She also let them know that she was unattached once again and wanted to have a girls' night out to scope something new to "wear." By that she meant a new man. When the seasons change, it's out with the old styles and in with the new.

Vanessa used those terms because all four of her friends were connected to the fashion industry. Two of them worked for designers in the garment district: Tonya, as a raw materials buyer, and Nikki, as a staff designer. Meme, an investment fund manager on Wall Street always researched, bought, and wore the latest designer fashions and accessories, as well as traded designer's stocks. She wore what the constantly changing trends dictated; needless to say, she lived paycheck to paycheck. Diane was a freelance fashion photographer; she shot all the top models for all of the top magazines in the fashion industry. Vanessa knew she would get replies of exceeding gladness from them all. As she clicked send, she exclaimed to herself, "Have jeans, will date!"

Vanessa closed her laptop and pushed it aside, got up and began removing her clothes while standing in front of her full-length mirror in the closet. She examined her body and said, "Hmmm. Not bad." Then a look of horror came over her face. She moved in closer to examine her find and discovered a long, gray pubic hair. She screamed and ran into the bathroom to find her tweezers. "Oh, don't think for a minute that you're gonna blow my twenty-five and holding cover. I look twenty-five now and I plan on looking twenty-five forever!"

She took the tweezers from her manicure kit that lay in a woven basket on the back of the toilet and ran back to the mirror. She grabbed the gray hair with the tweezers, held her breath, and yanked as she squeezed her eyes shut. It yielded without too much pain; this ritual was becoming an all too frequent habit, so she made a mental note to call the spa to set up a bikini wax appointment. "I'm going Brazilian this time. That will teach those pesky little gray hairs a lesson!"

Satisfied with her extraction, Vanessa sterilized her tweezers with a cotton ball drenched in rubbing alcohol and returned the tool to its leather case. She then wrapped herself in a warm terry cloth robe and lay down across her bed staring up at the crystal chandelier hanging from the coffered ceiling. She knew it was time to come clean with herself about her three-year relationship with Damon. She had always known their break-up was inevitable, but she didn't want to face up to it. She had always hoped she could change his mind about commitment. Their courtship had been fraught with red flags from the very beginning, but she chose to ignore them. Damon had never introduced her to his family. Sure, there were some attempts to get together with them for the holidays, but something always came up, which left Vanessa sitting at home, alone, under the mistletoe or watching the ball drop on TV.

There was the time when she found a brown bobby pin in the passenger seat of Damon's car and his story about giving a co-worker a ride home after working late one night. Vanessa knew the bobby pin was a sign from another woman to let her know she was marking her territory. It was one of the oldest tricks in the book. Then of course, there were the recurring yeast infections that she never said anything to Damon about. She'd never had a yeast infection until she started sleeping with him. She knew he transmitted it to her from other women. Using a condom was the right thing to do, but Damon wouldn't hear of it. She always gave in for fear that he might stop seeing her. As a consequence, she took an HIV test every 3 months and constantly popped pills and used creams to alleviate the yeast infections. She was thankful that she hadn't contracted anything serious, and prayed that she never would.

Yeah, she knew he was a cheater, and just like many other women, she put up with it in hopes of changing his wandering ways. He was a rare find and he knew it: tall, dark, handsome, degreed, professionally employed, well-off, well dressed, well read, and well, just fine. The perfect package. Well, except for the minor flaw that he couldn't, or more correctly, wouldn't be satisfied with just one woman. She sat up and said out loud while executing the black woman's neck roll, "I've put up with way too much for too long. I ain't puttin' up with nothing, no more! From now on, if a man wants me, he's gonna have to sweep me off my feet, not with a broom, but a huge street sweeper!" accentuating her words with the wave of her index finger and a snap for punctuation.

Vanessa rolled over to grab the cordless telephone, but as usual, it was missing from the base. She pushed the page button so that it would emit a beeping noise. After about twenty seconds of searching, digging, and pulling through the covers, she finally found it. She decided it was time to call

Monica, Maria, and Anne to come clean. Then she remembered Maria's accident; she would have to get an update from Monica on Maria's condition.

Monica was sitting in her office catching up on her email before leaving for the day. Her mind began to wander to the point of distraction as she did an inventory of Steve's body, while her panty shield absorbed the results of her thoughts. An unexpected knock came at her office door, which startled her and made her cross her legs. It was her assistant, Julie.

"I know you didn't want to be disturbed, but I thought you'd want to take Ms. Baldwin's call."

"Oh, thank you! Yes, I'll take it." Monica waited for Julie to close the door before she picked up the phone.

"Vanessa!"

"Hey Monica."

"What's going on? I've been on pins and needles waiting for an update from you. I thought I was going to have to call the fire department to come and knock your door down."

"I'm sorry I didn't get back to you. But, before I go into that, how is Maria?"

"Oh, she's getting better. She expects to be back to work by Monday."

"Great, I'm glad she didn't get seriously hurt."

"From the sound of your voice, it sounds like you did."

"Yeah, you're right. It's really over this time."

"What happened?" Monica inquired with an empathetic tone.

"I can't go into it right now. Why don't we get together for dinner tomorrow and chat? I want to invite Anne, too."

"Okay, sounds great. Sangritas?"

"Sangritas it is."

"How about six o'clock?"

"See you then."

"Why? Aren't you coming to work tomorrow?"

"I have an off-site meeting all day tomorrow, so I won't be coming into the office. Monica, I know you are really concerned about me, but seriously, I'll be fine."

"You'd better be!"

They both laughed and said their good-byes. Monica immediately called Anne and filled her in on the breakup and their plans for dinner the next night. They both agreed that Vanessa was really hurting. Monica expressed to Anne that she hoped Vanessa wouldn't fall into depression like she had after the break-up of her relationship with the guy she dated before Damon. It had taken several cases of tissues and months of therapy to pull her out of that one. They agreed that it would be better if Vanessa didn't know that they had talked; Anne would act surprised when Vanessa called her to invite her to dinner, and when

Anne and Monica met at the restaurant they would act as though they had never spoken to each other before.

Vanessa went into her home office to check her email. All of her sistah-girls had replied to her email about the jeans. They were excited about getting together soon, so Vanessa composed a reply to them to meet for drinks on Saturday night. All four responded within minutes with an affirmative. Vanessa said to herself, "Past experience brings on future assurance, therefore Tonya and Meme will be on time, Diane will be late, and Nikki will probably be a no show."

Vanessa looked out of the window at the skyline and thought to herself, *Five beautiful sistahs with degrees, careers, condos, and plenty of confidence to go around, but not one of us has a man, well, not a real man to speak of. What is wrong with this picture? Single men of this world are just wasting our time, trying to be players, trying to screw as many of us a possible without truly committing to us.*

Vanessa jumped to her feet with her hands on her hips and screamed, "All you Damons out there, I hope your dicks rot off!"

She took a deep cleansing breath, brought her hands together and whispered, "Namaste."

CHAPTER

5

The start of the day was not unlike any other weekday, except for one thing: it was moving day. José had left for work on time for a change. Ever since the "car accident," José had stayed sober, quiet, and helpful around the house. To Maria, this was just another one of his feeble attempts to get back into her good graces. She knew from past experience that as soon as she would begin to warm up to him, he would begin to slowly remove the mask to reveal his true self, again. The self that had a face red as crimson from alcohol, hands cut and bruised from bar fights, and a urine-soaked body that stumbled into the house at dawn to come to rest next to her in bed. She had spent many a night curled up on the living room sofa to escape the stench that filled their bedroom.

The girls had been fed breakfast, escorted to school, and were oblivious to the surprise that awaited them. The movers arrived promptly at nine-thirty and began moving out the furniture while Maria finished packing clothes and dishes. As she finished taping up a box filled with shoes, she looked over at her bed. That was one of the items that would not be making the move, along with all of the linens. She had no desire to sleep another night on the sheets or in the bed she had been raped in. She also left all of her sexy lingerie in a pile on the bed. She wanted to leave behind all of the memories of what had been. In addition, she left the kitchen table, on which she had served him, for the past nine years. The memories of being slapped across that table were not welcome where she was going.

When the movers had taken all of her belongings down to the truck, she placed four items on the kitchen table: the bride and groom topper from her wedding cake with the bride removed, her wedding album from which she had cut her face out of every photo, the groom's champagne glass, and the keys to the apartment. She closed the door behind her for the last time and proceeded to the garbage chute with a bag in her hand. It contained the plastic bride from the cake topper, the smiling faces cut from her wedding photos, and the crushed bride's champagne glass. She listened as the bag slid down the chute. When she was satisfied it was gone, she closed the chute door, and pulled her sunglasses from her tan canvas and leather Ricky bag, as she strode confidently down the steps.

When she came out into the sunlight, she perched the sunglass on her nose, raised her arm and shouted, "Taxi!"

Sparks were dancing and flying across a steel beam when José was startled by a tap on his shoulder from his foreman. José turned off his torch, lifted his visor and shouted, "What?" over all of the construction noise in the background.

"Someone's here to see you in the office," the foreman shouted back.

"Who is it?"

"Don't know."

As José removed his visor and gloves, he said a quick prayer under his breath while following the foreman to the office. He was hoping that his number had not come up for the random drug test, for he was certain alcohol would be detected. Although he hadn't been drunk in the past few days, he did keep a bottle of liquor in his locker at work to take the edge off when he needed it. José reluctantly approached the man waiting for him. He was dressed in a brown Carhartt jacket, blue jeans, and work boots. He wasn't dressed like the guys who normally administer the drug tests.

"Yeah, what's up?" José said with an annoyed look on his face.

"José Cabrera?"

"Yeah?" The man handed him a manila envelope and said, "You've been served," and walked away.

José looked at his foreman with a puzzled look on his face and began to open the envelope and pull out the documents contained inside. The first of the two documents was a restraining order stating that he could not come within 500 feet of his wife and children. The second document was notification of divorce proceedings. José tried to maintain a poker face in front of his foreman saying, "This is some shit from my landlord about a damned bounced check. What a fucking waste of my time!" he said as he walked back to his welding.

The foreman knew better. He had heard every excuse under the sun from many a construction worker being served on the job. He knew José's marriage was coming to an end. He also knew that his chronic drinking and calling in sick were about to begin.

José couldn't leave work; he had to put up a brave front. He'd show them that he was a man, a real man, not a wimp or a pussy-whipped husband. No, he would stay for the rest of the day and even do overtime if it was offered. José returned his visor to his head and flipped it down over his face. He put on his work gloves and lit the torch. Sparks began dancing and flying again, reflecting off his mask that hid the tears rolling down his face.

Anne had taken a little extra time to pick out just the right outfit for work that morning. She had another meeting scheduled with Brad to continue where they had left off. She had purposefully chosen a translucent cream-colored silk blouse with a red camisole underneath, tucked into a mid-thigh length skirt of a red and black Chanel suit. She made sure that a hint of red lace peeked out at the décolleté to spark interest. She had also taken a long hot bath that morning with a delicious honey and cream bath foam, and then finished off with a luscious body spray and a dash of expensive perfume.

At the office, Anne would make sure to burn an aroma therapy candle at lunch time so that when Brad showed up for their meeting at two o'clock the office would smell as inviting as she did. She had also asked Connie to order bottled water on ice and a fresh fruit tray. She needed the cold water to keep her body temperature normal and the fruit to keep from getting lightheaded. Anne would be ready and waiting to do "business."

Vanessa had begun her morning with her routine of hitting the snooze button multiple times and then emerging from under her mound of covers in overdrive. She began to peel off her pajamas in the closet while brushing her teeth and scanning the racks for something to wear to her off-site meeting, and to dinner later that night with Anne and Monica. She chose a pair of black Calvin Klein slacks with a custom-made pale gray oxford shirt. Vanessa went back into the bathroom to spit and rinse. When she grabbed her shower cap from the cabinet underneath the sink and stood up to put it on, she remembered that she was supposed to call and make an appointment to have her roots touched up. The gray around the edges of her hairline stood out boldly against her jet-black shoulder length hair. She quickly showered, dressed, combed her hair, and strategically placed hair-mascara on her side part to cover her gray. She slipped on a pair of black suede Manolo Blahnik pumps, grabbed her Ricky bag, a navy Ralph Lauren trench coat and ran out the door.

When she emerged from her building, the car service was waiting. As was her usual practice, she put her makeup on while in route. She decided she had better make the phone call to her hair stylist now while she was thinking about it.

"Hey Vince, it's me, Vanessa!"

"Oh, hey girl. What you want?"

"I need a big favor. I have a hair emergency."

"Yeah, every time you call me it's an emergency."

"I know, I know. Can you please fit me in on Saturday morning for a color touch-up? I promise I'll give you a big tip!"

"Now you know I been booked up for at least three weeks."

"I know, but I'm really desperate. Damon and I broke up and I am going out hunting with my girls on Saturday night.

"Oh, y'all ain't together no more. Huh, it's about time. Girl, I'll work you in and give you the 'I done dropped that Nigga and got a new attitude' hair-do. Get here at eight."

Vanessa laughed. "Thanks, Vince. I owe you one."

"Girl, you owe me so many, I ought to put a lien on your condo."

Vanessa laughed and breathed a sigh of relief as she hung up and began applying her makeup. Fifteen minutes later she emerged from the car relaxed, fierce and ready to start her business day.

Maria found a nice two-bedroom apartment in El Barrio, Spanish Harlem, at East 102nd and 2nd Avenue. The rent was a little high, but manageable on her ample six-figure salary. She was lucky because the apartment was in move-in condition with freshly painted walls and beautiful hard wood floors. The previous tenant was transferred by his employer to another state shortly after moving in, so he was eager to sublet. The girls' new school was four blocks away, right on Maria's way to work. Initially, she had second thoughts about leaving José, but when she started her apartment search and divorce proceedings, everything just seemed to fall into place effortlessly. That gave her a sense of calm and reassurance that she was doing the right thing for herself and her girls.

José knew the gossip had spread about being served. He kept working through lunch because he wasn't ready to face his co-workers. He always knew this day was coming. Maria was beautiful, smart, successful, and a great mother. "What does she need me for?" he muttered under his breath to himself. He knew he wasn't worthy of her. He couldn't control the monster that lurked within. He had tried to quit drinking several times without success; he needed it to dull the pain he had endured since childhood. But, the alcohol also pointed out his inadequacies and his unworthiness, which fueled his inner rage.

Deep in his heart, José was afraid of what awaited him at home. He didn't know what to expect when he walked through the door. Would there be smiles from his girls and a cold stare from Maria to greet him or would there be a dark, lonely silence? Another round of tears rolled down his face as the sparks continued to dance and fly across the cold, dark metal.

Maria arrived at her new apartment before the movers. They were undoubtedly taking a lunch break and she wanted to do some cleaning before they arrived. As she went from room to room, she envisioned where everything would go. That way, when the movers arrived, she could direct them where to put the furniture without wasting a lot of time. She had to be mindful of the clock, so that she wouldn't be late picking the girls up from school at 3:00.

A knock at the door startled her as she scrubbed the kitchen sink. She went to the door to ask who it was, as she was not expecting the movers back from lunch so soon.

"Furniture delivery!"

"Oh, you're here!" she said as she unlocked and swung open the door with a big smile on her face. The new bed and kitchen table Maria had ordered arrived earlier than expected. She directed the delivery guys where to put the new furniture and tipped them as they left. She ran and jumped onto her new queen-size bed like a giddy child. She rolled from one side to the other and screamed with excitement, "It's mine, all mine!"

The movers arrived just as she finished cleaning the master bathroom. She had asked them to put the girls' stuff on the truck last so that it would be the first to come off. That way, she could begin setting up their room while the movers brought in everything else. Maria wanted the girls to come home to their new room and feel comfortable and safe, so she worked feverishly to get their curtains up, beds made, and clothes and toys put away. Her room could wait. All she needed for tonight was to make her bed, for which she had bought new Egyptian-combed cotton sheets. It was a luxury, but she was worth it! She knew that she deserved to be treated like a queen, even if she had to treat herself.

By the time the movers finished unloading all of her belongings, she had the girls' room pretty much squared away just in time to go pick them up from school. Maria freshened up and grabbed a cab. On her way, she rehearsed how she was going to tell the girls about what she had done and how their lives were going to change. She hoped that they would not be too devastated about leaving their father, living in a new apartment, and going to a new school. She would promise to let them see their father often and go back to say a formal farewell to their friends and classmates. First, she would take them to McDonald's, which is every mother's secret weapon. Hopefully, it would help soften the blow she had to deliver to them.

Connie appeared at Anne's office door and leaned against the doorframe with her arms folded across her chest. She looked around the office and said with a smile, "Would you like me to put on some Maxwell?"

Anne rolled her eyes and said with a playful tone, "Ha, ha! Please let me know when Brad arrives, make sure we're not interrupted, and close the door behind you on your way out. Oh, and please put on a poker face when you greet him. Thank you!"

"Sure thing, Boss," said Connie as she laughed wickedly and closed the door.

Anne pulled out her mirror to freshen her lipstick and ensure that every hair was in place. She couldn't tolerate flyaways. Her intercom buzzer rang and startled her, sending her lipstick tube flying across her desk and onto the floor. She hopped up, ran around her desk to retrieve it, and ran back to answer the call.

"Yes, Connie?" she announced with frustration in her voice.

"It's Ms. Baldwin on line two."

"Oh, thanks! Stall Brad if he shows up early while I'm on the phone." Anne picked up line two.

"Vanessa! I guess congratulations are in order. I want to know all of the details!" Anne said trying to sound like she didn't already know Vanessa and Damon had split up.

"There's only one big detail. It's over."

"What's over?"

"Damon and I."

What! What happened to the proposal?" Anne said convincingly with shock and concern in her voice.

"It's too much to go into right now. Can you meet me for dinner tonight? I've invited Monica too. I'll fill you both in on the drama at the same time tonight."

"Well, I may have to stay at the office a little late. I'm meeting with a patent attorney this afternoon, but I'll try to get away as soon as I can. What time and where are you meeting Monica?"

"Sangritas at six."

"Okay. If I'm a little late, start without me. I'll join you when I can. Hey, are you all right?"

"I'm fine, really. See you later."

"Okay, take care!"

As Anne replaced the receiver, she detected Vanessa was putting up a brave front. She hoped Vanessa would pull through without a repeat of depression, as Monica had mentioned. The intercom buzzer rang and Connie announced Brad's arrival. "Thanks. Send him in please," Anne said as she raked the cosmetics off her desk into her top drawer, just in time to stand and greet Brad. They exchanged pleasantries and she offered to take his jacket. Hers was already off and the red lace was ready to work magic. As she walked over to the credenza to offer him some refreshments, she stopped dead in her tracks and in mid-sentence as she caught a glimpse of his left hand. It donned a thin, gold wedding band, which had conveniently been missing the day before. All she could manage to say was, "Would you excuse me?" and made a beeline for her office door. She quickly opened it and closed it behind her, and stood with her back up against it. Anne opened her mouth to speak as Connie looked up at her. With a devilish grin on her face, Connie said, "Yeah, I know. All the good ones are."

Maria sat on a bench near the school entrance as she waited for her girls. The bell rang and the doors to the school burst open with laughing, chatty faces emerging into the sunlight. The children shielded their eyes as they searched for the familiar faces that would escort them home. Christina and Elizabeth exited the school holding hands as always. All of a sudden, broad smiles broke out on their faces as they ran to meet their mother. They hugged and kissed her, each joining hands with her to make it a threesome, and turned towards home. Maria stopped and the girls looked up at her with a puzzled gaze. "Girls, I have a surprise for you!"

"What is it?" they exclaimed with excitement in unison.

"Well, I actually have several surprises for you today, and the first one starts with a trip to McDonald's!" The girls screamed with glee. "And, we are going to take a taxi to get there!" The girls jumped in the air. They loved riding in taxicabs. Normally they walked or went by car everywhere they went. Riding in a taxi made them feel grown up.

Maria had left the car she and José shared at her old apartment. It was in his name and he drove it most of the time. She didn't like to ride in it anyway; it reeked of beer and urine. She used a car service to get back and forth to work, so she wouldn't even miss it. Besides, when the day came for her to buy a car, she would get what she wanted: something cute and sporty, not a minivan like José had bought for her. But most importantly of all, it would be in her name, Maria Vasquez, her maiden name.

They hailed a taxi and made their way towards their new home that would soon be revealed to the girls. After a quick meal at McDonalds, Maria grabbed their hands and said, "Let's take a walk." The girls skipped along and sang, "Oh, Sing Sweet Nightingale" from *Cinderella*. All of a sudden, Maria stopped and said, "I have another surprise for you two. It's right up there" Maria pointed up to the window of their new apartment.

"What is it?" the girls begged.

"You'll have to follow me to see." They cheerfully followed their mother inside the building.

Christina yelled out first, "I want to push the button on the elevator!" They rode up to the 7th floor giggling all the way, and then cautiously entered the apartment with their eyes stretched wide.

"Hey, is this our furniture?" Elizabeth asked as they entered the living room.

"Yes, you are right. It is our furniture," Maria answered.

"Did we move?" Christina asked.

Maria bent down to meet their eyes, "Yes, we did!"

"But what about our room?" Christina said in a confused voice.

"It's right down that hall, the last door on the left." The girls ran as fast as they could to check it out. They reached the doorway and stopped.

"Wow!" they said in unison.

"It's has all of our stuff!" Christina announced.

"This room is bigger than our old room," Elizabeth noticed. They ran in screaming and began jumping up and down on their beds. They were so happy.

Maria clasped her hands together, looked up, and whispered, "God, give me strength." She walked in and told the girls to settle down. "Okay it's time for girl talk."

Elizabeth looked at Maria and said, "That means without Papi, right?"

"That's who we need to talk about." Maria sat down with the girls on the fluffy pink rug that lay in between the girl's twin beds. Maria braced herself for the sobs that would surely follow her announcement. "Girls, Papi won't be living here with us."

"What do you mean? Is he divorcing us like my friend Michelle's father did to her?" said Elizabeth with despair in her voice.

"No, Sweetie." Maria cleared her throat and took a deep breath. "Mami is divorcing Papi. He will always be your father. He just won't be my husband anymore."

"You mean he won't be here at night after we go to sleep?" Christina asked.

"No honey, I'm sorry, he won't." The girls looked at each other and started to scream as they reached over and hugged one another; then they hugged their mother. Maria was shocked, almost mortified, because their screams were filled with joy.

"Wait, wait! I said Papi wouldn't be here when you go to bed. He won't be living here with us at all."

"Thank you so much, Mami! This is the best surprise in the world," Elizabeth said.

Maria looked at them confused. "But, why would you say that?"

"Well, we're not supposed to tell, but I guess it's okay since Papi won't be living here with us anymore," Elizabeth whispered.

"Elizabeth, what are you talking about?"

"Papi told us not to tell or you would get really mad at us and leave us forever." The hair on the back of Maria's neck stood up on end.

"He asked you to keep a secret from me?" Maria asked searching for answers from both of her girls' eyes.

"Yes," they answered in unison.

"What was the secret?"

"He made us do it. We didn't want to do it," Elizabeth said with her head bowed in shame. Christina began to cry.

"Do what, Sweetie?" Maria said, raising both of their chin's with compassion.

"Mami, I'm sorry. He made us pull on his pee-pee," Elizabeth admitted.

"What!" Maria screamed. "You mean, down between his legs?" she whispered and pointed.

They nodded yes through their tears. Maria grabbed her girls, one in each arm, and rocked them as they cried together.

A million questions raced through Maria's mind. "How did this happen? When did this happen? Did he rape my niñas? What did he say to them? Where was I? Oh, my God how could I let this happen? Okay, okay, okay. I've got to calm down, reassure them, and get as much information as possible, so I can nail that son-of-a-bitch." She took a deep breath.

She had them kneel down in front of her, took their hands in hers, and looked them in their precious little eyes. "I love you both so much, more than anything in this entire world. I am so sorry that he made you do that. You will never, ever have to do that again!"

"Mami we're sorry we didn't tell you. We were scared," Christina said through her tears.

Maria raised their chins again and looked into their eyes and said,

"It is not your fault! Never, ever, ever be afraid to tell me anything, because I will always be here for you and love you no matter what.

"Okay, Mami," they said in unison.

"How many times did he make you," Maria paused, "touch him?"

"I don't know, Mami. Lots of times," Elizabeth answered.

"Do you remember when the last time was?"

"Yes. It was the night before you and Papi got in the car accident." It was all Maria could do to keep from screaming.

"Did he make you do anything else with him?" The girls looked at each other and said, "No."

"Did he touch either of you down there or anywhere else?"

The girls looked at each other again. Elizabeth spoke up,

"He would hold our hands to make us pull on his pee-pee harder and faster." Maria closed her swollen red, black-and-blue eyes and took a deep breath.

"Is that the only place he touched you, just on your hands?" The girls looked at each other again and said, "Yes." Maria breathed a little sigh of relief.

"Okay, this is what we are going to do. I want both of you to come in the bathroom with me, one at a time. I just want to take a quick look at both of you all over to make sure everything is okay. I want you to remember that it is not okay for anyone, I mean anyone, to look at or touch you up here," Maria pointed to their chests, "or down there," Maria pointed at their laps, "Except for Mommy or the doctor." They nodded their heads in agreement.

"Now, after I take a look at you both, I am going to take you both to the doctor for a little check-up. She is going to take a look at you from head to toe, but it's okay for her to look and touch you because Mommy will be right there with you. Okay?" They nodded their heads as they looked down at their hands. Maria lifted both of their chins up once again and met their eyes. "Girls, you didn't do anything wrong. I am just so thankful that you told me."

"Is Papi going to get in trouble now?" Elizabeth asked.

"Oh baby, don't you worry about a thing. Papi is going to get exactly what he needs; he will be just fine! Okay, Christina do you want to go first?"

"Okay, Mami."

91

"Elizabeth, you wait right here. We'll be back in just a minute." As Maria walked Christina to the bathroom, she made up her mind that she was going to prosecute José to the fullest extent of the law. Her next call after the pediatrician would be to the police.

Vanessa arrived at the restaurant a little after six that evening. She had a habit of always running fashionably late for everything. She headed for the bar and ordered a Sangrita. She took a long sip, tilted her head back, closed her eyes, and said,

"Where were you when I needed you last night?"

"At home with my wife, two point two kids, and the dog," Anne's voice answered.

"Vanessa cracked up as she turned to greet Anne with air kisses towards each cheek.

"Well, it sounds like you've been living a double life!" Vanessa commented.

"Yeah, and I need to get liquored up first to make sure I get all of the facts straight. Hey Bartender, give me one of these cute little drinks she has, but make mine a double."

"And speaking of double, you're talking my language." Monica interrupted.

"Hey Monica! I want you to meet my new friend, Anne."

"Pleased to meet you," Monica said as she extended her hand to shake Anne's and gave her a wink.

"Likewise, I'm sure," Anne said, while trying to sound formal like she had never spoken to Monica before.

"Hey Bartender, I'll have a double also. No, on second thought, super-size mine!" Monica ordered. They chuckled and settled in at the bar.

"So Vanessa, are you really okay about the breakup?" Monica inquired.

"I'm fine. It was a wake-up call and I'm thinking much more clearly, especially now that I have a Sangrita in my hand." They all smiled.

"Well, I'm glad you are all right and in good spirits. I didn't know what to think after I didn't hear from you. I thought maybe you had run off to Vegas to get married," Anne added.

"Yeah, right! I'm sorry I didn't respond sooner. I went out shopping yesterday after finishing up my pity party. Monica knows that shopping has always been the answer to my blues and I've got another maxed-out credit card to prove it."

"Hey, shopping is better than doing something mentally or physically destructive. You can always pay off your credit cards, but you can't get your mind back if you lose it or your life back if you take it," Anne added. They all agreed on her sobering point.

"Well, ladies, let's eat. I'm starving. I'll go see if our table is ready," said Vanessa.

"Yes, Ms. Baldwin, we have a table for you, however I'm sorry, but the private booth is not available. It was already reserved before you called in for a reservation this afternoon," the hostess explained.

"Oh, no problem," Vanessa responded.

"Please come this way."

Vanessa motioned to Monica and Anne at the bar to follow her. They were led to a window table with a view of the bustling street.

"Okay, time to come clean. What happened?" Anne said as she sat on the edge of her seat.

"Well, in a nutshell, this is how it went: I didn't receive a proposal, so I told him good riddance. He sent roses to my office and asked me to meet him for dinner, so I thought it was to propose, but I was wrong, dead wrong. It was an ambush, a bait and switch tactic. Would you believe he had the audacity to say he wanted us to get back together, as well as see other people! And Monica, before you say, '*I told you so...*'"

"Me? Oh, I would never say that," Monica said sarcastically as she raised her glass to her lips, leaned back, and took a sip with a sly grin on her face.

"I know, I know, I should have started playing the field a long, long time ago. I couldn't get him to fully commit to me, so I should have started dating other guys. But that's all water under the bridge now. He really threw me for a loop, so I just broke it off all together, again. This time forever!"

"You know, you should have agreed with his request to see other women and then just used him for

94

sex," Monica exclaimed. "If it's good, why throw it away?"

"Vanessa, I agree with Monica. Why shouldn't we use men? They use us all the time."

"What? Anne, I can't believe I'm hearing this coming from you. I figured you would have said, '*you should have dropped his ass after the first six months if he didn't want to commit*,'" Vanessa countered.

"Yes, I agree with that, but only if the sex isn't any good. If the sex is good, you'd better hold on for dear life until you find something better in your travels," Anne explained with a reminiscent smile.

"Hummm, sounds like someone got her groove back while on vacation," Vanessa offered as they cracked up.

"Look, men have a woman for every need: one to have sex with, one to have freaky sex with, one to cook and clean, one that gives good massages, the list goes on and on. Why shouldn't we have the same luxury? We should have one to have sex with, one to give us oral sex, one to buy us gifts, one that gives good foot rubs, one to discuss our man problems with, and one to get good fashion advice from. Of course the last two are gay," Monica said as they all cackled.

"Monica has a good point," Anne agreed.

"I guess instead of holding out for Mr. Right, we need to be dating a plethora of Mr. Right Now's," Vanessa said as they all clinked their glasses.

"Here's to Mr. Right Here, and Right Now!" Monica said as she pointed to her lap."

They laughed so hard their eyes began to tear, as they drank a lot and ate very little, well into the night.

The key slowly turned in the lock as José opened the door to the apartment. It was pitch-black inside. All he could see was his shadow projected across the floor from the light in the hallway. He moved toward the kitchen from the foyer flipping the light switch on as he made his way, but nothing happened. It remained dark. He knew that the electricity was on because he heard the hum of the refrigerator. He stumbled over the leg of a kitchen chair and felt around until he found the button to turn on the exhaust hood light above the stove top. The light didn't come on. He pulled the door of the refrigerator open. He was only met with coolness; no light came on from within. Finally, he pulled a lighter from his pocket, flicked it, and held it up to examine the light fixture above the table. All of the light bulbs were missing. He opened the door to the oven, but the light didn't come on. He opened the freezer and was met with darkness. The freezer was empty and the only thing in the refrigerator was one, lonely bottle of insulin; José was a diabetic.

He made his way through the dark apartment only to discover that all of the furniture was gone. The girl's room had been stripped of its contents; only the bright pink walls remained. The only things left in the master bedroom were the king-sized bed, his belongings, and Maria's lingerie on the bed. He made his way back to the living room; a cold chill ran down his spine as he stood staring at the dangling cable wires that were once attached to a flat screen television that hung on the living room wall. He went back to the kitchen and sat down heavily at his place at the head of the table. It was then that he noticed the items that Maria had left behind; the apartment and car keys, the brideless cake topper, the headless wedding photos, and the lone champagne glass that simply read, 'Groom.' He hung his head in silence with the darkness looming all around him.

Then all of a sudden, a loud crash echoed through the apartment as José rammed his two clenched fists through the wooden table. It cracked in half, right down the middle, and the items it contained flew in all directions. He stormed out of the apartment in a rage, slamming the door behind him without even locking it. What was the point? There was nothing left to protect anymore. His family was gone; his life was gone. José jumped in the minivan and headed for a dark, smoky bar, some place where nobody knew his name.

Maria, Elizabeth, and Christina had experienced an emotional roller coaster ride that day.

Feelings of freedom, joy, apprehension, heartache, grief, and relief had passed through them. The girls had been checked, poked, and prodded by medical personnel all evening. They had also given individual statements to the police. When they finally arrived home, their new home, they were exhausted, but elated to be together without the threat of the boogieman, José. Although their mental and emotional innocence had been stripped and stolen from them, Maria was relived to find out that Elizabeth and Christina were still virgins, physically.

Maria held them tight, one on each side, as they lay in her arms in the comfort and security of her new queen-size bed. As she read them their favorite story, *The Cat in the Hat*, they drifted off to sleep. Maria swept the hair back from their faces and kissed their foreheads while she said a prayer of thanks. Tears streamed down her face like raindrops onto the pages written by Dr. Seuss. She knew that she had failed to be the kind of mother her girls deserved; one who would and could protect them. She had loved and feared José too deeply to see clearly, and cared too much about what others would think if she left him. So, she stayed, and she tried too hard to love a man who didn't love himself.

During their marriage, Maria had stopped being who she knew herself to be, in order to please José. She had stopped loving herself and began loathing the person she had become. She had taken too much for too long and vowed to God, herself, and her sleeping angels that she would return to her former self: a woman with dignity, grace, and pride.

Maria would never let any man use and abuse her or her girls ever again.

"Ring!" A loud bell sounded to signal the beginning of the round. José came out fighting like a champ. It was round three and he had already put a nasty cut over the eye of his opponent. He would go in for the kill in this round. He began to smile with confidence through his mouth piece as he danced around the ring throwing soft jabs at his opponent's good eye. José was arrogant enough to drop his guard and simply duck punches that were thrown at him. He was waiting for just the right moment to throw all of his power and might into a left uppercut, right-cross combination. It would assure him another knockout to add to his record. He danced, bobbed, and weaved until the right moment arrived. Just as he was about to attain his victory, his jaw snapped and his right eye went dim. The boxing ring began to rotate. His head hit the mat and bounced several times as sweat and saliva sprayed in every direction. The referee began the count as his fist pounded the mat: One, two, three, four, five, six, seven, eight, nine, "Noooooooooooo!"

José screamed as he bolted upright on his urine soaked bed, waking from a dream that had once been a reality. A loud knock came from the door. José struggled to stand and staggered to the bedroom door.

"Who is it?" he shouted with a drunken slur.

"Mr. Cabrera, this is NYPD. If you don't open this door immediately, we'll break it down!" José tried to shake the drunkenness from his head. "I'm coming!" he said in an annoyed tone as he stumbled through the pitch-black apartment in his soggy shorts. He unlocked and opened the door, shielding his eyes from the light streaming in from the hallway. Two of New York's finest were waiting with their shields displayed and their hands on their weapons.

"What the hell is going on?" José shouted.

"José Cabrera?"

"Yeah?"

"Hey, didn't you used to be a boxer? I think I saw one of your fights in Atlantic City," said the younger of the two cops.

"I know you didn't knock on my door to ask me that! What the hell is going on?"

The older officer cleared his throat and said, "Ah sir, we have a warrant for your arrest." They entered the foyer and drew their flashlights. José's bloodshot eyes were wide with shock as he backed up.

"For what?"

"You name it… sodomy, child molestation, child endangerment, rape, assault and battery, the list goes on and on," the officer said as he waved the warrant in José's face. José stared blankly into the officer's flashlight as if in a trance. This was the sobering moment he had been waiting for. He always knew it would come eventually. The young officer took out his handcuffs and began administering Miranda rights. José interrupted and asked in a monotone voice, "Can I put some clothes on?"

The two officers looked at each other and shrugged. "Make it quick." The young officer escorted him, while the older remained behind.

As they made their way to the bedroom, José began to have flashbacks of kneeling in his white, altar boy vestment while lifting the Father's regal robe as commanded. He remembered the sounds vividly because he always kept his eyes shut so tightly; he would not dare to look upon the flesh of a holy man of God. He remembered the touch of the cross on his forehead as it dangled from the Father's neck. He remembered the tight grasp of the Father's hands around his head. He remembered the cracking of the Father's knees as he thrust himself back and forth. He remembered the taste of the holy water when it came forth as the Father called out, "Mary, Mother of God!"

The older officer began to radio in his report. José pulled on a pair of jeans that lay on the floor next to the bed. The young officer said, "Remove the belt. You won't need that where you're going." José took the belt off and threw it onto the bed. He then reached for a white dress shirt hanging in the closet with his right hand and a forty-five millimeter handgun with his left.

The older officer finished his report with a ten-four as he heard a single shot ring out from the bedroom. He immediately drew his weapon and shouted in his radio, "Code 421, shots fired, possible officer down!" He then shouted out his partner's name.

"I'm all right," the young officer answered in a weak and trembling voice. The older officer ran through the dark to the bedroom and discovered his partner standing with his gun drawn and his flashlight shining down. There on the closet floor he found José with half of his face missing. It had been rearranged all over the white shirt José still clung to in his right hand, while his left hand had a death grip on the gun.

The ladies ended their night with Anne telling her story about the married man she had all but thrown her panties at earlier that day in the office. They all laughed hysterically as they downed their last Sangrita.

"Well girls," Monica said with a slur, "I hate to be a party pooper, but I need to get home at a respectable hour and in a respectable condition. You know I'm a mother and all."

They all burst out laughing as they rose and grabbed their Ricky bags.

"Well honey, I hate to be the bearer of bad news, but it's after midnight," Vanessa said, "and the only things open after twelve are bars and legs, and believe me, there is no respect in the morning." They cackled as they slowly swerved their way out the door to grab two cabs: Vanessa and Anne in one and Monica in the other. They said their good-byes and zoomed off in opposite directions.

The taxi dropped Vanessa off first and waited while she stumbled her way to the door of her building. She waved good-bye to Anne through the glass door once she was safe inside with the doorman. On the way up in the elevator, her head began to spin as she climbed higher and higher. Vanessa pulled a pair of Fendi sunglasses from her bag to shield her eyes from the bright hall lights as the elevator doors opened on the 13th floor. She felt her way along the chair rail to her penthouse apartment and said aloud, "Thank goodness my door is close to the elevator."

She unlocked the door, stepped inside and let her coat, bag, and keys fall to the floor in the foyer. She locked the door behind her, dragged herself to the bedroom, and stood in the middle of the darkness undressing with her eyes shut as she let everything fall to the floor. Normally, everything would have been thrown across the already overloaded slipper chair in the corner, but she was too drunk and too tired to expend the energy to throw anything. She crawled up on top of her rumpled, mound of bed covers and wrapped her grandmother's quilt around her. She was fast asleep before her head hit the pillow, still wearing her sunglasses.

Anne arrived home shortly after dropping off Vanessa. She was in better condition than her two new friends were; Anne knew how to hold her liquor. She made her way up to her penthouse apartment and logged onto her laptop immediately. As usual, she wanted to see how the markets around the world had performed that day. She placed her black patent leather Ralph Lauren pumps in an empty slot on the shelf of her shoe closet and threw her nylon stockings in the wastebasket next to her vanity; she never wore them more than once. She meticulously folded her clothes and placed them in a canvas-lined, wooden hamper labeled 'cleaners' and placed her bra, panties, garter belt, and camisole in another hamper labeled 'delicates.' She grabbed something from her top left vanity drawer and stepped into the shower. For the next twenty minutes, the steam hugged her body as multiple showerheads drenched her from every direction from breasts to thighs. The only audible sounds were from her moans of titillation and pleasure as her surrogate man worked its magic.

The bell on the elevator rang and Monica stepped off. She gingerly made her way towards her penthouse apartment, using the wall to steady herself. She stopped abruptly at Mrs. Florence's apartment and checked the time on her Movado. "Shoot! She already hates me," Monica whispered to herself as she rang the doorbell. The door swung open within five seconds. Mrs. Florence stood there with her hands on her hips and an annoyed look on her face. Monica began to stutter an apology about the lateness of the hour while looking down at her hands. Mrs. Florence cut her off and said in a low and serious voice,

"You're drunk! Come back and get Lizzy in the morning." Then she slammed the door in Monica's face.

Monica hunched her shoulders as if to say, "Oh well" and stumbled down the hall to her door. Monica was used to being reprimanded by Mrs. Florence because she had been her nanny while she was growing up. Now she was Lizzy's nanny. Mrs. Florence adored Lizzy as she once had adored Monica. When Monica became pregnant, Jeff, Monica's husband, bought them an apartment, as well as the apartment next-door. They allowed Mrs. Florence to stay in the apartment rent-free for as long as she took care of Lizzy. She had been a part of Monica's life, for all of her life and they wanted her to be a part of Lizzy's life as well. Jeff's time had been cut short; he was killed a year earlier. That's when Monica's relationship with Mrs. Florence began to sour.

When Monica was in high school, her mother died from breast cancer, therefore, Mrs. Florence knew Monica better than anyone, even better than her own mother. Mrs. Florence had practically raised Monica and her younger brother. Mrs. Florence's husband died just before Monica found out she was pregnant with Lizzy. Jeff and Monica rescued Mrs. Florence from her sorrow with the anticipation of Lizzy's birth. Monica's pregnancy gave Mrs. Florence a new hope, a new focus, and something to live for. Monica had the utmost respect for her and knew Lizzy was being well taken care of.

Monica also knew that Mrs. Florence had a special place in her heart for Jeff, because whenever Monica went out on a date or brought a man home, Mrs. Florence would give her disapproving looks and comments. She felt that if a widow had the means to support herself and her family, she should remain unmarried and devote her life to her children. Monica was born with means, more than she could ever spend in a lifetime, but she chose to work and date. Monica knew her nanny didn't approve of her lifestyle, but the men were just diversions, an escape from the secrets and bitter memories of her past. However, unbeknownst to Monica, there were no secrets that Mrs. Florence didn't already know about. Mrs. Florence knew all the secrets of Monica's childhood, marriage, widowhood, and even some that Monica didn't know.

CHAPTER

6

It was 3:00 a.m. by the time Anne mustered up enough energy to get out of bed, after expending it all in the steam shower. She emerged from her stark, white silk sheets and pulled on a cashmere robe as she headed for the living room. She checked the overseas stock markets and the outlook for the U.S. Markets. After some deep thought and a few deep breaths, she picked up the phone and dialed a Hong Kong number as she strolled over to her chaise lounge. Anne gazed out at the view of the city through the floor to ceiling windows. A male voice answered and said, "Hello?" in Chinese. Anne was shocked. She hadn't expected her father to be home in the middle of the afternoon. She didn't respond to his salutation. After a few seconds of silence, her mother answered in Chinese as well.

"Hello?"

"Hi Mother!" Anne responded in English.

"Oh Darling, it's so good to hear your voice," she returned in English. "Where are you?"

"In New York. I just bought a place here. It's across the park from yours."

"Anne, you didn't have to do that. You could have moved into the Stanhope. It's been empty since the end of August. Our friends only stayed there for the summer."

"I know. I thought about it, but decided that five bedrooms was a bit too much space for me. Besides, I really wanted to have a place of my own."

"Well, I am certain it is a good investment."

"Exactly. I'll email you my new address and phone number."

"How's your new job?"

"Okay, just working on the merger; it's been pretty smooth so far."

"So, have you met anyone since you've been in New York?"

"Of course. I've met a lot of new people."

"You know what I mean."

"No, not really. There was one prospect, but he turned out to be married."

"Oh well. I'm sure in a city that large and diverse you will meet some really nice, well-educated, Chinese men, of course. In fact, a couple of my friends at the club have sons living and working in New York. Perhaps I can inquire and..."

"Mother, please don't. You know it would be a waste of your time."

"Oh, don't say that! You just have to give someone a chance!"

Anne desperately needed to change the subject before tempers began to flare.

"How's the firm?"

"Just fine; profitable as ever. Your father just added two new partners. Hopefully, that will allow him to spend more time at home and on the golf course. You'll be surprised to hear that he's been hinting about retiring."

"What? I don't believe it! I didn't think anyone or anything could tear him away from the firm. It's in his blood. When he gets cut during his morning shave, he bleeds jurisprudence." Anne's mother laughed in a soft and controlled manner.

"I don't know what has come over him lately, but he's been taking me out to more than just the obligatory social engagements. He even took the afternoon off today to spend it at home with me, just the two of us. He even gave the servants the afternoon and evening off."

Anne was in shock; she couldn't speak.

"Also, he wants to take a month-long vacation this winter, and he even plans on spending one of the weeks in New York. He hasn't been to New York with me since the late nineties. And most surprisingly of all," Anne's mother said in a hushed voice, "he asked if I thought you would agree to get together for dinner while we are in New York?"

"What?" Anne bolted upright from the chaise and began pacing. "I don't believe it!" She had fury in her voice

"It's true!"

"Mother, is this another one of your little ploys to get me to talk to him? Because if it is, it's not going to work."

109

"No, I am telling you the truth. I was as shocked as you are."

There was a pregnant pause, and then Anne spoke.

"Mother, I've got to go. It's late."

"Oh, okay. Please don't forget to email me your contact information."

"I won't forget. I love you. Good-bye."

As usual, Anne hesitated before she hung up to let her mother hang up first. To her surprise, she heard a second click after her mother hung up. Her father had been listening. She finally hung up, but couldn't move. She was in shock. In all the years she had wanted to hear the second click, it had never happened. Now that it had, she stood frozen with fear, for her father had never, ever listened to a word she had said in her entire life. Anne didn't know what to think of it or his peculiar behavior that her mother spoke of.

She knew she needed an emergency visit with her therapist. She called his answering service and left an urgent message for him to call her back. Her heart was pounding so hard she could hear it in her ears. She began to break out in a cold sweat as she made her way towards the bedroom. She climbed into bed and balled up in the fetal position, cradling the phone as she waited for the return call in the darkness.

After fifteen minutes, which seemed like an eternity, the phone rang.

"Hello, Dr. Porter?"

"This is Dr. Porter. How may I assist you?"

"Dr. Porter. I'm so sorry to disturb you at such an early hour, but I need to see you."

"Are you all right?"

"No. I, I don't know?" Anne began to cry.

"Did something happen?"

"Yes, and it scares me."

"Are you having thoughts of hurting yourself?"

"No, no nothing like that."

"Do you think you can cope on your own until later this morning?"

"Yes, I believe so. Just hearing your voice makes me feel a lot better."

"Good; I'll see you in my office at nine-thirty sharp."

"I'll be there. Thank you so much."

"Try some deep breathing exercises to relax. Hopefully, that will help you to get some rest. We'll talk in a few hours."

"Okay. Good-bye Dr. Porter, and thanks again."

Anne sighed as she hung up the phone and began taking some deep breaths. When she felt her anxiety diminish a bit, she snuggled with a body pillow underneath her white down-filled comforter.

She continued her breathing exercises to slow her heart rate and ease her mind until daylight, for no sleep came to provide her any peace.

Maria had gotten up early that morning to do some more unpacking in her kitchen while her girls continued to sleep soundly in her bed. She returned to her room and stood, looking down over them, smiling. They looked like two angels sleeping in a cloud.

"Good morning, my Princesses!" Maria sang out sweetly.

"Good morning Mami," Maria's girls said in unison while rubbing their sleepy, little eyes.

"I've got more surprises for you two today." Their eyes popped wide open. "We're going to IHOP for strawberry pancakes this morning. And, no school today!"

The girls erupted with squeals of joy as they hopped up and down on the bed.

"Okay, okay settle down. We've got a lot of things to accomplish today, so go brush your teeth and wash your pretty faces. I've already laid your clothes out on your beds."

The girls raced off to the bathroom to get their day of adventure started. Maria had made an appointment with a therapist that their pediatrician had recommended. She wanted to get the girls into counseling as soon as possible in hopes of minimizing any possible long-term psychological effects from the molestation by their father. She also contacted an attorney to represent her and the girls in a civil case against José. She was going to see to it that he paid for everything that he had done to her and the girls. And she wouldn't rest until he was behind bars for a very, very long time and penniless.

As she watched the girls devour their strawberry pancakes, she smiled and said a little prayer thanking God for providing them with a safe, new home where the only hands her girls would feel at night, would be their mother's as she tucked in the covers they kicked off in their sleep.

Maria sat lost in thought as she sipped her coffee and imagined what could have been if her girls had not still been virgins. She would have seduced José. And just before he was ready to enter, she would have pulled a knife from under her pillow, decapitated his penis, and watched him wallow in his own blood. While he experienced the excruciating pain, she would have explained to him that the pain he was feeling did not compare to the pain he had inflicted on her and her girls. And when he would have tried to speak, she would have silenced him with a knife through his throat, and finally, stabbed him through his heart. He would have been found with his penis protruding from his mouth.

Maria was glad that she didn't have to follow-through with that drama: not because of the violent act of murder, not because of the certain death sentence, but because she couldn't stomach the idea of seducing José.

Monica dragged herself into work by nine, which was truly a feat for her considering how drunk she had been the night before. She had a brief opportunity to say good morning to Lizzy at Mrs. Florence's apartment before she left for work. As usual, she received a look of disapproval from the Mrs. Florence and felt the claws of guilt rip at her soul. She needed a diversion to ease her conscience, so she picked up the phone.

"Hello?"

"Hi Steve, it's me!"

"Oh, hi! Is it burning?"

"Oh, it's hot, real hot!" Monica said with a devilish grin. She loved it when he made references to his profession as a firefighter. "So, got any fires to put out on Saturday afternoon?"

"Just yours!" Steve answered eagerly.

"That's just what I wanted to hear. I'll expect you at one."

"I'll be there with lights and sirens blazing!"

"Ciao!"

As Monica hung up the phone, she realized that she knew every inch of Steve's body, from the mole on the right side of his neck to the scar that ran along the left side of his foot. However, she knew nothing of his background, where he was from, or even how old he was. Ten years ago, when Monica was single and childless, she would have never called a man up for an afternoon of luxurious sex. But a lot can happen in ten years: a lot of heartache, betrayal, and grief caused her to do and say things that she never would have thought she would do or say. Everyone has their own type of pain reliever: Ben & Jerry's, golf, poker, work, prescription drugs, illegal drugs, shopping, or shoplifting. Her pain relievers were sex and alcohol. She had suffered some of the greatest losses of her life: her self-esteem and her self-worth. She used sex as a way to seek restitution for her betrayed and broken heart, and alcohol to numb the pain. They weren't the cure-all, but they helped to transport her away from the memories that haunted her.

Her next phone call was to Lizzy's paternal grandparents; she arranged for Lizzy to spend Saturday afternoon with them. Monica had overtaxed Mrs. Florence enough for the week and knew better than to ask her to keep Lizzy on the weekend. Monica knew she was being self-indulgent, but she felt compelled to satisfy the addictions that helped her cope with her unfinished business. After a Saturday afternoon of sexcapades with Steve, she would be ready to spend Saturday evening and all day Sunday with Lizzy. She would be able to focus and give Lizzy what she needed: her undivided attention.

Vanessa sipped a cup of coffee as she tried to concentrate on the reports spread out across her desk.

The sales figures she pored over seemed to jump from the pages and dance a jig on her desk. She looked, and felt like, death warmed over. She'd woken up late and was in such a hurry to get ready that she'd forgot to apply her hair mascara to hide the gray around the edges. She discovered her oversight in the car on the way to work while she was applying her makeup, so she used her eye mascara as a substitute. She made a mental note to buy an extra hair mascara to carry in her makeup bag for emergencies.

Vanessa was so glad that all of her meetings that day were conference calls. She couldn't bear the thought of having to sit in a meeting face to face with anyone. She just wanted to sip coffee, take Aleve, and keep her feet up on her desk for the rest of the day. Just then her phone rang, but she let Francine pick it up; Vanessa didn't want to take any unnecessary phone calls. Her intercom buzzed; she picked up.

"I know you didn't want to be disturbed, but I thought you would like to take this one. It's Mr. Patton."

"Who?"

"Mr. Patton of Dave's Place."

"Oh, Dave! Thanks Francine, I'll take it," Vanessa said with a puzzled look on her face.

"Vanessa Baldwin," she answered with uncertainty in her voice, wondering why he would be calling her.

"Hello, Ms. Baldwin. This is Dave Patton from Dave's place."

"Hello, Dave. This is a bit of a surprise," Vanessa said with a cautious tone.

"I apologize for calling you at work, but I don't have your cell phone number. This is the number you usually give us when making reservations."

"Oh, okay..." Vanessa said still waiting for an explanation for the call.

"You left your scarf in the booth at my restaurant. I discovered it as Damon was leaving, but I assumed you didn't want me give it to him for the purpose of returning it to you."

Vanessa smiled a broad smile. "Yes! You assumed correctly. Thank you, Dave. I'll stop by after work to pick it up on my way home tonight."

"Are you okay? You looked extremely upset when you ran out of the restaurant the other night."

"Oh, I'm fine, really. Thanks for asking. I'll see you later this evening. In fact, I might as well have dinner while I'm there. Would you put me down for a six o'clock reservation; I'll be dining alone."

"Sure thing," Dave said with a hint of excitement in his voice.

"Thanks again for tracking me down, Dave. That was awfully sweet of you!"

"No problem. I'll see you tonight at six," Dave responded, trying to sound all business, but feeling a little pleasure.

"Bye!"

Vanessa smiled as she hung up the phone and thought about how nice it was to know that there were still some real gentlemen left in the world. The only problem is that they are all married. She refocused on the task at hand and returned to the dancing figures on her desk.

Anne sat in Dr. Porter's office nervously picking at her cuticles while Sara looked on.

"He should be here any minute," Sara explained.

"Oh, I'm a little early. I don't mind waiting."

Just then Dr. Porter walked in and smiled at Anne. "Hello Anne. I'll be with you in just a moment."

Anne watched his gate as he moved towards Sara's desk with his briefcase and keys in hand. Suddenly, Anne felt flushed and broke her eyes from the gaze she had on him. The last time she saw him he had on a business suit and tie, but not today. He wore beautifully tailored charcoal gray slacks with a crisp white dress shirt open at the neck and a handsome black and gray tweed sport coat. His shoulders seemed as broad as the South China Sea. She knew he was attractive, but he was more handsome than she had realized. She put on a serious face and tried not to stare as they exchanged greetings when he welcomed her into his office. As Anne contemplated where to sit, chaise or chair, she did a quick finger check: no ring, no tan line. She stifled a smile. All of a sudden her crisis didn't seem so urgent. However, she was glad she had come to see him while he sported his sexy, business casual look.

Anne settled on the chaise because she had on a cute little pleated skirt and she wanted Dr. Porter to get a full view of her long, lean legs.

"Anne, you seemed very distraught when I spoke with you earlier this morning. How are you feeling now?"

She thought to herself as she crossed her legs, *I feel like doing you right now, right here on this chaise.* However, she responded, "Oh, I'm feeling much better now that I've had time to get over the shock and clear my head. Needless to say, I haven't had any sleep."

"Would you like to talk about the event that shocked you?"

"Sure. I called my mother and she told me that my father asked her if she thought I would have dinner with them when they come to New York to visit this winter. And he eavesdropped on our conversation. He even mentioned to my mother that he was thinking about retiring! But he built his law firm from the ground up and has always said that the last moments of his life would be billable. He's even spending more leisure time with my mother now! I just don't know what to think of this dramatic shift in his behavior. All my life he has been distant to the point of being absent while present, and now all of sudden he's changing. I don't know how to react. Should I be glad, angry, or indifferent – I don't know? But what I do know is his attitude shift really scares me."

"What are your theories for his change in behavior?"

"Good question! I really don't know? I guess it could be any number of things. Perhaps he finally realized after all these years that he has been a terrible father, or his mistress threatened to tell my mother about their affair and he is trying to butter my mother up before she finds out. I just don't know? I'm grasping at straws here."

"Do you know for a fact that your father has a mistress or are you just speculating?"

"It's just speculation."

"I see. Well, I can tell you one thing for sure. Major behavioral changes similar to what you've described are usually brought on by guilt."

"Guilt? He's never felt guilty before. Why now?"

"Well, no matter what the catalyst was, the outcome produced guilt, which in turn promoted a change in quote/unquote normal behavior. It could have been an affair, but it could have been something else as simple as a fender bender. Whatever it was, it appears that it made him do some soul searching."

"Hmmm, now I am dying to know what the catalyst was."

"You may never find out, but what you do need to know is how you will respond to him if he wants to begin to build a relationship between the two of you. However, you should not get your hopes up, because this change in him may be temporary. He may revert back to his usual behavior tomorrow. His inquiry about you may be just that, and his talk of retiring may be just talk."

Anne flew off the chaise with the pleats in her little skirt circling her legs at mid-thigh. With fire in her eyes, fury in her heart, and hands on her hips she yelled, "If he thinks for one minute that I am going to just throw away all of my resentment towards him that has been building up and hardening my heart for my whole life, he's got another damn thing coming!"

Dr. Porter tried to stifle a chuckle, but was unsuccessful. Anne's mouth fell open with disbelief as she crossed her arms over her chest and said," Okay, that was completely unprofessional of you to laugh."

Dr. Porter removed his glasses, looked her right in her eyes and said, "Anne, you have to admit, what you said was pretty amusing." Her serious look turned into a giggle as she flopped down on the chaise - her skirt instantly becoming a parachute.

"You're right. That did sound a little silly, didn't it?" she laughed even harder.

Dr. Porter composed himself. "Anne, you have a valid point and the way you feel is natural. So much of your life has been spent trying to get approval from him. You even went so far as to go to law school and became an attorney so that he would hire you on at his firm, but he refused."

Anne interrupted, "Yeah, who the hell does he think he is? It's his damn fault that I'm so screwed up! He is the reason it took me so long to speak. I left China to attend Julliard and I never went back, not even for a visit. And I hate Chinese men; I won't date one or marry one. I think I'm slowly killing my mother; she really wants me to marry a Chinese guy.

And the chances of me marrying an American are slim to none. The only guys that want to date me are either looking for some action outside of their marriage or think I will do some freaky shit in the bedroom because I'm Asian. No one is interested in my mind, my capabilities, or my loving spirit. No one is interested in just me." Anne paused to gain some courage. "I know what you're thinking, *with a foul mouth like that, how can she have a loving spirit?* I know it is hard to believe, but I do, I really do." Anne pleaded with tears in her eyes. "Hey, wait a minute! How did we get on the subject of me? We're supposed to be talking about my father. That asshole!"

"Anne, does it make you feel good to call your father names?"

"You know, it does. It really does! All my life I've talked to shrinks. Oh, sorry. I didn't mean to show disrespect towards your profession."

"None taken."

"I've talked to psychologists about my life growing up, but I've never been able to express my anger, my hurt, my feelings of abandonment, my longing, my insecurities, my desperation and utter anguish." Anne paused for what seemed like forever. It was as if someone had stolen her voice. Finally, she managed to speak again as tears continued to stream down her cheeks. "This is the first time in all my years of therapy that I've been able to truly vent my feelings and shed tears. I've never told anyone, not even my mother, why I don't speak to my father."

She looked up and met Dr. Porter's eyes. He was by her side in an instant with a box of tissues in hand. She blotted her tears and blew her nose. Anne looked up into Dr. Porter's concerned eyes.

"My father never held me or spoke to me as a baby. When I was a little girl, I would frequently go over to him to try and get his attention. When my mother was in the room, he would just get up and walk out, but when my mother wasn't in the room he would push me away, sometimes even pushing me down without saying a word to me."

"Anne, I'm so sorry you had to experience that. I'm also sorry that our time is up," Dr. Porter said with regret in his voice.

"Oh, can I stay an additional thirty minutes?"

"I wish I could accommodate you. I'm sorry Anne, but I have another appointment."

"Okay, well I have another appointment to see you on Tuesday anyway."

"Anne, I'm sorry. I'm going to have to cancel our Tuesday appointment."

"Cancel? Why?"

"Anne, I need to refer you to another psychologist, one of my colleagues. I don't think I can assist you any further."

"But, but Dr. Porter, I just made a major breakthrough. It was because of you. No one else has been able to get me to this point, ever!" Anne pleaded.

"Anne, it wasn't me. It was you. This just happened to be the right time and the right circumstances. You are definitely going in the right direction. Hanging onto all of these feelings without expressing them all of these years has been slowly chipping away at your ability to love and to be loved. That's why you have insomnia and you always feel the need to be so busy. That's why you're obsessive and compulsive about certain things."

"But, Dr. Porter," Anne said practically begging, "I need you!"

"Anne, I think it is in your best interest to see one of my colleagues. He is equipped to assist you further in your progression. I will have Dr. Felder's assistant call you to set up an appointment." Dr. Porter paused to collect his thoughts. "Before you go, I want to point out to you that you are who you are, in some very positive ways, because of your father's abuse. You excelled in music and became an accomplished violinist, graduated at the top of your class from law school, and became a successful attorney all because you were seeking recognition from your father. Although he failed to acknowledge you, you still prevailed and became a beautiful, smart, talented woman. You are a survivor!"

"Well, thank you," Anne said blushing through her tear stained cheeks. "You know, I, I guess I've never thought of my circumstances from that angle. I guess I am a survivor. I don't know what to say except thank you so much for the time we've spent together and for all of your help," She said as she put her hand on Dr. Porter's. "I just wish you could continue to see me, but I understand if you feel like you're in uncharted territory. I appreciate you being open and honest with me and putting my needs first."

Anne stood and extended her hand to Dr. Porter. They shook hands, looked each other in the eyes, smiled at one another, and then Anne exited through the back door. As she rode the elevator down, she felt lighter in spirit as though a weight had been lifted from her shoulders. She felt a calm and contentment that she had never felt before.

Dr. Porter took a few moments to collect himself in the washroom located next to his office. He returned and asked Sara to send in his next patient. Maria and her two girls were ushered into his office.

Anne smiled all the way home in the taxi, gave the driver a big tip, and even winked at her doorman. When she reached her apartment, she stripped and slipped into some white silk pajamas. She began the process of folding her clothes to put them in their prospective hampers and then she stopped. She threw the clothes down on the upholstered bench in her dressing room, left her shoes in the middle of the floor, took off running, and dived into her bed. She snuggled under the down comforter, lay back with her fingers laced behind her head, looked up at the vaulted ceiling and whispered with a giggle, "I'm free!" Suddenly Anne felt exhausted. She rarely got more than four hours of sleep at night and never, ever took naps; however, she turned over and slept like a baby for the rest of the entire day.

After a long morning with the psychologist, Maria and the girls were emotionally drained. Dr.

Porter listened as Maria walked him through the years of abuse she suffered at the hands of José, as well as the trauma she suffered as a child seeing her father repeatedly beating her mother. Maria also assisted the girls with walking through their molestation experiences, but Dr. Porter was unable to determine exactly how long José had been abusing them. Perhaps in time, and with more sessions, he would be able to construct a more detailed timeline.

Maria decided they needed a diversion, so they jumped on the train and went out to Coney Island. They went to Nathan's for hotdogs and sat out on the boardwalk to enjoy the sunshine of the unusually warm fall day. The girls chatted about Barbies, nail polish, and what color earrings they wanted to wear when their mother finally felt they were old enough to get their ears pierced. They also visited the New York Aquarium and ate pink and blue cotton candy as they skipped and hopped along the way.

Evening was drawing near so they caught the train back toward the city. While Maria sat in deep thought about the new direction her life had taken, the girls chatted about how much they loved their new room and how much they missed their friends. They were both a bit shy, so they were worried about the new school and making new friends. Maria assured them that they were talented, smart, and beautiful girls and that all of the kids would want to be their friends. They seemed satisfied with her words of encouragement and began drifting off to sleep as the train rocked them in their mother's embrace.

Maria enjoyed the beautiful skyline from the train as the sun set over Manhattan. The lights began to twinkle as darkness fell. As she rode along she noticed how empty the skyline looked without the twin towers. She reflected on where she could have been when the airplanes hit. She remembered how close she had come to being in Tower One that day. Maria had called her client and left a message in the wee hours of that morning to say that she needed to cancel the meeting they were supposed to have at 9:00 a.m., and that she needed to reschedule for the following week. Just then her cell phone rang, breaking her reminiscent thoughts. She fumbled through her Ricky bag until she found it.

"Hello?"

"Is this Mrs. José Cabrera?"

"Who is this?"

"This is NYPD Ma'am. Are you Maria Cabrera?"

"Yes, I am," Maria said rolling her eyes.

"We need you to come down to the precinct."

"What for? My lawyer is handling the filing of the charges against my husband."

"Ah, Ma'am, there's been an incident involving your husband and you need to come down to the precinct."

"Look, if he's been picked up for another DWI, I am not bailing him out again. Leave him in lock-up. It's over between us and I've taken my kids and moved out already."

"Ah, Ma'am, he's not technically under arrest."

"Then why are you calling me? I am not coming down there."

"Well, Ma'am..."

"Would you please stop calling me Ma'am!"

"Ah, sorry Ma… ah, Mrs., ah, Ms. Cabrera. I've tried to spare you this over the phone, but I regret to inform you that your hus... ah, Mr. Cabrera is dead."

"What did you say?" Maria said in a low whisper.

"Ma... ah, he committed suicide in front of one of our officers when he was being picked up on a warrant."

There was a long silence. Finally, Maria said in an expressionless voice, "Thank you for the information, but I won't be coming down to the precinct. You might want to call his mother, Rosita Cabrera. I'm sure you have the resources to find her phone number since you were able to find mine."

With that, Maria hung up and turned her cell phone off. She laid her head back and relaxed as she had been doing before the call came. Her body felt numb, not from the crisp fall evening air, but from the indifference she felt about the news of José's death. Her thoughts jumped back to 9/11 and tears began to stream down her face with a shocking realization. If José had not beat her on September 10, 2001, she would have gone to that meeting in Tower One on the eleventh and been murdered. She would have left this world on that day with the child she was carrying and left her first-born daughter in the hands of a molesting father. She hugged her two girls closer as they slept oblivious to it all, and she whispered to herself, "All things happen for a reason. Now, I'm truly free."

"Hello, Ms. Baldwin," Dave said in his deep, bass voice. Vanessa looked up from her menu.

"Well, aren't you just the ultimate gentleman this evening. You know, you don't have to be so formal," she said with a smile.

"Fair enough, Vanessa," he said with a sexy grin. "I heard you had arrived."

"Yes, and I'm really hungry too."

"I'd be glad to take your order. What would you like?"

"Mmmm, I guess I'll have what I didn't get a chance to eat the other night: Chicken Dijon over rice with broccoli..."

"And no mushrooms, right?"

"Right! You remembered."

"I'll put that in for you right away. Oh, and here is your scarf."

"Thanks so much for being so intuitive and not giving it to Damon. I hope I never have to lay eyes on him again," Vanessa said with attitude.

Dave smiled. "No problem. I'll put your order in and send a server over with a glass of white wine and a bread basket."

"You remembered my drink order from last time too! Thank you, Dave," Vanessa said with a warm smile.

Vanessa had brought some reports with her to review while she ate her dinner and did so with much more concentration than she had been able to muster up at the office. She ate leisurely and began to feel like her old self again after the delicious meal and soothing wine. Her headache had subsided and she felt recharged. While eating a fabulous piece of tiramisu, Vanessa thought back to the days before Damon. Her life had been so happy, carefree, and drama-free. For so long, she had longed for those days of not waiting by the phone for Damon to call, of not having to shave her legs above the knee if she didn't feel like it, and of not having to constantly run to the drug store for Monistat.

The idea of being single again was starting to feel good. She was finally free and couldn't wait to celebrate her newfound freedom with her sistah-girls on Saturday night. She would be armed with her new jeans, some killer man-catching pumps, and a discriminating eye. She had spent three years of her life chasing after a man that didn't want to be caught and really wasn't even worth the chase. She was determined to never put herself, her morals, or her dignity second to any man ever again.

"May I bring you anything else?" Dave asked.

Vanessa jumped. "Oh, you startled me. I guess I was deep in thought. Everything was delicious as always. I think I'm all set. Just the check please."

"This evening it is on the house."

"What? What are you talking about?"

"My treat."

"Dave, you don't have to do that!"

"It is my pleasure; I insist. You deserve to be treated well."

"Well, thank you! In that case, I accept your generous gift. The meal was nice, but the compliment was even better."

They both laughed as Vanessa grabbed her things and headed for the door, with Dave right behind her. He helped her put on her coat and flashed her a bright, sexy smile and said, "Come again!"

"Oh, I will! Thanks again, Dave," she said as she stepped out of the door onto the sidewalk and said aloud to herself, "Now that's how a man should treat a woman. Damn, why does he have to be married?" She smiled and raised her hand to hail a taxi. On her ride home, she realized that she had not felt this calm and relaxed in years. She felt as if a burden had been lifted and she was on top of the world again. She silently reprimanded herself for not breaking free from Damon years ago, but quickly thanked God for giving her the strength to finally do so.

Although she felt free physically, her subconscious mind was still entangled, snared in a net from the past. She was reminded of her demons as she slept that night. The recurring dream revisited, haunting her once again.

7

Friday was supposed to be a make-up day for Vanessa, Anne, and Monica. Vanessa needed to make-up for taking a day off to have a pity party and mourn the loss of a loser. Anne needed to make-up for the time she spent making up for sleep she hadn't gotten in years. And Monica needed to make-up for all the time she had spent daydreaming about how her Saturday afternoon sex-a-thon with Steve was going to play-out. They all worked through lunch, however Vanessa was ready to skip out of the office by 2:30 in the afternoon.

Monica's telephone rang. She grabbed it when she saw Vanessa's office phone number come up on the caller ID.

"Hello Ms. Young, Single, and Free!"

Vanessa laughed. "Hey Monica! I'm out of here; I can't take it anymore."

"Me too! I've been working my fingers to the bone all day and I'm ready for a cold one. Are you game?"

"Sorry, no can do. I've got an errand to run, so I'm getting ready to leave right now. I'm logging off my laptop and grabbing my Ricky bag as we speak."

Monica looked up when she heard a knock at the door. "Come in." The door opened and it was Anne. Monica motioned to her to have a seat.

"Vanessa, I've got someone in my office. I'll chat with you later, okay?"

"Okay. I just wanted to say have a great weekend!"

"You too. See you on Monday! Bye-bye." Monica quickly hung up the phone.

"Hi Anne! You almost busted me. That was Vanessa on the phone."

"It was? Do you think she suspected anything?"

"No, I don't think so. So what's up? What brings you to my neck of the woods?"

"Oh, I was just wondering if you've been able to gage how Vanessa is really doing?"

"She seems to be doing remarkably well. I think she finally realized that Damon was an opportunist. Anytime he had the opportunity to get some from anyone, he took it. Vanessa is a one-man kind of woman. She can only date one man at a time and gives her whole self to the relationship, even if she doesn't get much of anything in return. I've tried to get her to date several guys at a time and just date for the fun of it, not with the intent of falling in love and marrying the guy. But, she just can't seem to do that. She said she would feel dishonest and guilty."

"Well, I guess I can kind of understand her point of view. You know, I think she'll be fine. Besides, she has us to lean on," Anne said with a smile.

"She's really a beautiful person with such a giving and trusting spirit, but unfortunately that is what a lot of men look for in women, so that they can exploit and take advantage of them."

"You're absolutely right! You have to let men think you are tough as nails and hard to get. It's all about the chase for them. They pursue and marry women who engage them in a game of chance. There's a chance that they might get some, and there's a chance that they might not. Men need to feel like acquiring you is a mental challenge or a hunt. They want it to be a sprint, but we have to turn it into a marathon. The faster you give it up to them, the faster they will be on their way to meet the next challenge. Damon was off to the next one, but kept coming back when he'd hit a dry spell because he knew Vanessa would allow it. He knew he could get it without making a commitment, because he knew she was head over heels for him."

"You seem to be the expert on these matters," Anne said with a laugh.

"Yeah, well I think I know men pretty well. They are all pretty much the same when it comes to sex. They always try to get the biggest bang for their buck. That buck could be their money or their time. Their ultimate goal is to give the least amount possible in order to get the most bang possible."

In the back of Monica's mind, she knew she was an expert because she and Steve were using each other. They both wanted sex without the price of a commitment, however in order to get something you have to give up something; there is always a price to pay and Monica would soon find out how much it would cost her.

"Well, like I told Vanessa, I wish I could get just one guy to date me for *me*; to just enjoy my company and not want me to jump into bed with him. I swear, guys look at my slanted eyes and think that I've committed the Kama Sutra to memory. And, if one more guy asks me to walk on his back, I think I'm going to scream. I keep telling them, I'm not from Singapore!"

Monica laughed hysterically and so did Anne. "Anne, I am so sorry, I don't mean to laugh, but you are really funny, and I do understand that your situation is really, real. I'm sure you meet very few people who look like you in the executive ranks. And being women at our level is tough enough when it comes to finding partners. Most female executives are single and childless or divorced. They've had to choose between having a career or having a family, because most men are intimidated by women who are ambitious and make more money than they do. And besides, most male executives are already married. As women, if we married young right after college, we might've lucked out and landed a husband that didn't get too jealous as our career blossomed and salary increased, and in some cases surpassed his. And if we waited to get married, like so many women do today in order to develop a career, then we end up with no man, no children, and a closet full of designer suits and handbags."

"I agree with you one hundred percent, and I have a closet full of both, including the designer shoes to boot," Anne affirmed. They both laughed as Monica looked at her watch.

"Hey, are you about ready to head out?"

"Yes, I've given this place enough of me for the day."

"I'm heading over to Sangritas for a drink. Would you care to join me? They have a great happy hour and a lot of cute, corporate guys hang out there."

"Why not? I might not meet Mr. Right, but maybe Mr. Right Now might be waiting to buy me a drink."

"I'll drink to that," Monica said as she did an air-toast.

They grabbed their designer coats and handbags and made their way out of the corporate jungle towards the "meet" market.

"Ms. Baldwin, Dr. Porter will see you now," Sara said as she held the door open to his office. Vanessa breezed past her with a quiet "Thank you," as she inhaled the sweet scent of lavender that surrounded Sara. It had a calming effect on the butterflies that fluttered in Vanessa's stomach as she headed straight for the chaise lounge and kicked off her heels. Dr. Porter rose from behind his desk to greet her and settled into a leather club chair next to her.

"Hello, Vanessa. It's been quite some time since you've been on my couch."

"Yes, I know, Dr. Porter. The recurring dream that disappeared has suddenly returned," she said sadly.

"Hmmm, do you know what might have triggered its return?"

"Yes, I believe so. Damon and I broke up," Vanessa confessed with a sigh.

"If I recall, your dreams stopped when you two began dating on a consistent basis."

"Yes, that's right."

"How was the relationship?"

Vanessa looked at him with a puzzled look on her face. "Are you asking me why we broke up?"

"No, I'm asking, how was the relationship?"

"Well, Damon had everything I wanted in a man: education, gainfully employed, ambitious, and handsome. . ."

Dr. Porter interrupted, "Vanessa, you're not answering my question. How was the relationship?"

"Well, he kept saying he wasn't ready to make a long-term commitment."

"Vanessa, you're avoiding the question."

Vanessa knew exactly what he was asking, but she was afraid to admit that they didn't have a real relationship.

"People in relationships talk about their future together, make plans in advance to go out, introduce each other to friends and family, have each other's home addresses, and give gifts that have real meaning," Dr. Porter explained.

Reluctantly, Vanessa finally admitted to Dr. Porter that the only talk about the future came from her, while Damon nodded his head in insincere agreement. The only plans made in advance were by her, of which Damon usually backed out of at the last minute. She had introduced Damon to a couple of her friends they had run into by chance when they were out on a rare date. She had also let him talk to her mother over the phone once, however Damon had not reciprocated. The only contact numbers she had of Damon's were his cell and work numbers. His gifts to her were never personal and always something she didn't really need, like a key chain or an umbrella. He gave greeting cards on occasion, but they never contained a personal note. They were just signed, *Yours truly, Damon,* which she knew was a lie.

Vanessa confessed that she had been kidding herself by thinking that Damon's spontaneity was so romantic and refreshing. Every blue moon he would call on a Friday night at 8:30 and say, *"Let's catch a movie,"* or call her on a Saturday afternoon and say, *"I've got this formal company event tonight I need to attend. Would you accompany me so I won't be so bored?"* Damon always knew just the right thing to say and had the most plausible excuses that Vanessa accepted without question. On a few occasions, he would call her the day before a quick international trip and ask her to tag along with him. They were always the only two passengers flying on his company's jet.

When they reached their destination, she would be confined to the hotel room or spa while he worked. All of their evening meals were served in their hotel room, followed by her servicing him all night long.

The admission of her sexual behavior caused anger to roil inside Vanessa. She continued to explain to Dr. Porter that Damon didn't even have the decency to make a "booty-call" before dropping by. He just assumed she would be home, available, and willing. He'd show up on her doorstep at nine o'clock on a weeknight with half-wilted flowers from a corner store, literally sweep her off her feet and over his shoulder as he entered her apartment door, take her directly to the bedroom, and rip her clothes off. Afterward, he would be off into the night with an, *"I can't stay. It's a work-night and I have an early morning meeting."*

Vanessa began to silently reminisce. Damon was such an incredibly good lover; she could only comply with his wishes. When he held her in his strong arms and gently stroked her from cheeks to toes, down the front and up the back, she felt transported to a place far away from the harsh realities of her non-relationship with him and the inner pain of her trauma from the past. Damon never spoke while they were having sex, not even a moan. He would just let out a sigh of satisfaction when he climaxed without truly making an intimate connection with her. Vanessa, on the other hand, screamed loud enough to wake the dead. She always played music to help camouflage her sex-induced sound effects as a courtesy to her neighbors that might inadvertently overhear her.

"Vanessa, are you okay?"

"Oh, yeah, sorry Dr. Porter! I drifted off for a moment," Vanessa blushed.

"Well, it doesn't sound like you and Damon really broke up, because there was no real relationship to sever. I know it hurts to hear this, but it appears to me like you've decided to start being truthful with yourself and stop trying to give yourself to a man who truly doesn't want you. And when I say 'you,' I don't mean your body. I'm talking about your heart, your mind, and your soul. Your body houses who you really are and Damon is only interested in having the external you, not the whole you. Vanessa, you are a beautiful gift. The right man for you will want to unwrap your whole being, cherish what's inside, as well as save the gift wrapping."

Vanessa's eyes began to well up and the tears began flowing. Dr. Porter handed her a tissue box. She graciously accepted and wiped her eyes and blew her nose without shame.

"I know. I've been fooling myself for three years. What a waste!" Vanessa said, her voice anguished.

"Vanessa, you haven't wasted your time. Life's lessons aren't learned from just reading a self-help book or watching a talk show. We have to live life's lessons to learn them. The last three years have prepared you and positioned you to make a change. It's time for you to go in a new and productive direction for the rest of your life. The key is not to forget the lessons. Remember the words of William

Shakespeare, "this above all, to thine own self be true." Do what you believe is right for you.

"Now, about your dream, I wish I had a magic spell to make it go away permanently, but I don't. This dream may be a part of your life, for the rest of your life. Being molested by someone you trusted and loved is one of the greatest obstacles to overcome, especially if you have not or cannot confront your abuser to bring forth some closure. Your molestation experience may affect your relationships for the rest of your life. If the day comes when you find yourself in a committed relationship, you need to share the dream and your past with your partner. It's important for him to know what you've survived. Open up to him and allow him to comfort you when you wake up screaming in the middle of the night.

"In the meantime, you may want to confide in someone you trust. You'd be surprised to know that one in four women have admitted to being molested yet only one percent of the perpetrators are legally punished for their crimes. I guarantee you that one of your friends has been molested or have faced a similar situation in their lives. You shouldn't continue to bear this alone; there is nothing for you to be ashamed of. On the contrary, you should be proud of the many accomplishments you've made over the course of your life thus far. You are one of the highest paid African-American executives in the country! You ran the New York City marathon in two-five-nine! You've triumphed over a major adversity in your childhood; you are a successful survivor! Don't be ashamed of a situation you had no control over or the subsequent mistakes that followed. Share your painful experiences with others to educate them and possibly help them heal from a similar experience. The burden you carry will not be as heavy if you share it.

Vanessa nodded in agreement as she smiled through her tears.

Maria and her girls spent the day unpacking the rest of their belongings and organizing their new home. Maria's cell phone kept ringing all day, but she didn't answer. She needed time to process everything that was happening, so she finally turned it off. She knew from the caller ID that her mother-in-law and the police were trying to track her down. Her home phone had been ringing too, even though she had just gotten a new unlisted phone number and had not yet given it to anyone except her mother. The police had acquired her number and left several messages on her voicemail. She didn't even bother to listen to them all. She just deleted them; however, there was one message that she had begun to listen to, but quickly deleted it when she realized who it was. It was her mother's hysterical voice. José's mother must have called her and broke the news. Maria knew she needed to call her mother and explain what was going on. She decided to wait until after she had put the girls to bed. She didn't want them to overhear her conversation.

With the dinner dishes done and the girls tucked peacefully into their own beds in their new room, Maria went into the living room to make the call to her mother. She lay down on her couch and dialed the number.

"Hello?"

"Hi Mami,"

Maria's mother instantly began to speak frantically in Spanish. "Maria, I have been trying to reach you all day! What a terrible tragedy! Where are you? Are you all right? Where are the girls?"

Maria switched over to Spanish also. "Mami, calm down. The girls are fine. They are here with me."

"But where are you? I sent Carlos over to get you and the girls and you weren't there. Just the police were there. They wouldn't let him in!"

"Mami, when I gave you my new phone number," Maria paused with a pang of guilt, "I wasn't truthful with you. I didn't change my phone number because of telemarketing calls. I changed it because I moved out. I left José on Thursday."

"Moved? Why, what happened?"

"It is a long story. I didn't tell you because I knew Carlos would kill José. As it turns out, José did us all a favor."

"Maria, you shouldn't talk that way about your dearly departed husband!"

"Oh, Mami please," Maria said with an attitude of disgust.

"Please what? Why did you leave him?"

"He beat me Mami. He's been beating me for years! I have been covering it up, trying to save my marriage for the girls' sake."

"Oh Maria, that is no reason to leave him. You know how men are. They lose their temper every now and then."

"Mami, I watched Papi lose his temper all over you, all of my life. I still remember the secret knock." Maria's mother fell silent as she remembered too. Maria made a fist with her hand and knocked on the end table next to her, one knock, a pause, two knocks, another pause, and then three. Tears began to well up in the eyes of Maria's mother as she listened. "Mami, I watched it until the day he died two years ago. I knew it wasn't right for you to put up with it from Papi and I knew it wasn't right for me to put up with it from José either."

"But Maria, I could not leave him. I had nowhere to go. I had five children, no money, and knew very little English. Your papi was a good man and a good provider. He took care of us, just like José took care of you and the girls."

"Mami, José was an alcoholic. Every time he went out drinking, I would end up with black eyes and bruises. I had run out of sick time at work and phony excuses to give my manager. But this last time, he just went way too far. He beat me, gave me two black eyes, and raped me too!"

145

"Rape? Maria, when you are married your husband cannot rape you. It is your obligation to give into his needs."

"Mami, this is a new day and a new time. Women don't have to give into men's demands. We don't have to put up with being a punching bag anymore either. You know José used to be a boxer. It's a wonder that he didn't kill me! If I hadn't left him, then one day he probably would have. I didn't want him raising my girls." Maria said with tears streaming down her cheeks. "Mami," Maria gathered all her strength, "he made my girls touch him." There was a long, silent pause.

"What? Noooooooo. Touch him? Where? You don't mean . . .?"

"Yes, Mami, sexually." There was another long pause.

"Well, Sweetie, you did the right thing by leaving him and not telling me. He had better be glad that he killed himself, because I would have killed that no-good son-of-a-bitch with my bare hands," responded Maria's mother calmly. Maria gasped and managed to crack a smile through her tears.

"Mami, I have never heard you talk like that before!"

"I know. Mary, Mother of God forgive me, but nasty words are called for in nasty situations! Now, did he hurt the girls? Tell me now, because I will beat his cold, dead corpse if he did!" shouted Maria's mother with conviction.

"No Mami, I took them to the doctor. They are both fine and I am going to be taking them to see a therapist on a regular basis."

"Oh, good! Okay, now where are you staying because I am coming over there to see all my girls tomorrow. And I will bring groceries and cook all your favorites. Do you have pots, pans, and dishes?"

"Yes, I took pretty much everything," Maria said with pride.

"Good, that's my girl!"

"Is Carlos coming?"

"Yes, call him in the morning and give him your new address and directions. I will have him drive me over there and carry in the groceries, but then he has got to go. I want this to be a time just for my girls. I assume you haven't told them that their father is dead yet, have you?"

"No. I do not know how to tell them, Mami."

"Do not worry, Sweetie. We will tell them together."

"I love you, Mami."

"I love you too!"

"Bye-bye."

Maria lay on her back looking up at the ceiling for a long time, going over in her head the words she would use to tell her daughters about the death of their father. She knew they were happy not to be living with him any longer, but she did not know how they would react to his death. On the other hand, Maria was relieved that she wouldn't have to go through a messy divorce and criminal trial. Her girls would be spared the anguish of testifying against their father. José was dead because he wanted to be.

"Looks like everyone got what they wanted," Maria said out loud to herself as she rose and strode confidently off to her bedroom. When she reached her bed, she gleefully fell backward onto it and whispered, "Now, I can be whatever I want to be!"

8

Anne rose early as usual. She followed her morning routine and checked her online investment portfolio to see how the market had treated her. Since she stayed out so late with Monica, she had not checked Friday's market closing numbers.

As she stared at the screen on her laptop, her thoughts drifted back to the previous night. What started out to be a couple of drinks at happy hour, ended up being last-call at two in the morning. Anne and Monica really bonded over a discussion on the single woman's plight in the corporate executive arena. They also checked out the corporate jocks, some of whom were in denial about their receding hairlines and trying to hide the tan line from the wedding band jingling with the keys in their trouser pockets.

Anne and Monica amused themselves by speculating about the men and creating personality profiles about why each jock was hanging out in the bar aiming to pick-up a corporate cutie. Quite a few men sent them drinks during the evening. They accepted them eagerly while having some polite conversation with each man, mentally sizing him up.

The professions they represented ranged from Wall Streeters and retail marketing execs, to entrepreneurs and techie nerds. Anne and Monica would let them down graciously after consuming their drinks and then exchange impressions about the men as they walked away with their tails between their legs. It was an amusing game and the assessments they shared became wilder with each Sangrita they knocked back.

Anne recalled one of their conversations.

"You know, Monica, I've never had this many men approach me in my life. I think the only reason is because of you. I guarantee you that if I had been sitting here by myself, one, maybe two men would have sent me a drink. And, I guarantee you that the drink would not have been a Sangrita. No, it probably would have been a Sex-on-the-Beach or a Singapore Sling."

"Anne, it's a shame that in this day and age, in this melting pot/salad bowl of a city, that prejudice and stereotypes still have a strong hold. Race, skin color, or nationality shouldn't matter. What's important is that people are honest, sincere, loving, supportive, and are one hundred percent committed to their relationships. I think the issue that a lot of married men face is that they want the fairy tale. They

want the perfect little woman, and I do mean little. They expect their wives to be able to fit back into their wedding dresses the day after giving birth to twins.

"Yeah," Anne chimed in. "They want to be "Daddy" with the two point five kids but at the same time, they still want to be free, juggling multiple women, using cell phones, email and social media to arrange sex; sometimes in the same bed they share with their wives or girlfriends. And it amazes me how many single women will date married men without any regard."

"I know, right!" Monica added. "Then the crap hits the fan. The wife finds a strand of another woman's hair and smells strange perfume in their bed, or she wakes up one morning and her husband tells her he doesn't want to be married anymore and he's leaving. When you choose to put up with men's unfaithful behavior and suffer in silence, you end up with ulcers, STDs and alopecia. If you confront him, give him an ultimatum, and he stays, then you can't ever trust him again. It's unfortunate that so many women chose to suffer in silence instead of leaving to preserve their self-respect!"

"Monica, you know I think that most of the problems women have with lines, wrinkles, and premature aging are not due to the sun. It's from the stress that the son-of-a-bitch they sleep next to is putting them through."

Anne laughed out loud as she finished her cup of morning tea, wondering what Monica's husband had put her through for her to have such negative views of marriage. Had he pushed her to the point where she needed alcohol to numb her obvious pain? She always sounded like she spoke from first-hand experience.

The heap of covers on top of Vanessa's bed jumped as the telephone rang, interrupting an old black and white movie playing on her television. As usual, Vanessa pulled the covers from over her head and began pulling through the blanket, top-sheet, comforter and quilt to find the phone and the TV remote. Finally, by the fifth ring, she found them both. She looked at the caller ID and rolled her eyes as she turned the TV off, which had been on all night. She conjured up the sunniest disposition she could and said, "Hello, Mama!"

"Hey Honey! What's wrong? You sound like you were still sleep. Do you know what time it is?

Half the day is gone and you're still in bed. I've washed three loads…"

"Mama, please! I'm not feeling well," Vanessa interjected.

"Oh, is it that time of the month?"

Vanessa rolled her eyes up at the ceiling and said, "Yes," with the tone of a question instead of an answer. Vanessa hated lying to her mother, but sometimes she just had to. If her mother knew she had been drinking, she would have a fit, since Vanessa's father had died at an early age as a result of complications from alcoholism.

After her emotionally draining appointment with Dr. Porter the day before, Vanessa had headed straight to the grocery store. She'd picked up all of her favorite comfort foods: Ben & Jerry's Chunky Monkey ice cream, microwave popcorn with extra butter, and Snickers bars. She'd popped the cork on a bottle of wine and had ended up passing out in the comfort of her own bed while watching, *Breakfast at Tiffany's*.

"Baby, get a hot cup of chamomile tea and put a hot water bottle or a heating pad on your tummy. You'll feel better in no time!"

"Thanks Mama. I'd better go put the tea kettle on and find my heating pad."

"Oh, okay Baby. I'll check-in with you later. Bye-bye."

"Bye, Mama."

Vanessa hung up and threw the phone over her shoulder onto the heap of covers as she crawled off the bed. She glanced at the clock radio but could barely see the time. She moved closer to the clock. It was just after nine. As she made her way to the bathroom, she thought it was odd that her vision was so blurry. She squinted at herself in the bathroom mirror. "Oh shoot," she shouted as she realized she had neglected to remove her gas permeable contact lenses before falling asleep. She had to practically scrape them off her eyeballs. She followed up with a cold splash of water on her eyes and blindly grabbed a towel from the rack beside the sink. She sat down on the toilet to pee as she dried her face and gently rubbed her eyes. When she finished, she opened her eyes and could see a little bit better. She grabbed her glasses from their usual resting place in the toothbrush holder next to the sink. As she looked in the mirror with her newfound vision she screamed, "Oh shit!" She saw her bangs sticking straight up in the air and the gray that was standing at attention along her hairline. At that moment, she remembered she had forgotten about her eight o'clock appointment with Vince to get her hair colored.

She grabbed her toothbrush, squeezed a little too much toothpaste on it, shoved it in her mouth, ran to the slipper chair in her bedroom and threw on the sports bra, t-shirt and hooded jogging suit that she had worn a few days prior. She quickly found a clean pair of socks in a laundry basket sitting inside her closet and put them on while hopping back towards the bathroom. She spat, toothbrush and all, into the sink, did a quick rinse, ran to grab her backpack and a red baseball cap that hung in the hall closet and darted into the kitchen. She grabbed two bottles of Aquafina from the fridge, a more-brown-than-yellow banana from the fruit bowl on the countertop, a couple of energy bars from the cupboard, and threw them all into the backpack. She knew she was going to be in the salon all day because she was late for her appointment. She prayed that somehow Vince could work her in or that maybe someone had cancelled.

She slipped into a pair of running shoes, put on the baseball cap, flipped up her hood, grabbed her Ricky bag, and ran out the door. The doorman hailed a cab for her and she hopped in and began applying her make-up as usual. As she applied her pressed powder, she kept readjusting her butt in the seat. She felt oddly uncomfortable. She tried to carefully apply her mascara as the cabby hit multiple potholes in the street. Suddenly she dropped her head and couldn't help but laugh out loud.
She realized that in her rush to get dressed, she had forgotten to put on panties.

"Good morning, Mrs. Florence," Monica said as she stood at her neighbor's door in her bathrobe, ready to collect her daughter.

"Good morning, Monica" Mrs. Florence said in a stone cold voice.

"Where's Lizzy?"

"She's still asleep. She was up half the night wondering when her mother was coming home."

Monica tried to ignore the comment, though she felt a stab of guilt. "Look, I'll cut right to the chase. I know you don't approve of my social life, but I have friends that I like to spend time with."

"It's your life, you're wasting," snapped Mrs. Florence.

Monica dismissed her comment. "Mrs. Florence, are you available tomorrow evening?"

"What? Again? Poor Lizzy," the nanny said with indignation in her voice. "She's going to start thinking that I'm her mother if you don't stop spending so much time away from her. You should be ashamed of yourself!"

"Yes, you're right," Monica said as she rolled her eyes and smiled. "Now, are you available or not?"

"Of course I am. I'm always available to care for Lizzy."

"Good. Please come by my apartment around seven."

"How long do you plan on being out? Because if you're going to be hanging out half the night and coming home drunk again, you might as well let Lizzy come over here and stay the night again with me."

"I would prefer that you come to my apartment this time."

"Fine!"

"Fine. Then I'll expect you promptly at seven tomorrow evening.

156

"I said, *fine!*"

"Good, then please bring Lizzy home within the hour when she wakes up."

"Fine!"

"Thank you, Mrs. Florence. Bye-bye," Monica said as she playfully waved while walking backwards towards her apartment.

Mrs. Florence slammed her door shut without responding further. She shook her head with a sad smile on her face. Although she hated Monica's dating habits, she still loved her unconditionally.

Maria's mother showed up the next morning as promised with a big smile and lots of hugs and kisses for her three girls. Carlos, Maria's brother, carried in several bags of groceries and pulled Maria aside while their mother fawned over her two granddaughters.

"Nice place! Hey, you know you my baby sister, right? I would do anything for you, including killing José," Carlos whispered with controlled anger. "He got off too easy with a bullet to the head. I know places where I could have taken him, tortured him and castrated him to let him bleed out. Next to my wife, you know you my heart. You better not let anyone ever hurt you again!" Maria reached out to take Carlos' hand with tears in her eyes.

"I won't, Carlos, I promise. I love you too."
They embraced, then looked each other in the eyes and
smiled.

"Hey Mami, call me on my cell when you are
ready for me to pick you up," Carlos yelled as he made
his way to the door.

"Okay, I will," she answered.

As Maria closed the door behind him, she
thought about the many times that she had picked up
the phone to call Carlos, but she knew if she had, she
would have spent the rest of her life visiting him
behind bars for having killed José.

When she found out what José had done to the
girls, she had regretted not having called Carlos, but
now she was glad she had let fate take care of her
problems.

"Mmmm, hmmm, I know yo' behind ain't
strolling up in here at some nine forty-five looking for
service!"

"Vince, I am so sorry. Something came up,"
Vanessa said with regret.

"Mmmm, hmmm, sounds like a personal
problem to me. I hope he was worth it. Nothing
personal, Baby, but this is business." Vince said with
his left hand on his hip and a color brush in his right
hand motioning to the sign on the window that read,
'Baldwin Salon and Day Spa.' At that point, everyone

within earshot stopped in mid-sentence, mid-braid, mid-relaxer and mid-weave to check out the brewing conflict going down. Even the ladies under the hair dryers tilted the hoods back, so that they could get a good listen.

"Vince, may I talk with you in private for a moment?" Vanessa begged.

"I don't think so! You expect me to stop in the middle of applying color to my client's gray new-growth to hear some ole tired excuse from you?" Vince said with a simultaneous roll of his eyes and neck.

"Okay, okay, I see your point. But Vince, I'm really desperate here!" Vanessa whispered.

"And so is everybody else up in here," Vince said loudly.

"I know that's right" came from somewhere close behind her.

Vanessa tried to ease her way closer to Vince to keep so many people from hearing their conversation. That didn't do any good. The receptionist grabbed the TV remote and hit the mute button as everyone leaned in closer.

Vanessa said, as quietly as possible, "I'll double what I normally pay you," but Vince loud-talked her anyway.

"Oh, I know you don't think that you can just throw money at this and I'll forget about your blatant disregard for my time, talents, and everyone else's time up in here."

"Mmmm, hmmm, I know that's right," was offered again by someone in the waiting area.

Vanessa's eyes got big as half dollars. She had no response. She dropped her head in shame. You could hear a pin drop.

Finally, one of the other stylists broke the silence and said, "Boy, you better take that money, 'cause if you don't, I will!" Everybody busted out laughing.

Vince looked at Vanessa out of the corner of his eye and said, "Well, we are cousins. Blood is thicker than water."

Someone from under the dryer said, "Family's, family, now."

Vince continued, "But ain't nothing thicker than them gray roots you got sticking out from under that baseball cap."

With that, the salon erupted in laughter once again and Vanessa knew she had been forgiven. The TV began blaring again as she meekly took a seat and waited for Vince to fit her in between a wet set and a relaxer.

"Okay Lizzy, it's time to go with grandma and grandpa. You'll have a great time! Now, if you ask real nice, I bet they'll take you to FAO Schwartz! And if you behave, I bet they will buy you a toy too!"

"I be good girl. Bye-bye Mommy."

"Bye-bye Sweetie. I love you!" Monica said as she kissed her daughter on the cheek and zipped up her jacket. "I'll see you in a little while."

Monica ushered them out of the door just in the nick of time. As she gave one last wave good-bye to Lizzy, the elevator bell rang and Steve stepped off as Lizzy and her paternal grandparents stepped on. Lizzy stared at the tall, blond man with her mouth open as he passed her by. Somewhere in the back of her little mind, she conjured up an image of her father. She whispered, "He looks like my daddy, but he's not my daddy."

"Where's my daddy?" Lizzy screamed just as the doors to the elevator closed. Her grandparents began to sob, because of the wounds reopened by Lizzy's question. Her grandpa picked her up and held her tight as her grandma rubbed her back and made promises of toys and McDonald's happy meals instead of answering her urgent question.

Monica was too distracted to hear the faint muffled screams of her daughter. All she could hear was the sound of Steve's boots on the marble floor as he approached her apartment. Just then, Mrs. Florence's apartment door flew open and she exclaimed, "Did you hear that?"

"Hear what Mrs. Florence?" Monica answered with an agitated tone. She just knew Mrs. Florence was trying to be nosy again.

"I thought I heard a scream, Lizzy's scream."

"Oh, that must have been Lizzy laughing on the elevator."

"Oh," Mrs. Florence replied flatly as she looked from Steve to Monica and rolled her eyes. She turned on her heels to go back into her apartment, but not before emitting a loud sucking sound from her teeth as she slammed her apartment door.

Monica fell into Steve's arms as they laughed and he lifted her up, carried her over the threshold, and shut the door behind him with a kick of his boot. From that moment on, there wouldn't be much conversation. Perhaps a few giggles, moans, and expletives, as Steve plunged his thick, hot tongue through Monica's glossed lips. She received his tongue and took a long, hard drag on it, as if it were a Cuban cigar. He gingerly put her down and then savagely ripped open her winter-white silk blouse while placing the toe of his boot to his other heel to remove it. White, mother-of-pearl buttons flew in every direction across the living room. She knew buttons would be found for months to come, just as her housekeeper often found pine needles from the Christmas tree when she did the spring-cleaning. She clawed at his navy blue turtleneck sweater and managed to get it up over his pecs. Her mouth was at just the right height to grab his left nipple between her teeth and massage it with little quick flicks of her tongue, as he pulled his sweater over his head and threw it to the floor.

He popped her Cs from her demi-cupped bra and used his thumbs to softly caress her firm nipples. They both moaned, then Monica giggled and moved to his right nipple. Steve began backing Monica down the hallway toward the master bedroom but paused at the hall closet. He opened the door while Monica unbuttoned his Levi's. His jeans quickly dropped to the floor from the weight of his keys and wallet. Monica wasn't surprised to find that he had nothing on under his jeans.

Steve backed her into the closet while pushing the coats aside to expose the brass bar and placed Monica's hands on it chin-up style. He then got on his knees, tore off her crimson, silk, wool-blend wraparound skirt and slipped off her French lace panties. He looked up at her eyes as he licked the crotch of her underwear and said, "Mmmm." The taste of her wetness unleashed something in him. He shouted, "Hold on!" and lifted her up by the back of her knees as she held onto the brass bar. He flipped her stiletto-clad feet up and threw one over each of his shoulders, then used his tongue with precision to pleasure her. He licked and flicked repeatedly as she began singing passion's song, each note going higher with each stroke of his tongue. Then he stopped, just before she climaxed, and waited for her to calm down while he enjoyed her aroma. Then all of a sudden he began again, but this time he drew circles around her pleasure center with his tongue, evoking passion's song once again.

Just before she climaxed, he stopped again. This time he let her legs down gently and rubbed her up the back of her legs with his hands and licked her up the front, over her belly button and between her breasts as he stood up. She dropped her hands and looked up into his eyes as she grabbed his ass and plunged her nails deep into his flesh, pulling him toward her. His stare locked onto her eyes as he placed her hands back up on the brass bar. Once again he lifted her by the back of her knees while gently spreading her legs. She threw her head back as he gently slid in and began to plunge in and out, over and over again, as he held her ass in the palms of his hands. She arched her back and spread her legs open wider as she sung with pleasure. She had never felt anything so good in her entire life. She forgot all of her problems and insecurities. They seemed to melt away with every thrust. She cried, moaned, and screamed, "Deeper! Harder!" He answered with intensity, pushing further and further.

Monica kept going in spite of the pain of the blisters that were forming on her hands from the friction on the brass bar. Steve grabbed her and pulled her away from the bar. She threw her hands around his neck and her legs around his waist as he backed out of the closet. Without missing a stroke, Steve put her back up against the closet door as he held her with his left hand and the top of the door with his right hand. Monica was suspended in ecstasy.

He thrust even deeper inside her. Their bodies glistened with sweat from their passion in the afternoon light. All of a sudden, Steve stopped and looked into her eyes and asked, "Had enough?"

Monica replied, "I'm just getting started."

He lifted her away from the door and she rode him into the bedroom. He carefully laid her down on the bed, all the while still tucked inside her. The fire continued to burn all afternoon and neither one of them wanted to put it out.

Vanessa finally returned home five hours later with her hair relaxed, her gray covered, and a freshly coiffed hairdo. She had a splitting headache and ransacked her medicine cabinet for a strong pain reliever. She knew she was on her way to a migraine; therefore, Tylenol wouldn't do the trick, so she chased down three Ibuprofen with a swig of Pepsi. Her slipper chair caught her clothes once again as she made a beeline for the shower. She was careful to cover her hair with not one, but two, shower caps to ensure the moisture wouldn't make her curls fall. She stood with her back to the pulsating water in hopes that it would help alleviate her tension headache and her fatigued body. After a few moments of letting the water cascade down her body, she turned around to bathe. The firm pressure from the water hit her nipples and they became hard instantly. She rubbed vanilla and cream body wash on her breasts, abdomen, and down between her legs. She closed her eyes and tilted her head back to enjoy the sensation. She was ready and felt hot liquid beginning to flow. She caressed her nipples with her left hand and her pleasure center with her right. Her thoughts wandered to Damon and the last time they made love. Her strokes became firmer and faster. She put her left leg up on the built-in marble shower bench to gain better leverage as she grabbed the towel bar to steady herself. She went deeper as she moaned with each stroke; her body gyrated with the motions of her hand. She cried out, louder and louder with pleasure. Then with one last scream, or so she thought, she reached orgasm. She clung to the towel bar while trying to catch her breath as she continued to pulsate from within. Finally, after a few minutes, she felt relaxed enough to open her eyes. Suddenly, she let out another scream. Not one of pleasure, because she saw red all over her hand. It was dripping down her legs and she was standing in a pool of bloody water.

"Oh, shoot!" she said with an annoyed voice. *My period, just what I needed. No wonder I have a headache*, she thought to herself. "Hmmm, wait a minute, my headache is gone. Nice remedy!"

Maria's mother sang in the kitchen as she cooked, while Christina and Elizabeth set the table with Maria's guidance.

"Mami, how much longer until dinner is ready?" inquired Maria.

"Oh, about fifteen minutes," Maria's mother replied.

"Well girls, why don't we all have a seat in the living room together and have a chat before we eat the wonderful meal that your grandmami prepared for us."

The girls both called dibs on the chaise lounge and began to argue over who should get to stretch out on it.

"Okay girls, settle down. You can sit on it together right next to each other." Maria knelt down before them on the floor, while Maria's mother wiped her hands on her apron as she made her way over from the kitchen.

"I'll sit on the chaise too with my girls, one on each side."

Maria reached up and took a hand of each of her girls as Maria's mother put her arms around them.

Maria took a deep breath before she began.

"Girls, do you remember when your grandpapi died a couple years ago?"

They both nodded their heads as Maria's mother's eyes began to well up with tears.

"And remember when we told you that he died because his heart was broken?"

They nodded in agreement again.

"Well," She paused, "Your papi has just died from a broken heart too."

The girls looked wide-eyed at their mother in silence until Elizabeth finally said, "How did Papi's heart get broken, Mami?"

"Well, he was very sad for a very long time, even before you two were born and before I met him. The sadness just weakened his heart to the point that his spirit didn't feel comfortable living in his body any longer. So, it flew away."

All of a sudden, a big smile came over Christina's face. "Is his spirit with Grandpapi's spirit now?"

Maria swallowed hard and reluctantly replied, "Yes, yes, baby he is." She would deal with the lie next time she went to confession.

Then Elizabeth said, "Well, now they can keep each other company!" Maria and her mother both looked at each other and thought about how a confrontation would have gone between the two men, had Maria's father known what José had done to the girls.

"Mami?" Christina said sweetly.

"Yes, Baby?"

"Can we eat now?"

Maria looked at her mother in shock and said with a broad smile, "Well, I guess that's it. Mami, let's eat!"

The girls ran to their places at the table for their favorite meal of Chimichangas and Chalupas with lots of beans and rice. No tears of sorrow fell that day from the girls' eyes as they enjoyed their dinner in the company of their mothers. The girls seemed to be satisfied with Maria's explanation of their father's death, so she just decided to let well enough alone.

As usual, Vanessa stood in front of her mirror naked while holding up different outfits to see which would best fit the occasion, weather, and her mood. Tonight was sistah-girl's night out and she wanted to look hot. Being back on the market meant she was going to wear a semi-revealing top, her new jeans that hugged her curves, and some man-catching heels. She had a red, deep V-neck, long-sleeved spandex sweater picked out with a red, French, lace push-up bra, along with some strappy, stiletto-heeled, pumps. She just needed to decide on the jeans. The darker ones were slimming and dressier, while the slightly faded ones would be more comfortable and easier to dance in. Needless to say, she went for fashion over function.

As she put on her eyeliner, she glanced at her watch and realized how late it was. She would put on the finishing touches of her makeup in the cab. She wanted to arrive earlier than her friends to scope out the guys first. She grabbed a small, Louis Vuitton, cross-body bag off the top shelf of her closet and threw in the essentials: pressed powder, lip gloss, Tic Tacs, two tampons, some Aleve, two panty shields, an unmaxed-out credit card for cab fare and a couple rounds of drinks for her sistah-girls, driver's license, and two hundred dollars in small bills for tips and incidentals. If the club was really jumping and she was up to staying out late, she would just run a tab. She took one last look in the full-length mirror; the booty was banging and the "girlz" were pumped up. Vanessa headed for the door, grabbed her keys, and sailed out into the cool evening. As the doorman blew his whistle to hail a cab, she took a deep breath and said,

"Look out NYC Boyz, Vanessa is back!" She stepped into the cab feeling sexy, giddy, and unburdened.

Vanessa walked up to the entrance of the club, which had a line going down the block. She flashed a blinding, bright smile and her hourglass figure said all the rest. The message was loud and clear to the bouncer who let her cut the line and to every man in the club when she walked through the door swinging her hair and her hips. Before she could make her way to the bar, she had three drink offers. She smiled and declined them all. She nudged her way through the crowd and placed a drink order. She always had to explain to the bartender how to make her second-favorite cocktail.

"I'll have a Cosmo, up, with Bacardi Limon instead of Vodka, and shaken vigorously with crushed ice." A gentleman nearby with his back toward her, over heard her instructions and turned around wearing a big smile on his face.

"Well, if it isn't Miss Table number 19."

Vanessa's face lit up. "Dave Patton," she said as she gave him a friendly hug.

"Hello Vanessa Baldwin. How are you? You certainly look well," he said with a playful hint in his deliciously, deep voice.

"Why thank you! I think my break up with Damon looks pretty damn good on me," she said with the tone of a Diva. "I am YSF: young, single, and fine!" They both laughed.

"I'll drink to that," Dave said as he lifted this old fashion. "So, are you here alone?" Dave inquired.

"For the moment. I'm meeting four of my girlfriends here for drinks. What about you?"

"Well, it's my birthday, so I'm meeting up with a few of my boyz.

Vanessa's man meter went off immediately at the mention of "my boyz." She knew that Dave wouldn't hang out with just anybody. His boyz were probably MBAs, Esquires, MDs, and CPAs. Hopefully, some of them were single.

"Well, happy birthday! Hey, maybe we'll have to introduce your boyz to my girlz. It should make for a better evening for all of us. And since it is your birthday, I'm going to buy you a drink." She lifted her hand to signal the bartender, but Dave gently grabbed it and pulled it down.

"Vanessa, thanks but I couldn't possible accept."

"Well, why not?" Vanessa asked with a confused look on her face.

"Because you're the one that deserves to be treated to a drink and much, much more," he said as he moved in closer.

Vanessa's mouth fell open because she realized that Dave, a married man, was trying to make a play for her. Before she could respond, Tonya and Meme let out simultaneous screams.

"Girrrrrrl, I see you arrived early to check out the goods," Meme shouted.

Tonya co-sign with a, "Mmmm, hmmm." The three of them cackled and exchanged hugs and air kisses.

"Oh, ladies, this is Dave Patton, an acquaintance of mine.   Dave, this is Meme and Tonya." Tonya said hello and shook hands with Dave politely, while Meme extended her arm for Dave to kiss the back of her hand and said in a sexy, raspy voice, "Hi, it's actually Melody."

Dave said hello and awkwardly shook her hand with a smile.

Meme blurted out to Vanessa, "Girl, I am pleased to meet your acquaintances."   They all laughed.

"Dave, you'll have to excuse Meme.   She hasn't had a drink yet. After a couple, she will mellow out a bit," Vanessa said to make Dave feel more at ease.

Dave flashed a smile and said, "No problem."

"Well, I know Diane will be fashionably late," Tonya predicted "Have either of you heard from Nikki?"

"Girl, now you know we ain't heard from Nikki. She is probably somewhere in the islands with a Pina Colada in one hand and a cute island boy in the other," announced Vanessa.

"Yeah, I bet she'll be a no-show," Meme added.

"Well, let's grab a booth over by the dance floor. Dave, I look forward to meeting your boyz. Bring them by our table when you get a chance," Vanessa insisted.

"I will," Dave said with a nod of his head and a mischievous grin on his face.

"Nice meeting you!" Meme and Tonya said in unison.

"The pleasure is mine," Dave politely responded.

"Boyz? Have you been holding back on us?" exclaimed Tonya as they made their way over to an open booth.

"No Girl. Dave is meeting up with some of his boyz for a drink. It's his birthday."

"Drinks ladies?" interrupted a cocktail waitress. Tonya ordered a glass of white wine, while Meme ordered a Diva-tini, a chocolate martini with a Godiva chocolate heart submerged in the center.

"Hmm, I'd like to see Dave in his birthday suit," Meme said lustfully.

"Meme, you know you ain't right. Look, he owns a fabulous restaurant that I used to go to with Damon all the time."

"So, he's still fine as hell! Girl, if you don't want him, pass me the leftovers."

"Girl, are you crazy? The man is married. Hello!"

"Well, he's not wearing a wedding band. Holla back!"

"Oh, he wasn't? I guess I didn't notice," Vanessa said with a perplexed look on her face.

"And, there's no visible tan line either! Besides, it's his birthday. If he had a wife at home, he wouldn't be out here meetin' up with his boyz."

"Yeah, I guess you could be right. Maybe his marriage is in trouble or something," Vanessa mumbled, even further confused.

"Yeah, or maybe it's over. Girl, wake up!" Tonya exclaimed with a neck roll.

"I never looked at him in that way, so if he hasn't been wearing his ring, I hadn't notice."

"Yeah, that's because Damon had your nose so wide open you couldn't see a damn thing," Meme teased.

"I know that's right," Tonya threw in.

"Forget Damon, let's get our drink on! Damon is past and forgotten," announced Vanessa.

"And Dave is the future and unforgettable," Meme said dreamily.

They cackled as their drinks arrived and toasted to an unforgettable night.

"Oh, you started the party without me?" Diane said with a fabricated attitude.

"Girl, sit your late behind-self down and order a drink. And what chu got on? That little, and I emphasize *little*, dress you got on is going to have all the brothas up in here barking," Vanessa scolded playfully.

"Oh, it's just a little something I found in the back of my closet."

"Yeah right! That's why your ass was late because you were out shopping for that little sling shot you wearing," Meme replied. They all cracked up and ordered another round of drinks.

Vanessa and the girlz were finishing up their second round of drinks when Dave and his boyz approached their booth.

"Ladies, I would like to introduce you to a few good men. I'm Dave and this is Raphael, Max, and Tyrone." The ladies swooned. Raphael was dark chocolate with beautiful locks and pearly white teeth. Max was white chocolate with hazel eyes and a deep, Barry White, bass voice. Tyrone was a tall glass of chocolate milk with luscious full lips and broad shoulders that seemed to go on forever.

"Gentlemen, I'm Vanessa, and these are a few good women." They all chuckled. "This is Tonya, Meme, and Diane." The men licked their chops. Tonya was milk with a hint of chocolate syrup and deep dimples with a demure smile. Meme was chocolate mousse with a short and sassy haircut that showed off her long regal neck. Diane was mocha choco-latte with a sexy cleft chin and green eyes. They all exchanged pleasantries as they checked each other out. Just then, the DJ played an old-school jam,

Kiss, by Prince. Dave's boyz asked Vanessa's girlz to dance. They were eager to hit the floor. Dave asked Vanessa to dance, however she was disappointed that one of Dave's boyz didn't ask her to dance first. She didn't relish the thought of wasting her time dancing with a married man. So, she just shrugged her shoulders and went to the dance floor with Dave to be polite.

After two Cosmos, Vanessa was feeling at ease. She let herself go as she danced and Dave showed her a side of himself she had never seen before. He was a great dancer and very sensual as they moved around the floor playfully. Vanessa couldn't remember the last time she had felt so carefree, happy, and tingly inside. As the last few notes of the song played, it ended with the sound of a kiss. At that very moment, Dave planted one right on Vanessa's neck. Vanessa stood there with her mouth hanging wide open and her hand on the spot where he had kissed her as the dance floor began to clear. After a few awkward seconds, Dave smiled and said, "I'm sorry, I just couldn't resist," as he led her back to the table. Vanessa was speechless. "You look like you could use another drink."

"I'd better not. I need a clear head right about now."

"Okay, I'll order us some bottled water." Dave signaled to the cocktail waitress and ordered.

"Dave, I really wasn't prepared for that kiss you planted on me."

"Well, just know that you need to prepare yourself for many, many more; that is, if you enjoyed it."

"Now, wait a damn minute. If my memory serves me correctly, aren't you married? Where's your ring? Did you take it off to prowl the clubs tonight?"

"Yes, I'm technically married; however, I've been legally separated for almost a year. In fact, my divorce will be final in a matter of weeks."

"Oh, I'm sorry. I had no idea."

"No need to be sorry, Vanessa, I admire your principles. Besides, the divorce will be a good thing for both of us."

"Wow, I don't know what to say. I, I guess you are back on the dating scene again just like me. Welcome back to the club." They both lifted their bottles of water to toast and smiled.

Just then a Luther Vandross classic ballad began to play, *'There was a time, when I didn't have no one, didn't have no love. Do you remember. . .'* Dave's eyes lit up as he nodded toward the dance floor. Vanessa took his perfectly manicured hand and said, "Why not?" He led her out onto the floor, spun her around and pulled her close, but not too close. He placed his hand firmly in the small of her back and laced his fingers between hers. Vanessa's knees began to tremble from the hypnotic scent that filtered through Dave's silk shirt. It showed off his muscular build, which Vanessa had never really noticed before. She nestled her arm lightly over his shoulder and almost fell off her heels when the inside of his knee rubbed the inside of her thigh. Vanessa felt moistness down below that made her thankful that she was wearing a panty shield.

While Dave and Vanessa danced, the others had gone back to the booth for another round of drinks and to joke about how close Dave and Vanessa were dancing, given they were only "acquaintances." As the song ended, Dave looked into Vanessa's eyes and said, "Would you like to share a cab home?"

Vanessa smiled and said, "Sure, why not?" They met back up with the boyz and girlz and were teased unmercifully. After they finished two more rounds of drinks and a few more dances, Dave stated he had to get back to the restaurant to survey the damage that had been done in his absence. He then turned to Vanessa and said, "Going my way?"

She answered, "Why not?" They were teased again and said good-bye to their friends. Vanessa knew her girlz were in good hands with Dave's friends. She would call them later to get the details on the remainder of the night's happenings. Dave and Vanessa stepped out of the club into a light misty rain; their ears were ringing from the loud music in the club. They instinctively grabbed each other's hands as they dashed across the street to catch a cab. Vanessa took shelter in a doorway trying to protect her hair from the moisture. Dave raised his hand to hail a cab, but it passed him by. This happened again two more times. When he was about to raise his hand for the fourth time, Vanessa grabbed his arm.

"Dave, let me. You're a black man trying to catch a cab after midnight, on a Saturday, in Manhattan, outside a club. Now you know they'll never stop for you, but they will for me."

"Yeah, you're right. If I want to get back to the restaurant before the night manager locks up, I'd better take you up on your offer." Dave stood back in the shadow of the doorway as Vanessa hailed an oncoming cab. It pulled over right away. She opened the door to get in and the cabbie smiled back at her, but he quickly changed his expression when Dave ran up and slid in beside her.

"Where to?" the cabbie asked with an attitude.

"Dave's Place, Wall Street and Front," Dave answered. The cabbie started the meter and they were on their way with a jolt.

Dave held Vanessa's hand as they made their way through the city traffic. She was speechless and began going over in her head the many, many occasions when she had seen Dave at the restaurant. He had never made any gestures indicating he was interested in her. He was always a perfect gentleman and host. She had a million questions for him but chose to keep them to herself. She didn't want to appear too eager or nosy. She decided to let Dave continue to lead the conversations to see where his head was and what his intentions were.

Dave didn't say a word. He just let his hands do the talking for him. He held her hand in several positions, each one more sensual than the last, pausing to give light strokes to her palm and the inside of her wrists. It drove Vanessa crazy to the point where she wanted to moan, but she didn't bat an eyelash; she kept a poker face the entire time. However, she did cross her legs. Dave smiled knowing his goal had been achieved.

Dave broke the silence. "So, do you go to church?"

Vanessa was shocked by his question. "As a matter of fact, I do."

"How about lunch tomorrow afternoon, after church?"

"Ahhhh, sure. Why not?" Vanessa said in disbelief. "Where would you like to meet?"

"What time do you leave for church in the morning?"

"About ten-thirty. Why?"

"I'll be at your door at ten-twenty to pick you up for church. We can go to lunch from there."

Vanessa couldn't believe what she was hearing. "What... I..." she stuttered. Then she shrugged her shoulders and said, "Why not?"

The cab pulled up to the curb in front of the red awning that read Dave's Place. Dave smiled and kissed Vanessa on the back of her hand. He gave the cabbie enough money to cover both of their fares and was gone.

"Where to?" the cabbie asked.

Vanessa announced her address and rode the rest of the way home in amazed puzzlement. She shook her head and smiled as if to wake herself from a dream. She shrugged her shoulders and said with a big smile to herself, *Why not?*

It was a clear sunny morning in mid-June. The wind was kicking the surf up a bit, which caused some concern for those who were revving up their engines in preparation for the New York City Powerboat Poker Run. The stands were filled to capacity with thousands of family, friends, and powerboat enthusiasts as flags and awnings flapped loudly from the windy conditions.

She sat in the VIP section of the stands with her daughter and the nanny by her side. There was excitement in the air as the toddler bounced up and down on her lap saying, "dada, dada" while pointing at the brightly colored speedboats. As they lined up for the race, they resembled pieces of hard candy floating on the surface of the water. She smiled with sadness knowing that this would be the last time she would be attending one of her husband's races. A loud horn blew interrupting her reminiscent thoughts and a green flag waved to signal the start. The sound of the roaring engines was deafening as the nanny covered the child's little ears.

The long slender boats sprinted away leaving a streak of white foam behind them as they made their way to the George Washington Bridge for the official start of the race, then on to Ossining Boat and Canoe

Club to collect the first playing card. While the boats sped out of sight, the bleachers began to empty as the crowds meandered around to check out the hundreds of vendors that had set up shop, and admire the beautiful boats on display at the Liberty Landing Marina. She fastened the child into the stroller and she and the nanny made their way through the crowd to grab some lunch in the Liberty House dining room.

As all moms do, she bent down to pick up a toy the child had thrown on the floor from her stroller. When she looked up, she spotted a woman across the room seated at the bar with her back towards her. An odd feeling came over her that made the hairs stand up on the back of her neck. She shook her head to dismiss the feeling and continued to play fetch with her daughter throughout lunch. As they rose to leave the restaurant, she glanced over at the bar. The woman had disappeared.

They spent the afternoon touring Ellis Island, experiencing the breathtaking view from Lady Liberty's crown, and checking out the latest boats, accessories and gear as the child napped on and off. As the crowds were getting settled back into the stands, anticipating the return of the speedboats, a horn sounded to signal the approach of the first team. Everyone stood and raised their binoculars to watch the speeding boats come into view. As she watched her husband's boat skipping along the surface of the water sprinting for the finish line, the child lay sleeping in the nanny's lap. All of a sudden, a strong gust of wind came up and lifted his boat from the water. It rotated, flipped upside down, and bounced along the water end to end, narrowly missing two other boats that were racing along just behind it. Finally, it came to rest after what seemed like an eternity and burst into flames. The crowd gasped and cried out in disbelief as the plumes of black smoke billowed up into the air. The child wailed inconsolable screams from having been abruptly awakened by the crowd's reaction. Sirens began to blare as the Coast Guard and emergency response crews made their way out to the scene. She dropped her binoculars as her hands flew to her heart. Instinctively, she turned to the nanny and said, "Take the baby to the car and have the driver take you both home immediately. I'll call you when I know something." The nanny obeyed her without comment, wearing an expression of deep concern while trying to quiet the child.

Monica gathered her things and ran down to the dock, but was stopped by security from running out to see some of her husband's crew that had remained behind. Just then another woman ran up screaming with anguish. As the security guards stopped her, she fought back with a vengeance yelling, "That's my boyfriend's boat!" It was the woman that was seated at the bar in the dining room from earlier that day. As the woman struggled with the security guards, her shirt inched up to reveal her lower back. What was revealed made the hairs stand up on the back of Monica's neck again and confirmed her uneasy feelings.

Monica reached out to the woman and put her arms around her in an effort to comfort her. "It's okay, it's going to be all right. Just let the emergency crews do their jobs and I'm sure that everything will be fine. Come on, let's step into the ladies' room for a moment so that you can collect yourself and calm down a bit."

The woman nodded as mascara ran down her cheeks and went along with Monica as she took her out of sight and earshot of the crowd. As they made their way to the restroom, the woman looked up into Monica's eyes and said, "Oh, thank you so much! You're so sweet, just like he said you would be."

"Oh, he told you about me?" She said matter-of-factly.

"Yes, you're Monica aren't you? "Monica Kennedy?"

She calmly replied, "Yes, I am," as she opened the door and led the woman inside. She turned as the door closed and locked it. She turned back to the woman and said, "For privacy," with a fake smile, barely hiding the rage building within her.

The woman went on to say, "He told me you would be here. I feel like I know you. He's told me so much about you and Lizzy."

At the mention of her daughter's name, Monica could no longer contain herself. She dropped her bag to the floor, grabbed the woman by the throat, clutched the back of the woman's long brunette hair, wrapped it around her hand and slammed her head up against the wall. The woman screamed with shock and pain as Monica tighten the grip around her neck, and with clenched teeth said, "Who the hell do you think you are?" The woman gasped for air and frightfully replied, "I'm Jeff's girlfriend. Aren't you his sister-in-law?"

Monica dropped her grasp of the woman's throat and hair as she stepped back in disbelief. All she could manage to say in a whispered tone was, "No, I'm his wife."

"What! What the hell are you talking about? Oh, oh my God, I didn't know!" the woman screamed. "He's married, to you? I'm going to kill that son-of-a-bitch!"

With a new resolve and an eerie calm, Monica said, "Oh, I don't think so. That's my job. If he's not already dead, he'll wish he was by the time I get through with his ass!"

"Daddy, Daddy!"

Monica, startled from her dream that was once a reality, jumped up with sweat soaked clothes and ran down the hall to her daughter's bedroom. She found her sitting up in bed shaking and crying.

"It's okay, Sweetie. It's okay. Go back to sleep." Monica scooped up Lizzy and carried her over to a rocking chair, while soothing her with reassuring hugs and strokes through her golden ringlets.

"I know you wish Daddy were here. I do too," Monica admitted; however, she wanted him back for a very different reason.

CHAPTER

9

At 7:00 p.m. sharp, the doorbell rang. Monica placed a freshly popped bowl of popcorn on the living room coffee table as she went to answer the door.

"Mrs. Florence, come on in. You're right on time."

Mrs. Florence nodded her head and entered the apartment and noticed the smell of popcorn in the air.

"I thought you were going out. I see you've prepared dinner for your date," she said gesturing at the bowl of popcorn.

"Cute, real cute," Monica answered with a smile.

"Why aren't you dressed yet?"

Monica was wearing a pair of light gray lounging pants, a white, V-neck t-shirt, and a white, monogrammed Ralph Lauren bath robe.

"I have a date tonight with two people."

Mrs. Florence held up her hand and stated, "Look, I don't want to hear about your perversions."

"My date is with two ladies," Monica said in a sensual tone.

"Oh my heavens! Monica, really?" Mrs. Florence said as her hand flew to her hips.

Monica couldn't stifle a laugh any longer. "The two ladies I am referring to are you and Lizzy. I thought it would be nice to get together and watch a movie and eat some popcorn." Monica grinned as Mrs. Florence's face flushed with embarrassment as she tried to stifle a smile. She straightened her posture, turned her nose up in the air and said, "Monica that would be lovely."

"Great! I'll go get the little lady. She's getting into her PJs."

Monica rescued Lizzy's head from the neck of her pajama top and the three of them snuggled together on the sofa under a large, camel-colored, cashmere blanket. The feature film was a Disney classic, the original *Cinderella*. Before Cinderella had a chance to sing the words, 'In my own little corner, in my own little chair, I can be whatever I want to be,' Lizzy was fast asleep between the two women she loved most. Monica picked up her little cherub and carried her to a canopy-topped bed, while planting multiple kisses on her forehead and chubby cheeks. When she returned, she paused the movie just as the clock began to strike midnight.

"Why did you do that?" Mrs. Florence objected. "I want to see the rest of it."

"We both know how it ends. She marries the prince with the foot fetish and they all live happily ever after." They both chuckled.

"I asked you to come over because I really need to talk with you, like we used to talk before Jeff died. You've always been there for me, my entire life. You've loved and supported Noah and me when Daddy was emotionally unavailable and Momma was unconscious from her drinking binges. You tried your best to make up for my parents' shortcomings."

"Well, your parents had a lot of issues that they were never able to work through. Your father escaped through his work and your mother escaped through the bottle."

"Issues? What kind of issues?"

"It's really not my place to reveal their private struggles."

"Well, they couldn't have been too private if you knew about them. Besides, they are both dead now. You're released from your confidentially agreement."

Mrs. Florence paused, cleared her throat and began. "Monica, your father was unfaithful to your mother. He had an ongoing affair that lasted for many, many years."

"What?"

"Yes, your parents' marriage was arranged by their parents. They both came from well to do families and their parents wanted to ensure that their fortunes didn't end up in someone else's hands that didn't know how to appreciate wealth."

"You've got to be kidding! I thought that kind of thing only took place in royal families and foreign countries."

"Oh, no. These types of arrangements still happen quite frequently with families of means."

"I can't believe my parents gave their consent."

"They did so to appease their parents, but the problem was that your father had fallen in love with a woman he had met in college. However, he married your mother to keep from being disinherited and continued his relationship with the woman he truly loved. Your mother knew of the relationship from the beginning, but married your father under pressure from her parents. She managed okay while you were small, because I think she truly believed that by having a family, your father would eventually end the relationship. However, all hopes were dashed when the other woman had a son two months after your brother, Noah, was born. She was married to another man, however your father admitted to your mother that the baby was his."

"My poor mother. She must have been devastated!"

"She was, and that's when her drinking started to get out of control. I basically took over the responsibility of caring for you and your brother. She confided in me, but forbade me to say anything."

"Why didn't you tell me when I got old enough to understand?"

"It wasn't my place. Your parents were my employers and if I wanted to keep my job, I had to keep my mouth shut. I couldn't bear the thought of losing you two. I cared for you both as if you were my own children."

"Oh Nanny, I truly thank you for being such a blessing in my life, as well as in Lizzy's," Monica said with tears in her eyes as she hugged Nanny tight.

"Well, it started out just being a job, but it developed into a labor of love," Mrs. Florence said with a reminiscent smile.

"You know, I never realized how much you sacrificed your own life to raise Noah and me until I had Lizzy. I am so glad you were there for us; otherwise, I truly don't know what would have become of us. But since Jeff's death, last year, you've become more and more distant. I know it's because you don't think I am acting like a widow should: working, dating, and spending so much time away from Lizzy. But there are some things I think you need to know." Monica took a deep breath and took Nanny's hand in hers.

"Over the seven years that Jeff and I were married, he was cheating on me for at least the last three years that I know of. After our fourth year of marriage, he became increasingly distant and emotionally unavailable like Daddy used to be, so I knew in my heart of hearts that something was wrong. Something had changed. One day Jeff said he was going to sleep out on the yacht, because he was going to be up late prepping his cigarette boat for a race. I thought I would surprise him, so I put on some lingerie and a trench coat and slipped on board that night." Mrs. Florence cleared her throat and looked away with embarrassment. "The light was on in the master cabin, so I peeked through the window from the deck and saw him with another woman, making love to her in our bed, on our sheets, on our yacht. They weren't just having sex. I could tell by the way their bodies moved and the way they looked at one another that he was emotionally tied to her. She had a birthmark that I will never forget.

"I left as quietly as I had come and for the next year, I suffered in silence. I blamed myself for his straying, thinking that I had put my career before his needs. I decided that having a baby would bring us closer together so I stopped taking the pill and got pregnant. Jeff was ecstatic. I thought Lizzy was going to be our saving grace. All his focus was on me during the pregnancy and then on Lizzy when she was born. Jeff didn't spend any nights away from home anymore and he was truly a great father. But, there really wasn't any direct communication between Jeff and me, unless it was about the baby. When Lizzy went to bed at night, it was as though a wall went up between us. We didn't speak to one another, or even look at each other. Needless to say, there was nothing going on under the sheets either." Nanny cleared her throat.

"I just figured this is what all new parents go through. I was always tired from constant sleep interruptions because Lizzy was so colicky. Jeff was racing full-time and preparing multiple boats for multiple races. But, he always came home at night, so I thought all was well and that our communication would improve over time. Boy, was I delusional!

"One Saturday afternoon when Lizzy was about eight-months-old, I fixed a nice picnic lunch and headed for the yacht, struggling with a diaper bag on my shoulder, the picnic basket in one hand, and Lizzy in her carrier in the other. Jeff's head mechanic, Nick, saw me coming and ran up to try and deter me from going on board. At that moment, I knew what was going on. I handed the basket, the baby bag, and Lizzy to him and left him standing on the dock while I tiptoed on board. I looked through that same window and was met with the same view as before, same woman, same position, and the same birthmark. I turned around, retrieved Lizzy and the diaper bag, and told Nick, "Enjoy the lunch! Oh, and don't bother to thank me. In fact, don't mention that I was here!

"I was so angry at myself for thinking that I had the power to change Jeff's behavior by throwing my birth control pills away. He had a big race coming up, so I decided to confront him and tell him that I was leaving him after the race. Needless to say, I never got the chance." The tears began to flow from both of their eyes. Mrs. Florence took Monica into her arms, and as she had done so many times before, Monica instinctively curled up into the fetal position.

Monica said through her sobs, "I wanted Jeff to know that I knew all about his love affair. I wanted so much to vent my anger and resentment. I wanted him to feel the hurt when I walked out the door with Lizzy, but I never got the opportunity. It's been eating at me every day since I watched him die in the boat crash. I never got to tell him how much he hurt me. It's so unfair!"

Monica began to wail. She had spent the year since Jeff's death medicating herself with sex and alcohol to keep her from feeling the anger, pain, and discontentment that eroded her spirit. Mrs. Florence gently wiped away Monica's tears with a handkerchief that she always kept tucked in her sleeve on the inside of her wrist.

"Monica, I need to tell you something." Monica sat up and looked her in the eyes.

"Nanny, why are you crying? I've never seen you cry before!"

"My child, I've cried for you and your brother many a night over the years. I've seen many things that you've never seen and heard many things that you've never heard." Mrs. Florence paused and took a deep breath, grabbed Monica's right hand and sandwiched it between hers.

"I knew about Jeff's affair."

"What!" Monica said in a shaken and bewildered voice. "When did you find out? How did you find out? Why didn't you tell me?"

"Remember when you lived in your old apartment and you were away on a business trip on your birthday? You had just found out you were pregnant. I remember how upset you were about being away from home on your birthday. So, I decided to come over and cook a big birthday meal and leave it in the refrigerator so you could have it when you returned home on the red-eye the next morning. I even had the bakery make your favorite cake for the occasion. I knew that Jeff wasn't home during the day, so I figured I would be in and out before he came home for the night. Well, when I opened the door, there was a trail of clothing leading down the hall to the bedroom. I could hear sounds, you know, of lovemaking. For a minute I thought that you had taken an earlier flight back until I saw a size nine shoe in the middle of the floor. I bought shoes for you until you were well into your teens, so I knew that shoe didn't belong to your size six and a half foot. I must have gasped because Jeff came running out of the bedroom dragging a sheet wrapped around his waist. Both the groceries and the chocolate tiramisu cake I was holding hit the floor as my mouth flew open.

"Nanny, why didn't you tell me?"

"Sweetie, you were pregnant, it was your birthday, and you were in the process of closing on this apartment. I didn't want to cause any physical risk to you or the baby, and most of all, I didn't want to give you news that would break your heart." Nanny paused before asking the question "Do you know why I live in the apartment next to you?"

"Yes. To be near Lizzy."

"No. It's because I told Jeff that if he didn't allow me to continue to be in your life and take care of the baby when it was born, I would tell you about the incident. He begged me not to tell. He said it was just a one-time thing, however I challenged him on that. Then he offered to buy the apartment next door and let me stay in it rent-free for as long as I wanted if I would keep my silence. I agreed."

"You blackmailed Jeff?"

"Oh, I wouldn't call it that. I was just protecting you and the baby because I knew that one day you would find out about his affair. I wanted to ensure that I would be nearby, to be your shoulder to cry on. It's what any mother would have done to protect her daughter and her grandchild. After Jeff died, I felt there was no need to bring it up. I just decided to let sleeping dogs lie."

Monica laid her head on her nanny's lap and cried herself to sleep. Mrs. Florence covered her up and quietly crept back to her apartment feeling light on her feet like Mary Poppins, because she had finally unloaded the burden she had been carrying for so long. Monica slept like a baby, better than she had slept in years. She dreamed that Cinderella's shoe size was six and a half.

CHAPTER

10

The opening bell for the stock market was about to ring as Anne sipped her green tea and rechecked the online financial news for any late breaking stories from her office laptop. Connie waltzed in casually and gently dropped a gold envelope on Anne's desk then headed back towards the door without saying a word. With a raised eyebrow, Anne picked up the envelope and said in an annoyed voice, "This had better be an apology from you for letting me make a damn fool of myself in front of that married corporate attorney!"

Connie snickered as she returned to her desk. That incident had been the comedic highlight of her career. There was no way she was going to apologize for that.

"Damn! I hate these stupid things," Anne exclaimed as she read the invitation to a company-sponsored event at the New York Metropolitan Museum of Art.

"I have to spend hours choosing and getting fitted for just the right gown, shoes, bag, and jewelry.

The dress can't be too provocative or too conservative, and not too bright or too flashy. Then I've got to spend half a day getting coiffed and made up like a china doll just so I can stand around all evening by myself holding a drink, smiling, making corporate cocktail party small talk, and praying that I don't trip over the train on my gown that I have to drag around all night long." Anne paused, took a deep breath, and shouted toward the outer office.

"Are you getting any of this?" Anne said with an attitude.

"I hear you loud and clear, Boss," Connie said sarcastically.

"Get Barney's on the phone and tell them I need a dress for Friday night, please. Make an appointment for me to go in this afternoon."

"Already called. Your appointment is at one o'clock," Connie replied.

"Figures. You just know every damn thing, don't you?" Anne shouted from her office. Connie laughed because she prided herself in being able to predict the wants, needs, and desires of her boss. She had gotten to know Anne like the back of her hand quite quickly. She also took great pleasure in knowing that it pissed Anne off that she could predict her every move. Although Anne deplored being predictable, she valued Connie for her intuition and proactive responses; however, Anne would never in a million years admit that to Connie.

Connie took a call and then quietly walked into Anne's office and closed the door behind her. She looked like she had seen a ghost. Anne looked up at her.

"What? Don't tell me you're pregnant!"

"Are you kidding! My kids are grown."

"Good, because I don't have time to fire you today."

Maria walked into her office and closed the door behind her. She threw her Ricky bag on a side chair and took a deep breath as she sat down at her desk. She knew there would be questions, lots of questions, about her return to work so soon after the death of her husband. She didn't care about the stares and whispers she witnessed as she made her way up in the elevator and through the halls to her office. She just kept her chin raised high and smiled as she walked by the onlookers. She leaned back in her chair, looked up to the ceiling and whispered with a broad smile, "I'm back, for good this time! No more calling in sick because of black eyes and bruises. I'm safe, my girls are safe, and I am ready to kick some corporate ass." A bewildered look came over her face as she spotted the mountain of messages, mail, and reports on her credenza that needed her attention. A beautiful gold envelope sitting on top of the stack caught her eye. She delicately picked it up and carefully opened it. When she read it, she got excited about the prospects of rubbing elbows with the senior executives. It was her time to shine and network for her next career move. José had never let her attend these kinds of events. Even when she begged him to come with her, he still said no. There was nothing holding her back now. She immediately picked up the phone and called Saks. There was no time to waste; she had to look perfect.

Vanessa dragged herself into work after her whirlwind weekend with Dave. She enjoyed his company and attention so much that she had been racking her brain for a creative way to thank him. A beautiful gold envelope on her desk distracted her thoughts. She grabbed her sterling silver letter opener and broke the seal open with an inquisitive look on her face, which quickly turned into a broad smile, accompanied by a high-school giggle. Vanessa pressed the invitation to her chest, and kicked up her heels as she leaned back in her leather executive chair.

"Perfect, just perfect," she said as she pulled her cell phone from the pocket of her Burberry trench coat hanging behind her office door.

"Dave's Place," a female voice announced.

"Yes, is Dave in?"

"Who's calling?"

"Vanessa Baldwin."

"Oh, one moment, please, Ms. Baldwin."

Vanessa was put on hold. She tapped her Montblanc pen on her desk blotter as she waited. A few moments later, Dave's eager voice greeted her.

"Well, hello!"

"Dave! It's Vanessa."

"Hmmm, it's been less than ten hours since we parted and you're hounding me already," Dave said with a sarcastic tone.

"Oh, you wish. I don't fall head-over-heels that easily. Well, at least not anymore." Vanessa said with a playful tone.

"So, to what do I owe the pleasure of this call?

"Look, what would you say to escorting me to a black tie event on Friday night at the MET. My company is sponsoring the opening of a new exhibit."

"I'd say, 'I would be delighted.' What time shall I collect you?"

"Oh, about six. We'll arrive fashionably late for the cocktail hour. And I'd like to treat you to a late supper afterwards."

"Well, in that case, I can't attend."

"But why? Do you have some important clients coming to the restaurant on Friday night?"

"No. As I've stated previously, you deserve to be treated, and treated well, therefore I will arrange for a late, intimate supper for two."

Vanessa smiled. "Well, if you insist! I look forward to spending the evening with you Mr. Patton. Until then. . ." Vanessa kissed the phone to end the call and did a fist pump in the air. As she pushed the intercom button on her office phone, Francine walked into her office and closed the door behind her.

"Oh, I was just calling. Can you please get my personal shopper over at Neiman's on the phone?"

With a solemn voice, Francine said, "I have something to tell you."

As part of her morning routine, Monica stopped by a newsstand to pick up the *Wall Street Journal* and the *New York Times*. She liked to peruse them as she drank her morning cup of Starbucks coffee. She sang a perky "Good morning" to Julie as she stepped into her office, which Julie always had unlocked and open for Monica each morning. She knew Monica's hands would be full with her newspapers, briefcase, morning joe, and her tan, croc-embossed leather Ricky bag. Monica's snail mail, daily reports and messages were neatly arranged on her desk next to her phone. In the center of the desk was a golden envelope. She put her Ricky bag in the lower left-hand drawer of her desk and plopped down in her khaki-tan, butter-soft leather chair. It was customary for her to read the newspapers first, but the golden envelope was too irresistible to pass up. She grabbed a letter opener from her crystal pencil cup and neatly sliced it open. She took a sip of coffee and read the invitation.

"Hmmm, the prince is giving a ball. I guess I'd better get my glass slippers shined up for the occasion. But, when the clock strikes twelve, I am out of there."

Monica summoned Julie into her office and asked her to call her personal shopper and send him over to Bergdorf's to find her a gown.

"Right away! Will you be needing a limousine as well?"

"No, I think I'll skip the limo this time. Just inform my driver that we'll be taking the Rolls out. I am sure the champagne will be flowing, so I'll need a designated driver."

Julie thought to herself, *she'll need a designated walker too.* As she returned to her desk, her phone rang.

"I'll need appointments to have my hair and make-up done, mani, pedi and waxing also," Monica instructed.

"Julie did you hear me?"

Julie walked into Monica's office and closed the door behind her.

"Well, did you hear me about the hair . . ." Monica stopped mid-sentence, because she could tell Julie was upset.

"What's wrong, Julie?"

"I just received a call with some terrible news. Maria's husband committed suicide," Julie said in a hushed tone.

"What!" Monica said with a gasp as she brought her hand up to cover her heart. "What happened?"

Just as Julie was about to recount the story reported by the corporate grapevine, someone knocked at Monica's door. Julie turned to open it and to their surprise it was Maria. She poked her head in and greeted them with a cheerful, "Good morning!"

Both Monica and Julie's eyes grew wide as their mouths fell open with shock. Neither one of them expected to see Maria for quite some time, at least not until after the funeral. Julie exited Monica's office quickly with an unusually high pitched, "Good morning," followed by a nervous laugh, and closed the door behind her.

"Did you receive your golden opportunity?" Maria said with a giddy smile as she waved her envelope and practically skipped over to Monica's desk.

Monica sat paralyzed as she stared at Maria in disbelief. Finally, she snapped out of it. "What? Ah, what are you doing here? We didn't expect you to return so soon after . . ." Monica searched for the right words to finish her sentence.

Maria rescued her from the awkward moment. "Well, I needed a distraction to keep my mind off the situation and work is the best one I could come up with."

"Well, we missed you," Monica said as she made her way around the desk to hug Maria. "Were just so glad that you and the girls are okay. The girls are okay, right?" Monica asked, still dumbfounded that Maria was standing in front of her.

"We're all doing fine. It's great to finally be back."

"Your bruises from the car accident are almost gone," Monica mentioned.

"Huh? Oh, yeah they are fading quickly. So, did you get the invitation?" Maria said, quickly changing the subject.

"Hmmm, oh, yeah. I've already summoned my Fairy God Shopper," Monica remarked sarcastically.

Maria giggled like a schoolgirl as she slid into a leather club chair in front of Monica's desk. "I cannot wait! This is such a great opportunity for me to cozy up with the senior execs."

"You are kidding, right? You don't plan on attending given your, your situation. Besides, you loath these corporate soirees more than I do," Monica said as she made her way back to her executive chair.

"No, I'm going! This is the first time that I'll be able to attend a company event. This is a really big deal for me."

"Able to attend? I don't understand. I thought you hated these kinds of events. That's the reason you always gave for not wanting to go."

Maria suddenly became interested in her cuticles. She couldn't look Monica in the face as she replied in a whisper of a voice, "I just said that because my hus... José never allowed me to attend. I was ashamed to admit it."

"Maria, I had no idea!" Monica said with concern as she leaned forward on her desk.

"Yeah, I know. I put up a good front for a long time. Needless to say, my career ladder climb was hindered because I couldn't mingle socially with the powers that be."

"Well, this calls for a celebration and a special meeting of The Sangrita Club. I'll call Vanessa and she'll set it up for tomorrow evening. We can get together and chat about who's wearing what designer. The last thing we need is for the paparazzi to have a field day because two of us show up in the same gown."

"Sounds like a very important business meeting that I cannot miss." They both chuckled as Maria stood to leave.

"Oh, Maria, how insensitive of me. Our celebration can be postponed if it interferes with the arrangements for your hus. . . José's funeral and burial?"

"Oh, no. Believe me it won't. See you tomorrow," Maria said as she exited Monica's office waving her golden envelope once again with the flick of her wrist.

Monica jumped up from her desk, ran to the door and spied as Maria rounded the corner toward the elevator. Monica closed her door, and hit number three to speed dial Vanessa's number.

"Hi, Monica!"

"Vanessa, did you hear about José?"

"Yes, I was just getting ready to call you. I was busy all weekend, so I didn't catch the news. I just heard about him a few minutes ago."

"Yeah, I just heard about it from Julie a few minutes ago."

"We've got to get together and go see Maria. She must be devastated!"

"Well, we won't have to go far because she's here!"

"Here! Where?" Vanessa said in a confused tone.

"She was just here in my office a minute ago, going on and on about the gala and how she can't wait to go."

"You've got to be kidding! I don't believe you. She's in mourning. Besides, she hates those things."

Monica went on to describe her unusual encounter with Maria and that she had wanted to ask more details about José's sudden death, but she was afraid to broach the subject with her just yet. They surmised that she might be in a fragile state, just putting up a brave front to keep her composure and keep her mind off the pain of José's passing. The office rumor mill was buzzing about his death being a suicide, but they both agreed to wait for Maria to bring up the subject before giving her the third degree.

As Monica asked Vanessa to set up The Sangrita Club fashion meeting, Monica knew in her heart of hearts that she had to begin showing some restraint when it came to her drinking. She had a new beginning with Nanny, and she didn't want to blow it by coming home walking sideways again. She used to drink to deaden the residual pain she felt from her husband's betrayal and her inability to confront him about it before his death. But now she felt she had gained back some control after her talk with Nanny, and could truly drink socially without going too far. Or so she thought. . .

"Hello, my name is Rachel and I will be taking care of you today," the personal shopper announced with a fake French accent.

"Okay, I want something sophisticated, figure hugging, and easy to walk in. I don't want to have to pull it up in the front all evening to keep my boobs from falling out. It needs to be floor length with a small train and no sequins! Chiffon, silk and jersey are okay, but no satin, pleats, gathers, or bows. So, do you have something that will fit my requirements?"

"Well Ms. Wu, you've certainly narrowed down our selection. Please have a seat and I'll send out the models with some of the items we pre-selected based on the criteria your executive assistant gave us. Please feel free to enjoy something from our beverage bar while you wait. Drew will take your order. I'll be back momentarily."

"I'll have an espresso straight up, no frills, thanks," Anne said with an attitude. Drew disappeared with a bow. "Connie's criteria. What the hell does she know about what I want?" Anne muttered under her breath.

Drew reappeared with Anne's coffee and a linen napkin. She sipped her poison as the first model emerged from the dressing room. She wore a flowing "red chiffon overlay gown with diamond encrusted spaghetti straps," Rachel explained.

"Red says whore," Anne commented under her breath as she took another sip.

Rachel tried to ignore Anne's response. The second model quickly appeared wearing a white strapless empire waist silk gown with an embroidered bodice sprinkled with multi-colored semi-precious stones.

"Great, if I were getting married, but that's not going to happen," Anne snapped as she sipped again.

The third model appeared.

"That's it! That's the one. It's sleek, conservative, with a little flair." Anne shouted as she jumped up and practically pounced on the third model. She was wearing a midnight blue jersey gown. The bodice was asymmetrical with one wide strap over the right shoulder, no sleeves. It was sleek, hugged every curve, and had a modest train that just swept the floor. It had a gorgeous jeweled broach at the waist and a smaller version was worn in the model's hair, which was swept up into an elegant chignon. "Can you provide alterations by Friday afternoon?"

"But of course, Ms. Wu! This is Leah, our seamstress. She will take your measurements and do the fitting. This way please."

Anne was so pleased that she almost skipped into the dressing room. Then she remembered, Connie had given them her requirements. Anne had to admit to herself, *Connie is good!*

"No. No. Nooooo. Oh, God no! No. No. I don't think so. Not in this life." Monica let out a big sigh as she pulled through a rack of gowns while waiting for Lance, her personal shopper, as he finished up a phone call with a client.

"Ah, Ms. Kennedy, please come this way," Lance directed in an octave that paralleled hers. "I have a selection of gowns and accessories already put aside for you. Would you care for some herbal tea?"

"No thanks, but if you have some champagne available, that would be nice."

"Coming up," Lance said with a smile. He snapped his fingers and a server appeared from nowhere. "Champagne for the young lady please." Monica chuckled at the thought of being called a young lady.

"Come sit, sit. I will show you." Monica plopped down in a comfy chair and waited for the parade to begin. Lance knew her color palette and her taste, so Monica knew it wouldn't take long to pick a gown. Two models emerged wearing champagne-gold gowns as the server handed Monica a glass of bubbly.

"Darling, this is your color and your drink! It will blend well with your hair color and look great against your residual summer tan."

The first model had on an empire-waist gown with spaghetti straps that crisscrossed down a dangerously plunging back, down to the crack. The low-cut bodice formed a deep V-shape and was hand embroidered with gold Swarovski crystals. The skirt was A-line with an overlay of flowing chiffon that ended in a train that lightly skimmed the floor.

The second model wore a simple sleeveless scoop neck gown with an empire waist. The A-line skirt was made of opaque silk with a sheer silk overlay in cream that parted with a slit up the front from hem to bodice. The overlay was adorned throughout with clear Swarovski crystals, with more of a concentration at the waistline.

"Hmmm, do I want to be a princess or a queen?" Monica asked Lance.

"Honey, go for the princess! You've got the rest of your life to be a queen." They chuckled and Monica chose the first gown. Next, they concentrated on shoes and accessories.

"Oh, my, God! I've never seen so many gorgeous gowns in my life!" Maria exclaimed. "I don't know where to begin!"

"That's what I'm here for," an eager voice said over her shoulder. "Hi, I'm Colin." Maria shook his hand violently.

"Hi, I'm Maria, Maria Vasquez!"

"Just tell me what you're looking for Ms. Vasquez." That sounded like music to Maria's ears.

After she discovered what José had been doing to the girls, she started the legal process of not only changing her last name back to her maiden name, but also her girls' last names. She wanted her girls to have a brand new start with new names, a new address, and a new school. Maria wanted a fresh start for herself also, with a new name, new gown, and if she played her networking cards right, a new executive position. This gown was going to represent her new direction: onward and upward.

"What is the experience you want to have in this gown? Based on your feedback, I will make a selection that will fit your ideal."

"Well, I want to be elegant, conservative, but not librarian-ish, formal, with a bit of whimsy."

"Do you have a color in mind?"

"Black is always good for corporate events, I guess."

"Hmmm, I believe I've got just the right gown for you. It's different and it's from an up-and-coming new designer, so keep an open mind. Now, help yourself to a beverage and I'll be right back. I guarantee you'll love it!"

Maria sat uneasily on pins-and-needles, munching on a tea cookie while flipping through the latest issue of *Vogue*. After a few minutes, a tall, beautiful, Latina woman approached and stopped right in front of her. Maria's mouth fell open and her half-eaten cookie fell to her lap.

"So, I was right. You do love it, don't you?" Colin gushed.

"Oh, my God, it's absolutely incredible," she said as she retrieved the fallen cookie and stood to brush the crumbs from her lap. "It's perfect, absolutely perfect!"

"Great, let's get your measurements and check out some accessories."

Maria felt like Colin had read her mind and knew just what she wanted to wear, just like Cinderella's fairy godmother. She couldn't wait for her little girls to see her all dressed up in that beautiful gown. She felt like she had finally crossed the threshold of a place that she had been forbidden to enter for so long. She fought back the tears as the seamstress took her measurements. She vowed to herself to never let anyone hold her back from realizing her dreams ever again.

11

It was Tuesday evening, yet the bar at Sangritas was packed by five-thirty. Everyone needed an hour or so to get happy before heading home after a grueling day at work. Vanessa introduced Maria to Anne as they walked over from the office. They entered Sangritas like a whirlwind.

"The name is Vanessa Baldwin. I have a reservation for the private booth," she announced to the hostess.

"Yes, Senorita Baldwin. Your table is ready." Anne, Monica, and Maria gave each other a "well, excuse me" look as they were led to a booth. The hostess seated them and closed the curtains behind her as she left.

"I'm scared of you, Miss Vanessa! No wait with a packed house? Usually, we have to wait at the bar and order a few rounds of drinks even if we have a reservation," Monica exclaimed.

"The keys to getting seated quickly are: getting in good with the owners, referring new, big spending customers, and having them mention your name when they come in. And last, but most importantly, tipping well, including the hostess!" They all screamed and cackled with laughter, but froze when the curtains suddenly flew opened. They thought they were going to be reprimanded for their loud voices, but instead the server announced, "Your drinks have arrived, ladies."

"But we didn't order yet," Anne said with a puzzled look on her face. Vanessa just sat back and smiled.

"Your drinks were pre-ordered at Senorita Baldwin's request." Once again, 'well, excuse me' looks were passed around.

The potions were given out and the curtains were closed once again.

"Vanessa, you really know how to work it, girl!" Anne offered.

"Thank you, Anne. And with that . . .," "Vanessa lifted her glass and said, "Let this meeting of The Sangrita Club officially begin." They all clinked glasses and sipped the potion.

"Now, our first order of business," Monica added, "is to officially welcome Maria back."

"Here, here," they chimed in unison as they clinked and sipped again.

"We are so happy that you've returned to us alive and well. We can't even begin to know what it must be like to be in a car accident, then turn around and lose your hus . . . José," Monica said tripping over her words, yet trying to sound as sympathetic as possible.

"Guys, I'm fine, really. Sometimes tragedy brings about immense clarity. Thank you all for calling and checking in on me. I really appreciate it."

Vanessa leaned over and put her hand on Maria's, "I think I can speak for all of us when I say, if there is ever anything we can do for you or the girls, just name it. We are here for you, even if you just need a shoulder to cry on or someone to listen."

"Thank you." Maria felt bad about not being open about what had really transpired in her life. She wanted to come clean, but needed more time to wrap her own head around all of her circumstances. Besides, she had only just met Anne and needed more time to feel her out.

"Now, let's get down to the real reason we are here: to talk about Friday night's fashions and celebrate Maria's coming out. This will be the first company-sponsored formal event that she's attending!" Monica announced. Congratulations were passed around.

"Oh, you'll have fun getting all dressed up. And an evening at the MET is always fabulous," Vanessa commented.

"Well, I'll start," said Anne as she dipped a crunchy tortilla chip into a hot and spicy sauce. "I'm wearing a beautiful navy, one-shoulder gown made out of this wonderfully soft jersey fabric, along with some strategically placed diamond jewels." Everybody "ooooed" and "ahhhhed" over her description.

"Well, I'm wearing - wait, hold on a minute," Monica said as she poked her head through the curtain to flag down a server. A server appeared immediately. "Can you be a dear and bring us another round of Sangritas please? Thanks!"

"And menus too, please," Vanessa blurted out. "We're starving!"

"Vanessa, you didn't pre-order entrées for all of us too?" Maria joked. They all cackled.

Vanessa was surprised that Monica had ordered another round so soon. No one else had finished their drinks yet. She had always been a social drinker, but it seemed to have gotten heavier and heavier since her husband's death.

"Now, where was I? Oh yeah, my gown. Well, it's a soft gold to match my natural blonde hair color," she said with a wink. "I'm going to be wearing a crystal encrusted, dressless, evening strap." They all hollered to the point of tears, then froze again as the curtains parted, the second round of drinks was served and menus presented. As the curtains closed, the laughter rang out again.

"Okay, okay, all jokes aside. It's an empire waist, crisscross back strap number, which exposes my back down to my ass crack." Laughter burst forth again.

"Well, what about you Maria?" Monica inquired as she took another swig of her second drink. "This is your first time, so I am sure you picked something to dazzle us."

"Well, to tell you the truth, I am really excited about going and would prefer to surprise everyone with my gown."

"What?" Anne and Monica exclaimed in unison.

"Oh, come on! You don't have to give us the excruciating details of the gown. You can at least tell us what color it is," Monica said with an attitude.

"All right, all right! It's black and white," to which Vanessa, Anne, and Monica all gasped and said, "Uh oh!"

"Uh Oh? What's that supposed to mean?" Maria asked.

Vanessa spoke up. "Well, it sounds a little brides-maid-ish."

"Oh, believe me, no bride would ever let her bridesmaids wear this gown. Otherwise no one would be looking at her. Words to describe this gown are class and sophistication."

"Well as long as it doesn't have any bows, I guess you'll be all right," Monica added.

"Uh, there is a bow," Maria said reluctantly. Anne and Monica looked at each other but looked away quickly while stifling smiles.

Vanessa fought to keep a straight face and said, "Well, as long as the bow isn't bigger than your butt, then you should be okay."

Monica put her arm around Maria and said with a sarcastic slur, "I'm sure it's just beautiful!"

Maria playfully pushed her away and said, "See, that's exactly why I didn't want to say anything. You just wait and see. My gown is going to blow all of yours out of the water."

"Let the contest begin!" Monica challenged. They all raised their glasses and said, "You're on!"

"Hey, wait a minute, Vanessa. What about you?" Monica interrupted.

"Well, I'm kind of in agreement with Maria. I want to surprise you all too, but I want to leave here in one piece, so I'd better at least throw you a bone. It's a two piece!"

"Vanessa, we're going to a ball, not the beach," said Anne. Monica and Maria sniggled.

"Cute, real cute. It's sort of a jacket and a skirt."

"You're wearing a suit? Oh, you have definitely lost the contest on that alone," Maria added.

"The skirt is a really beautiful metallic fabric."

"Hmmm," Maria, Anne, and Monica said simultaneously.

Monica leaned over and attempted to take a sip from her already empty glass and said, "The last thing you want to do is show up with a shiny ass. I hope that skirt doesn't cup your butt!" The laughter erupted again but ceased as the curtains flew open again.

"Are you ready to order?"

"Yeah, another round of Sangritas for the senoritas, please," Monica exclaimed with laughter, and a slight slur. No one laughed except Monica. Vanessa broke the silence and gave her order. While the others made decisions about their entrées and offered up their orders, Vanessa made a decision to confront Monica about her drinking. She would set up an intervention if needed, because unlike most New

218

Yorkers, Monica had several cars and had a tendency to drive quite often. Vanessa didn't want her to get pulled over for a DUI, DWI or get into an accident and hurt herself or somebody else.

The Sangrita club spent the rest of the evening joking about each other's work wardrobes and the fashion choices of their colleagues, as well as discussing how easy men have it when it comes to business attire: suit or trousers and sport coat, white or blue shirt, black shoes and belt – you can't get any simpler than that.

Monica took a cab home from the restaurant. She knew she was in no shape to drive, aside from the fact that Vanessa had practically snatched the keys out of her hand when they got up to leave. As the city lights passed by, she grew melancholy because she knew that she had gone too far and crossed the line with her drinking once again. As her cab pulled up to her building, the doorman opened the door, helped her out, assisted her through the front door of her building, and to the elevator.

"Shall I see you up to your penthouse, Ms. Kennedy?" Ralph offered, with chivalry not being the purpose of his asking.

"No thanks, Ralph. I'm fine."

"Yes, Madam," he replied respectfully as he pushed the call button for the elevator. When it arrived, he escorted her on, inserted a key, pushed the penthouse button, and said good night as he stepped off the elevator.

"Boy, I must really look like I'm drunk. Ralph has never asked me if I wanted to be escorted to my apartment before. I don't feel drunk. I know I had too many drinks to be able to drive, but I'm not falling down drunk," she said out loud as the elevator made its way up. She fished around in her Ricky bag for a compact to assess the damage. She wanted to make an attempt at looking semi-sober for Mrs. Florence.

"Hmmm, I don't look too bad. A little lipstick will do the trick," she said as she rummaged through her bag again. She finally found it and began applying it when a familiar tone rang out, indicating that she had reached the penthouse floor. Monica straightened her posture and checked to see if she had applied her lipstick straight. She was so busy checking her bloodshot eyes in the mirror that when she stepped off the elevator, she stepped short and the heel of her stiletto went down through the crack in between the car and the floor. Since she was wearing pumps, her foot slipped out of the shoe easily, however she lost her balance and fell forward into the hallway. Her lipstick went skidding across the marble floor hitting the wall and her compact mirror hit the floor and shattered into a thousand pieces. Luckily, she caught herself with her hands and her bag swung around and hit the floor instead of her head.

The doors began to close behind her, so she scrambled to her knees and tried to pull her shoe out of the crack; however, before she could get a good grip on it, the door hit her shoe and bounced back. She tried with all of her might to free the heel from the crack, however the doors began to close once again, and this time the alarm sounded. She crawled into the elevator with one shoe still on and started pushing buttons to stop the alarm bells, but to no avail. She then began again tugging feverishly on her shoe but it still wouldn't budge. In the midst of all the mayhem, she looked up and saw the all-too-familiar slippers of her Nanny. She froze, put her head down, and covered her eyes with her hands and began weeping uncontrollably. Without a word, Nanny knelt down and grabbed Monica's bag and helped her stand up. At that moment Nanny had a flashback. There had been many nights when she had helped Monica's drunken mother up off the floor and into her bed after the kids had gone to sleep. They made their way down the hall with Nanny supporting Monica as she limped with one shoe still on and her hands still covering her eyes and sobbing.

"Nanny, I'm so sorry. I don't know what happened. It got stuck. I fell down. Oh, Nanny . . ."

A security guard emerged from the freight elevator and ran to see what was going on. He stopped when he reached the elevator and stood there with a puzzled look on his face as he stared at the shoe and the shards of glass from the mirror. He looked up and saw the two women making their way down the hall.

"Ms. Kennedy, are you all right?" he inquired.

"She's fine." Nanny responded without turning around as Monica continued to sob. They reached Nanny's apartment where Monica removed her remaining shoe as she entered and flopped down on the nearest couch to assume the fetal position. After a while, the slippers reappeared, this time with a box of tissues and a cup of strong black tea. Monica blew her nose and sipped her tea as Nanny sat in silence in a wingback chair across the room.

"You could at least say something!" Monica shouted as she dabbed her raccoon eyes.

Silence followed.

"Just give me your usual lecture about how I'm an irresponsible drinker and I am turning into my mother! Just tell me that I'm imposing on you by assuming that you can care for Lizzy anytime day or night! Oh, and don't forget the part about you having a life too! Just say that you hate to see me in this condition and what a bad example I am for my daughter."

Silence followed.

"Just tell me!" Monica shouted with rage and remorse in her voice.

The slippers shuffled closer as Nanny sat down beside her. "It sounds like you told yourself quite well."

Suddenly, a little voice said, "Mommy, what happened?" Nanny quickly rose and scooped Lizzy up in her arms and took her over to sit next to Monica. Monica grabbed Lizzy's little hand and stroked it softly.

"Princess, it's okay! You see, one of Mommy's shoes got caught in the elevator and she fell down. She lost her shoe just like Cinderella! But she's going to be okay. Do you know why?" With wonder in her eyes, Lizzy shook her little head of tousled curls." Because just like Cinderella, she still has the other shoe and we know how that story ends don't we?"

"They live happy ever after," answered Lizzy, sleepily.

Monica's eyes welled up with tears as she smiled and hugged Lizzy. She looked up at Nanny and mouthed the words, *thank you*.

"Mommy, I give boo-boos a kiss!" Lizzy leaned over and gave both of Monica's bruised knees a kiss and said, "All better!" The three of them laughed and held each other. At that moment, Monica knew she needed to seek professional help; she had denied it for far too long, but now it was too evident. She was an alcoholic, just as her mother had been.

12

"Dr. Porter's office, Sara speaking."

"Hi Sara, this is Monica Kennedy. My daughter was a patient of Dr. Porter's about a year ago."

"Oh yes, of course. How is little Lizzy? I bet she's so big now!"

"Yes, she's growing like a weed and doing just fine, thank you. But I'm not. I need to see Dr. Porter as soon as possible." Monica took a deep breath for this was the first time she had said it out loud, "I'm an alcoholic and I have some issues that I need to address."

"Monica, you're in luck! I just had a cancellation. I can fit you in this afternoon at three o'clock. Can you make it?"

"I'll be there. Thank you very much."

"No problem. We'll see you at three."

Monica hung up the phone with a smile on her face. She had taken the first step. She leaned back in her office chair, kicked her stiletto-clad feet up on the desk, and buzzed Julie.

"Yes?"

"Please clear my schedule for this afternoon from two o'clock on. I will be out of the office and unavailable."

"Okay. What time shall I tell the valet to bring your car around?"

"Two-fifteen will be fine. Thanks!"

Vanessa returned to her office from a meeting. As she placed her Ralph Lauren Purple Label portfolio case down on her desk, Francine appeared in the doorway.

"Julie called. Monica is clearing her schedule from two on; therefore, your three o'clock with her has been cancelled. Do you want me to reschedule for tomorrow?"

"No, that might be too late," Vanessa said with urgency in her voice. Francine looked at her with a puzzled look on her face.

"Ah, let me try and give her a call now. Thanks, Francine. Would you please close the door on your way out?"

Vanessa took a deep breath as she dialed Monica's extension.

"Ms. Kennedy's office, Julie speaking."

"Hi Julie, this is Vanessa. Is Monica available? It's urgent."

"She's on another line right now. Would you please hold and I will see how much longer she … Oh, wait a minute. She just hung up. Hold one moment please." Julie buzzed Monica on the intercom.

"Yes, Julie?"

"Ms. Baldwin is on line two. Would you like me to take a message?"

"No thanks, I'll take it." Monica took another deep breath.

"Yes, Ms. Baldwin. What can I do for you?"

"Hey, you canceled our meeting for this afternoon. What's going on?"

"Sorry Vanessa, but I have a personal matter I need to attend to."

"Oh. I hope it's nothing serious. Are you okay?"

"Well, I am hoping with time, I will be okay."

"Monica, you're scaring me! What's going on?"

"Oh, you worry too much. I wasn't even aware that you were on my schedule for this afternoon. What did you need to see me about?"

"Well, I asked Francine to schedule our meeting through Julie this morning. Ahhhh, do you have a couple of minutes to meet right now? I can come right over to your office."

"It's about my drinking, isn't it?"

"Ahhhh, yeah. How did you know?" replied Vanessa with a stunned voice.

"Well, after last night, I finally admitted I have a problem. I'm going to seek professional help. In fact, I have an appointment today. So, you can call off your little intervention; there is no need," Monica said with a sarcastic tone.

"Wow, Monica, I'm shocked and elated! I was starting to get really concerned and, frankly, a bit scared."

"Yeah, I scared myself too. It took falling off the elevator last night to really open up my eyes. It's funny, your perspective is altered significantly when you're looking up at the world from the ground."

Vanessa laughed. "I hope you didn't hurt yourself!"

"Yes, as a matter of fact I did, but just my knees and my ego were bruised. I thought I had it all together, but when I hit the floor, it was a real wake-up call."

"Monica, I am so happy you've made this discovery on your own."

"Oh, I think some divine intervention was involved. I'm just grateful that the divine intervention didn't come in the form of something like a horrible car accident."

"That's exactly what I was afraid of. I'm so glad you're seeking professional help. If there is anything that I can do to help, please let me know."

"Thank you, Vanessa, you are a true friend and I don't use the term *friend* loosely."

"You're welcome, Monica. I consider you a true friend as well. Take care and I hope your afternoon is productive."

"Thanks. I'll chat with you later."

"Bye."

"Bye-bye."

Monica hung up the phone with a sigh of relief. She had admitted her problem to Vanessa. Although she was a dear friend, she was also a colleague; therefore, Monica had always felt that she needed to project a perfect image to Vanessa, as well as the other executives. In the tough corporate arena, she had to check her emotions, weaknesses, insecurities, and imperfections at the door. Monica had played the game well for a number of years, but now her demons were gaining on her. The chink in her armor was beginning to show and she knew it was time to do something about it.

"Okay, Maria are you there?"

"I'm here."

"Anne, are you still there?"

"Yes, I'm still here."

"Great, I wanted to have a quick conference call to update both of you on the Monica situation. I just got off the phone with her. Get this: she admitted that she has a problem with alcohol."

"She did? Wonderful! Admitting you have a problem is one of the most difficult hurdles to recovery," Maria stated.

"Oh, I am so relieved," Anne exhaled.

"Absolutely! She even said that she is going to seek professional help. She has an appointment this afternoon," Vanessa relayed.

"Wow, I am so glad we didn't have to do an intervention. I was afraid that she was in deep, deep denial about it," Anne added.

"Yes, I agree. And I do think she was in denial about it until last night," Vanessa admitted.

"Why? What happened?" Maria asked.

"Well, apparently she fell getting off the elevator when she got home last night."

Anne and Maria gasped.

"She said it was a wake-up call."

"Is she okay? She didn't break anything, did she?" Maria asked with concern.

"No, she's fine. Just a few bruises."

"Hmmm, I know how that feels," Maria mumbled under her breath.

"What was that Maria?" Vanessa asked.

"Oh, I was just saying that bruises can be pretty painful," Maria said in a reminiscent tone.

"Yeah, well, I'm glad that was all it took to make her realize she had a problem. It's better to have a few bruises than to be facing criminal charges for vehicular manslaughter," said Vanessa.

"You're right about that, for sure," Anne agreed.

"Well, if either one of you hears her say or sees her do anything that is contrary to her recovery efforts, let's do another conference call and figure out a

229

course of action. We have got to keep each other informed and do whatever we can to support her."

"Deal," both Maria and Anne said in unison.

"Great. Talk to you guys later."

Vanessa hung up the phone with a sigh of relief. She felt as if a burden had been lifted. She just hoped and prayed that Monica could pull herself through the arduous task ahead. Vanessa knew it had been tough for Monica to admit to her that she had a problem, because she always wanted to appear to be the perfect female executive. As a woman in corporate America, especially for women-of-color, the pressure to be perfect is oppressive. Women are expected to say the right things, make the right decisions, work longer hours, wear the right clothes, have the right hair style, never let a gray hair show, always be on point, and knowledgeable on every topic discussed. The pressure to outperform male counterparts to get noticed is always at the forefront of women's minds. But the disheartening part is, men don't have to work as hard or long to climb the same ladder, and they have higher salaries, bigger bonuses, and better perks. And what's most frustrating is that they can do it all while wearing the same 4 or 5 suits, two pair of shoes and never have to cover a gray hair. Well, so much for equal rights and a level playing field!

Monica nervously picked at her cuticles as she waited for Dr. Porter to finish up a conversation with Sara.

"I'm sorry to keep you waiting." Dr. Porter said as he ushered her into his office.

"Oh, no problem. It's only two minutes after three. I won't dock your fee," Monica joked facetiously as she took a seat on the chaise. Dr. Porter smiled briefly, but immediately got down to business.

"How's Lizzy adjusting?"

"Oh, she's doing pretty well. She still calls out for her father sometimes, but usually a soothing diversion helps her to recover quickly. Thank you for asking!"

Dr. Porter switched to a more serious tone. "What brings you in today?"

"Well, I'm sure Sara filled you in on what I told her, as to why I am here."

"As a matter of fact, she didn't. We make it a habit not to share information we receive from patients. Patient confidentiality goes both ways around here."

"Oh, well, I guess I need to fill you in." Monica took a deep breath and looked Dr. Porter in his eyes as she sat across the desk from him. "First of all, I am an alcoholic, and secondly, I have some unresolved issues I need to address. Whew! I said it!"

"Congratulations, Ms. Kennedy," Dr. Porter offered with a smile.

"Oh, please call me Monica."

"Monica, how's your work life?"

Monica answered haltingly, wondering why he asked. "Ah, fine."

"What about your home life? Are you eating well, caring for your daughter, paying your bills on time, etcetera?" Monica thought the questions were strange but answered anyway.

"Yes, I'm fine. Everything is fine."

"What makes you think you are an alcoholic?"

"Good question," Monica said as she began to formulate an answer. "Well, when I go out with my friends for drinks or dinner, no matter how much I try to restrain myself, I always come home a little tipsy. Well, more than just a little tipsy," she said with a sarcastic tone. "I pretty much need a designated driver every time I go out. If I'm in an environment where liquor is being served, I feel compelled to drink. I used to be able to drink socially without a problem, but now I'm just out of control. I'm constantly having to leave my car when I go out and take a cab home."

"Do you drink alone?"

"Yes, but not when my daughter is around. If she's not with me, she's usually with my, I mean, with her nanny or with her paternal grandparents."

"What are you trying to escape from?"

"Well, there are a few unresolved things," Monica said almost laughing. "I began drinking alone and more heavily when I found out my husband was cheating on me with another woman," Monica said. She suddenly felt uncomfortable looking Dr. Porter in his eyes. "I truly believed he was in love with her. I saw them making love, twice; once before I had my daughter and once after."

"You saw them?"

"Yeah, I saw them."

"What happened?"

"Nothing."

"Nothing?"

"Nothing. I didn't do anything."

"Well, what did you say? What did he say?"

"He didn't say anything because I watched him through a window from outside on the deck of our yacht. I was in such shock that I didn't do or say anything. I blamed myself for his straying. I thought that having a baby would be the cure-all, so I got pregnant. I quit drinking during my pregnancy, but started up again when I saw him with the same woman a second time. I had to quit nursing my daughter cold turkey because I just couldn't stay away from the liquor. Lizzy and I both suffered – she cried for my breasts and I cried because my breasts were engorged, and my heart was shredded. Lizzy finally took to formula from a bottle after a couple of days and my milk gradually dried up. Oh, sorry, I guess that was a bit too much information." Monica laughed nervously.

Dr. Porter ignored the comment and moved on. "Do you know who the other woman was?"

"No. Well, yes and no. Yes, I do know she is quite limber and has a birthmark on her back shaped like a boot," Monica said with a sarcastic tone and a laugh. Dr. Porter cleared his throat and leaned back in his chair to cover his urge to laugh.

233

"And no, I don't know her name."

"Did you confront your husband after the second incident?"

"No, I had planned to confront Jeff and tell him I was going to take Lizzy and leave him, but he was killed in the boating accident before I had the opportunity. I never had the chance to shred his heart like he did mine," Monica said with regret and anger.

"Did you ever confront the other woman?"

"Well, I guess you could say I did."

"Would you care to elaborate?"

"Sure!" Monica took a deep breath. "She was there at the marina the day of Jeff's accident. I saw her, she told me who she was, and I slammed her head up against a wall."

"I see," Dr. Porter said with a raised eyebrow. "How did that make you feel?"

"Pretty damn good at first, until I realized that Jeff had told her I was his sister-in-law. Evidently, she didn't know he was married. I guess we are both victims of his deceit."

Dr. Porter nodded his head in agreement. He wasn't surprised, he had heard it all – *he told her I was his sister, the nanny, the housekeeper, his personal trainer...*

"Hummm, let's shift gears a bit. Do you have a history of alcoholism in your family?"

"Yes, my mother. She died from breast cancer when I was getting ready to graduate from high school. It turns out she had liver disease too, but the cancer got her first. I didn't even know she was dying. My parents kept it from me. I just thought she was a depressed drunk. I never even got a chance to say good-bye," Monica said with sadness in her voice as she got up and walked over to the window to survey the skyline. "We were never really close. Well, except for when I was very young. I remember she used to read me bedtime stories and tuck me in at night, but gradually that became my nanny's job. I was closer to my nanny than I ever was to my own mother. In fact, my nanny is now my daughter's nanny."

"It sounds like she became your surrogate mother."

"Yes, she did. My mother used to spend her evenings passed out in her bedroom with an empty bottle of liquor on her nightstand and the TV blaring. I rarely saw my father. He would come home late at night and go to his bedroom, a room he did not share with my mother. Then he would be up and out early in the morning. Sometimes I would see him at breakfast with his head buried in the morning newspaper. But most of the time I'd see him running out to his helicopter for the morning commute to work. He died from a heart attack two years after Jeff and I got married."

"Monica, I see several issues that need to be addressed: the alcoholism, abandonment by your parents, the betrayal of your husband, pent up anger, and the lack of closure." Monica nodded her head in agreement as she turned to face him with silent tears streaming down her cheeks. She knew he was right.

"Others may manifest themselves as we continue our sessions. You've acknowledged that you cannot control your drinking, therefore, you must quit, period. You appear to be a functioning alcoholic, so I wouldn't recommend disrupting your life for several weeks to check into a rehab facility, but I will recommend an outpatient program that requires daily meetings, frequent drug testing, and health monitoring. I'll have Sara set everything up and provide you with the logistical information. We have a lot of work to do; however, you will be setting the pace. You can break this cycle. You have to for your health and for your daughter's sake. I'm sure you don't want your nanny to become her surrogate mother also, and I am also sure that you don't want Lizzy to become an alcoholic or a promiscuous teenager." Monica cried out and burst into more tears because she knew she needed to reveal her own promiscuous behavior to Dr. Porter.

She moved over to the chaise with her head in her hands. He handed her a box of tissues. "Dr. Porter, I have a problem in that area as well."

"Which area?"

"To put it bluntly, I engage in what you might call serial monogamous encounters."

"Encounters?"

"Well, I can't really call them relationships because there's no emotional attachment. I meet a guy and I call him whenever I want to have sex. I see him for a few months, then I move on to someone else when he gets too attached," Monica said while picking her cuticles and avoiding eye contact.

"How long have you been engaging in this type of behavior?"

"Ever since Jeff died."

"Are you practicing safe sex?" Monica took a deep breath.

"No, and I know what you're going to say. Believe me, I already know about the dangers of HIV and various STDs. The guys I choose aren't needle sharing drug addicts, and they most certainly aren't bisexual."

"Monica, men with HIV don't wear scarlet letters. I know the men in your circle have great wealth, advanced degrees, perfect white teeth, and wear white collared shirts, but that doesn't mean they don't carry HIV or STDs. And besides, sexually transmitted diseases are not the only things you need to worry about. You need to be concerned about your dignity and self-esteem, as well as your well-being. Monica, you are a woman of great financial means. You need to be concerned about your safety, as well as your daughter's. In addition, you should be concerned about the possibility of theft of your possessions and your identity."

"I guess I hadn't really thought about that," Monica said shamefully.

"Why do you feel that you need to be with these men?" Monica lifted her eyes up to the ceiling as tears began to stream down her cheeks once again.

"I, I don't know. I guess I just want to feel like I'm someone else and somewhere else. I just want to be transported away from the pain. Sex whisks me away to another place with no boundaries and no sadness. The sex I'm having now is nothing like the sex I had with my husband. I always felt like he was absent when we made love."

"So now you are the one who is absent."

"What? What do mean?" Monica said looking at Dr. Porter with a puzzled look.

"Well, you take advantage of the physical pleasure without investing your emotions. Isn't that what your husband did when he had sex with you?" Monica stared at Dr. Porter with shock in her eyes. She broke down again.

"Oh my God, I'm doing exactly what Jeff did to me."

"Monica, I think it would be in your best interest to suspend all sexual activity for the time being."

"Yes, Dr. Porter," Monica whispered as she blotted the mascara from under her raccoon eyes. "Dr. Porter, I want to protect my daughter, be there for her, and love her.

"You have and you will. Just stick to your plan. Don't let anything or anyone stand in the way of your recovery. Now, stand up. Take a deep breath, step forward, and leave the past behind." Monica stood up, closed her eyes, took a deep breath, and stepped forward. She opened her eyes with a smile through her tears.

"The first step is always the hardest. Just make sure that you don't step back into the world that you just left."

"I won't, Dr. Porter! I promise."

"Don't make the promise to me. Make the promise to yourself.

"I will."

"Monica, our time is up for today."

"Thank you, Dr. Porter. I'll see you next week," Monica said as she extended her hand.

He shook her hand and said to himself as she left the room, *You'll be seeing me sooner than you think.*

Maria's mother started taking care of Elizabeth and Christina after school because Maria had moved closer to her. Previously, they went to afterschool care. Nothing gave her more joy than to spend time each day with her little angels for a few hours in the afternoon. She would pick them up from school and spoil them with chocolate milk and fresh, homemade cookies that they enjoyed baking together. When José was alive, Maria's mother had very limited access to her granddaughters. Because of his selfishness and possessiveness, she only got to see them on major holidays or an occasional weekend. Sometimes Maria would sneak them by for a quick visit while José was working overtime; Maria swore the girls to secrecy.

They never told José because they loved spending time with their grandmother, aunts, and uncles. They were treated like princesses when they came around, and there were lots of cousins to play with.

"Hi, Mami," Maria announced as she let herself into her Mother's apartment with the key she had had since high school. It was still on the same *I Love New York* key chain that used to be attached to her backpack many years ago.

"How are Mommy's girls this afternoon?"

"Fine," they both said in unison as they ran to give Maria a hug.

"We made cookies today," Christina announced.

"Again? Mami, are you trying to fatten up my niñas."

"Nooooo. These cookies are good for you. They are oatmeal with raisins and cranberries."

"Is that so? Well, in that case, let me have one." The girls giggled and Elizabeth handed Maria a cookie.

"Mmmm. You're right. They are good, but being good for you is up for debate." They all smiled. "Girls, go get your coats and backpacks. It's time to go."

"Awwwww," they whined simultaneously and reluctantly went to gather their things.

"Maria, you know the funeral is tomorrow," Maria's mother whispered in Spanish. "Are you planning on going? What about the girls?"

"No, I'm not going and neither are the girls. I'm taking the day off from work and keeping the girls home from school. I don't want to raise any suspicions at my job, so I've told my manager and friends not to attend because it will be for family only. Everyone will assume we're attending. I'm keeping the girls out of school on Friday as well. Would you please take care of them?"

"Oh, of course I will. You know I welcome any opportunity to spend time with my little girls."

"I'll bring them by around eight on Friday morning. Remember, I have a formal affair to attend Friday night, so I'll be spending the day getting ready. Most likely I won't be picking them up until Saturday afternoon."

"That's right! Don't you worry about a thing! They'll be fine. You go out and enjoy yourself. You deserve it!"

"Thanks, Mami. I love you," Maria said as she leaned over and kissed her mother on the cheek.

"You're welcome, my sweet niña. You know, José's mother has been bugging me to give her your phone number."

"Yeah, I know. She's been calling me at work, but I have my assistant screening my calls. I refuse to talk to her. I know all she wants is José's money. The insurance company won't pay because he committed suicide," Maria whispered softly while checking to make sure the girls were out of earshot. "All the money we saved toward buying a house has been deposited into educational accounts for the girls.

241

When they're ready to go to college, they will be able to afford any university they choose. And the money in his personal account is mine. I'm taking you and the girls on a Disney cruise next summer. Nothing can make up for the pain and suffering inflicted on us all of those years and nothing can bring back my girls' innocence. We have been used and abused for so long; we deserve to treat ourselves like we should have been treated all those years, like princesses."

"Mommy, we're ready," Elizabeth announced as she and Christina reluctantly strolled into the kitchen. They all said their good-byes and Maria hailed a taxi out front for the three of them.

"Well, let's go," Maria said as she ushered her girls into the cab. "We've got a lot on our agenda. Since you'll be out of school for the next two days, I say we have a slumber party tonight, just the three of us." The girls screamed with joy as they bounced up and down in the back seat of the taxi.

"We'll stop at the store on the way home and pick up some groceries, like microwave popcorn and candy bars! Oh, and ice cream too! What kind should we get?" Maria asked with a straight face, trying to hide her smile.

"Chocolate," Elizabeth screamed with laughter.

"No, strawberry," objected Christina with an attitude.

"Neapolitan it is, because I want vanilla," Maria added. They giggled and tickled each other all the way home.

It would be a time that the girls would remember well; well enough to tell their children about the time when grandma let them skip school; two full days of treats and laughs, tummy aches and Pepto-Bismol, healing hugs and tender kisses, and discovering the hidden beauty of triumphing over tragedy.

CHAPTER

13

Monica pored over a mound of papers on her desk, trying desperately to compile information to finish up the report she had committed to submitting to the Board of Directors before the end of business. Her cell phone rang, but she was too engrossed in her work to notice it. A few moments later, her office phone rang, but she chose to ignore it. Then came a knock at her door.

"What?" she answered with frustration. Julie opened the door and stuck her head in. "I thought I told you I didn't want to be disturbed?" she said peering over her reading glasses with an annoyed look on her face.

"Yes, Ms. Kennedy, but I thought you would like to take this call."

"Who is it? Vanessa?"

"No, it's Dr. Kelsey's office."

"Oh yeah, I bet they want to know when I'm scheduled for a mammogram. I forgot to ask you to schedule that for me after my exam. Would you call and set it up, please?"

"Will do." Monica returned to her work. A moment later, another knock came at her door.

"What the hell is it now?" Monica demanded. Julie opened the door and stuck her head in again.

"Sorry, but Dr. Kelsey's administrative assistant said that she needs to speak with you directly."

"Oh, give me a break. What line is she on?"

"Line two," Julie said with an apologetic tone and closed the door behind her.

"Yes, this is Monica Kennedy," she said with an attitude.

"Ms. Kennedy, Dr. Kelsey would like to speak with you. Hold please."

"I can't believe she put me on hold, like I have nothing else better to do," Monica said as she heard the Carpenters singing, *"I'm on top of the world looking down on creation and the only explanation I can find..."*

"Hello, Monica!"

"Dr. Kelsey. What is so urgent? I'm really tied up at the moment."

"Monica, are you sitting down?"

"Yeah. Why? Don't tell me I'm pregnant!" Monica gasped.

"No, you're not pregnant."

"Oh, thank God!"

"There is a bit of a problem."

"Problem? What do you mean?" Monica said as she put her pen down.

"You've contracted an STD."

"What!" Monica shouted as she jumped to her feet. "Oh my God, please don't tell me I have HIV!" she said with panic in her voice.

"No, no nothing like that."

"Oh, thank God!" she said bringing her hand to her heart. "Then what is it?"

"It's HPV."

"H what?" Monica bellowed.

"HPV. Human Papilloma Virus."

"What the hell is that?" Monica whispered, suddenly becoming aware of her surroundings.

"Some abnormal cells were detected in your PAP smear, which tested positive for HPV. It's a very common virus. Nearly all sexually active women and men contract HPV at some point in their lives; however, most don't realize it because of the absence of symptoms. In some cases, genital warts and/or abnormal cells can develop on the cervix and surrounding vaginal tissue. And it is now known that HPV is the leading cause of cervical cancer."

"Cancer! Do I have cancer? Am I going to die?" Monica screamed.

"No, no. Monica, just calm down and let me explain. The good news is that we caught it early. There is no sign of cancer and there is treatment. In the meantime, until you can get an appointment to see me again, I want you to come into the lab for bloodwork. I'd like to test you for other STDs that you may have contracted that we didn't test for during your annual exam two weeks ago. It's also important for you to know that you may not have contracted HPV from your current sexual partner. This virus can lay dormant in your system for years. You could have contracted it five or ten years ago. There's really no way of knowing exactly when. And Monica, no more unprotected sex, okay?"

All Monica could manage to whisper was, "Yes, Dr. Kelsey."

"Do you have any questions for me now?"

"I don't know. This is a lot to absorb. I guess I need to go online and do some research. But you are sure I'm going to be okay?"

"Monica, you'll be fine. We will provide you with more detailed information on your next visit. I'll transfer you back over to my assistant to make your next appointment. Try to come in as soon as possible and don't forget to visit the lab for your bloodwork."

"Okay. Thank you, Dr. Kelsey." This time she heard the jazz rendition of *"Burn Baby Burn, Disco Inferno..."* while on hold. Monica made her appointment for three weeks out, which was the first available, but asked to have her name put on the cancellation list.

"Why the hell is this happening to me?" Monica seethed in a whispered voice. "That bastard!" Monica yelled as she felt rage building inside of her. The only problem was she didn't know who to direct her anger at. It could have been her husband, Jeff. He may have picked it up from his mistress. It could have been her current on-call lover, Steve, or a number of other men that she had been with over the past year. Jeff had been the only guy she had ever been with before and during her marriage, but after he died she began her sexual healing binge. The only thing is, what she thought would heal her, had turned out to harm her – or so it seemed.

Monica twirled around in her chair to her computer on the credenza behind her desk. She did a search on HPV. Over five million hits came up on the subject. She could not believe there was so much information out there. She began scanning and reading articles and commentaries. Monica found some information that said a preventative vaccine had been developed and is available for preteens. Young girls can receive it just like vaccinations for mumps, measles and rubella. The objective: to significantly reduce the number of cervical cancer cases in the long run. After a half an hour had passed, she sat back in her chair, exhaled heavily, and said, "Damn, why didn't I know about this virus?"

She felt a little bit more at ease after reading some of the information and vowed this would never happen to Lizzy. She was going to make sure that Lizzy got vaccinated against it and know the dangers associated with unprotected sex. Monica hadn't received any guidance from her mother about sex, or anything else for that matter. She wanted to break the cycle and have an open and honest mother-daughter relationship with Lizzy.

Monica picked up the telephone and reluctantly dialed the number.

"Hello Sexy!"

"Hi Steve," Monica said with a sad tone in her voice.

"Hummm, sounds like you need a warm-up. I'm free tonight!"

"That sounds great, but I have a bit of bad news."

"What happened? Is Lizzy all right?"

"Oh, yes, she's fine. Thanks for asking. No, this has to do with you and me."

"Don't tell me you're cutting me loose? I don't think my heart can take it," Steve said with a playful tone.

"Steve, I don't know any other way to tell you this except just straight out."

"Okay, you're scaring me, Monica."

"I have an STD."

"Oh, God, not HIV?" Steve said with panic in his voice.

"No, nothing like that. It's HPV."

"H… what? What the hell is that?"

"It's a sexually transmitted virus and is one of the leading causes of cervical cancer in women, but usually doesn't have any effect on men."

"Shit! Should I go get checked out?"

"I would advise you to call your doctor for advice. Look, to be honest with you, I don't know if I got it from you or someone else. It's so common that almost all sexually active men and women end up with it, most not even knowing that they have it. Because most people don't get symptoms, they're not aware that they have it and become carriers as they continue

249

to spread it without knowing. My doctor says it's not life threatening and the symptoms are treatable. She told me not to worry."

"Oh, man, that's good news. Well, I appreciate you letting me know. I've never even heard of it before."

"Yeah, I hadn't either. A lot of people haven't."

"Wow, I don't know what to say. I, I guess I won't be getting any more calls from you?"

"Yeah, you guessed right. But not because of the HPV, I need some time to deal with some issues that I haven't addressed in my life."

"Yeah, I know what you mean. I've got some ghosts from the past that I need to sit down and have a talk with, also."

"Well, Steve, It's been nice fighting fires with you."

"Yeah, you too Monica. I'm gonna miss you."

"Likewise." Monica hung up the phone, took a deep breath, rose from her desk and made her way out to Julie's desk. "Julie, I'm sorry for snapping at you earlier. I know I can be a real diva-bitch when I'm under a lot of pressure."

"No problem boss, I already know you're a diva and a bitch," Julie said, her smile cancelling her sarcasm.

"And don't you forget it," Monica said with a straight face. She put her nose up in the air as she turned on her heels to go back into her office. But she stopped dead in her tracks and turned back to Julie.

"You know, Julie, life is too short to spend it stressed out. I'm leaving for the day to spend time with Lizzy."

"But what about the report you owe the board of directors?"

"Screw the board of directors. And since I'm such a diva-bitch, you can have the rest of today off and all of tomorrow too. See you at the gala!" Monica said with a smile.

She went into her office, turned off her computer, swept all of the reports and papers she had been working on into her top drawer and locked it. She grabbed her Ricky bag and trench coat, and pulled the door shut behind her. "Good riddance," she said as she waved good-bye to Julie.

"Are you really leaving?" Julie inquired.

"Yep, and you should do the same."

Julie stood at her desk in shock as she watched Monica walk down the hall and disappear into the elevator. She couldn't believe what she had just witnessed, but she wasn't going to stand around like a fool and wait for Monica to change her mind. Julie password-protected her computer screen, grabbed her coat and purse and slid into the service elevator. She didn't want one of the other executive assistants to see her leaving right behind her boss. As the large, noisy, dimly-lit elevator made its way down to the lobby level, Julie wondered what in the world the doctor could have said to Monica to cause her to have a 180-

degree attitude adjustment from her workaholic ways.

"Hi, Dr. Porter," Vanessa said as she kicked off her Italian leather pumps and stretched out on the butter-soft leather chaise lounge.

"Hello, Vanessa! How are you doing this week?"

"I've been better."

"Has your dream recurred?"

"Unfortunately, yes. I can't seem to shake it. I try to think pleasant thoughts and distract my mind by reading before I go to bed. I even pray for pleasant dreams, but I always wake up screaming and soaked with sweat each time the dream recurs. The only good thing is, once I've dreamt it, it doesn't recur again the same night."

"Vanessa, things have a tendency to come back and haunt us when we're sad, depressed, or have idle time on our hands. In addition, I really believe that you're holding on to your dream."

"Holding on! I'm not holding on to it! I want nothing more than to be rid of it, forever!" Vanessa said angrily. "I want it out of my mind and out of my life!"

"Have you confronted your mother about it?"

"No," Vanessa said quietly. She dropped her head in shame.

"Then you're still holding on. You've expressed to me how you feel about your mother because she didn't protect you. You need to address it with her so you can begin to repair your damaged relationship with her. In addition, you've never told me who the perpetrator was or what he actually did to you. Vanessa, you need to release your demons or they will continue to haunt you."

Vanessa's eyes began to well-up and overflow. Dr. Porter handed her a box of tissues and said softly, "I really want to help you, but you have to be willing to shed your fear of revealing your abuse and your abuser."

Vanessa took a deep breath as she dabbed her eyes. She sat up and folded her legs Indian-style. She began to resurrect those painful moments from her childhood.

"I was six years old and my brother was eleven. We always came home for lunch because we lived so close to our school. Normally, we'd make lunch for ourselves because my mother was at the university. When I started first grade, she started law school. She had always wanted to be an attorney, but took a hiatus when my brother was born. Her plan was to start law school soon after I was born, but her dream was derailed when my father filed for divorce to marry another woman, while she was pregnant with me. I can only imagine how difficult that period in her life must have been, being the loving and devoted wife of her high school sweetheart, only to be cast aside for an older, rich, white woman. Oh, I digressed. Sorry!

We're supposed to be talking about me, not my mother."

"Vanessa, it is appropriate that we discuss the experiences your mother had that relate directly to you. Any background information that you can provide from your childhood about the relationship you and your mother had just prior to, during, and after your period of abuse will help give me insight into why you've become who you are."

"Oh, okay. Well, my relationship with my mother was pretty typical before the abuse. Our only points of conflict were about me wanting the hemlines of my dresses shorter and my pigtails lower. When I was a kid, if I wore my pigtails up too high on my head, I ended up getting teased and called Pippi Longstocking.

"Uh, where was I? Oh yeah, lunch. Every day my brother and I would make our peanut butter and jelly sandwiches, eat, play for a few minutes, and then walk back to school. To this day, I won't eat peanut butter and jelly sandwiches. I think it's because I ate too many of them as a kid and they remind me, in some way, of what happened to me that day. But anyway, on this particular day something went terribly wrong." Vanessa paused as her eyes welled-up once again. She took another deep breath, laid down with her eyes closed tightly, and curled up in the fetal position.

"We had finished eating and I was sitting on the third or fourth step of the stairs that led up to the second floor of our house, and my brother was sitting across from me a few feet away in a chair by the front door. I remember being so happy sitting there laughing and talking, when all of a sudden my brother lunged at me. He started tugging at my white cotton panties from underneath my little plaid school dress. I began to kick, scream, and laugh; I thought he was playing some kind of game with me. I didn't know what game he was playing; I thought perhaps he just wanted to tickle me. But before I knew anything, he had pulled my panties down around the ankles of my white knee socks. It was then that I realized that he wasn't playing. I screamed at him, "What are you doing?" and tried to pull my panties back up, but he grabbed them and held them down. After a few moments of playing tug of war, I realized it was no use. He was a lot bigger and stronger than I was." Vanessa paused to catch her breath.

"Before I knew it, he had forced my legs open and shoved his middle finger up inside me. I remember not being able to make a sound as he tore into me. My mouth was wide open, but no sound emerged. I looked into his eyes with anguish on my face and he had the look of a monster on his. After a few seconds that seemed like minutes, he ripped his finger out of me and held it up to look at it, then ran out the front door. I don't know where he went. I assume he ran back to school. He left me home, alone, and bleeding. I finally caught my breath and began to scream and cry as I slid down the steps to the floor. I didn't understand what he had done to me or even why I was hurting. He robbed me of my innocence that day. I was no longer a child," Vanessa cried out. Her body shook with overwhelming emotion as she relived the pain.

"Vanessa, I am so sorry this happened to you. I understand why you've been so reluctant to share this with me."

Vanessa sat up and noisily blew her nose. "Dr. Porter, there's more!" she said with even more anguish.

"Would you like some water before continuing?"

"Yes, please."

Dr. Porter handed Vanessa a bottle of water from the beverage refrigerator next to his coffee bar. She took a long drink, dabbed her eyes, and continued.

"Somehow I made my way upstairs and onto my mother's bed. That's where she found me sometime later. I guess I was drawn to her bed because when children are sick or in pain, there is just no other place that is more comforting than their parents' bed. I assume the school must have called her when I didn't return after lunch. She asked me what happened. I told her in the best way I knew how. I remember the exact words I used and how I said them. I answered, "Kenny stuck his finger up a hole," in an almost sing-songy voice. My mother said, "What?" I repeated, "he stuck his finger up a hole." She said, "Where?" I pointed down between my legs and said, "Down there."

Vanessa's tears began to well up and flow again. She looked Dr. Porter in his eyes and said in a voice racked with hurt, "Do you know what she said to me? 'Well, that's not a reason to stay at home. You should've gone back to school.' I couldn't believe it! I was hurt, confused, and emotionally distraught, yet she acted as if my brother had just punched me in the arm or something. I never spoke another word about it and neither did she." Vanessa broke down with heart-wrenching sobs.

"Vanessa, I am so sorry she reacted that way," said Dr. Porter with concern in his voice.

After a few moments, Vanessa dried her eyes, blew her nose, straightened her back, pushed her hair behind her ears, and continued. "From that moment on, I loathed my brother for what he had done to me and I despised my mother for letting him get away with it. I wanted to get him back, but I was afraid if I confronted him or did something to him he would hurt me again. I wanted to kill him, but as fate would have it, he died the next year - his appendix burst. Needless to say, I didn't shed a tear. I was so glad he was gone. I felt like God had answered my prayers. My mother was terribly crushed by his death, but I couldn't offer her any comfort. I figured she got what was coming to her for not protecting me and for not punishing him for hurting me."

"What type of relationship did you have with your brother before he abused you?"

"The usual. I was his kid sister and he didn't want me around him. He used to call me names, push me down, and throw my dolls down the stairs. I think he was resentful when I came along, because he had all of my parents' attention for five years to himself. But as soon as I was born, my father left us and pretty much severed all ties, not only with my mother, but with my brother also."

"Were you ever able to confront your father or establish a relationship with him before he died?"

"No, not at all. When I was about ten, I saw him and met his wife and their eight-year-old daughter; my mother and I ran into them at the mall. Needless to say, it was pretty awkward. That was the only time I ever saw him. Five years later when I was fifteen, my mother told me he had died from a heart attack. He was 44. So, no, I never got the chance to confront my father for dumping my mother and abandoning my brother and me. If he had been a real father to us, maybe my brother wouldn't have done this horrible thing to me," Vanessa broke down once again. Dr. Porter came over to the chaise to comfort her.

"Vanessa, I know you've been avoiding it, but you need to confront your mother. You have a right to be angry, but you also have a right to confront her and let her know how her actions and those of your brother have affected you your entire life. Because you have never spoken of this incident, it's been like an open wound that refuses to heal. It's just been festering all these years. In order to heal, you need to talk to your mother and hopefully get some answers to your questions."

"Questions? What questions? I don't have any questions," Vanessa said with an indignant tone.

"Oh, but you do. How about, 'Why didn't you show some compassion towards me? Why didn't you take me in your arms and hold me, and tell me you loved me and that everything was going to be all right? Why didn't you punish him? Why didn't you take me to a doctor?

Why didn't you make him go to counseling?' Vanessa, these are the questions that you deserve answers to."

Vanessa nodded her head as a new flood of tears burst forth. Dr. Porter stood and said softly, "I'm sorry, our time is up for today." Vanessa nodded as she blotted her eyes and blew her nose once again. She stood, slipped her heels on, grabbed a couple of tissues for the road, and exited through the back door without saying a word. She dug down deep into her Ricky bag for a pair of sunglasses to hide her swollen red eyes as she rode down in the elevator. Right then and there, Vanessa decided to choose freedom over the prison she had been living in for most of her life. She would confront her mother and be prepared to completely sever their relationship if it came down to it. As she stepped from the elevator, she thought about the three words her heart had ached to hear from her mother since she was six years old. *Baby, I'm sorry.*

CHAPTER

14

All of The Sangrita Club members had taken the day off work to get ready for the gala. It was noon and Vanessa had already had an exfoliation treatment, a hydrotherapy Vichy shower, full body massage, and a fabulous up-do done by none other than her his-bark-is-worse-than-his-bite cousin Vince. He had taken his job seriously that morning and turned out a style on Vanessa that he had seen on Beyoncé in a magazine. He had washed, conditioned, blow-dried, trimmed, molded, set, flat ironed, curled, and spritzed Vanessa without so much as one crack of a joke. He had created a fierce masterpiece; he was a force to be reckoned with.

If anyone could knock off a hairstyle by one of New York's famous hair stylists, it would be Vince. All you had to do was show him a picture, or even just describe a hairstyle that you'd seen on T.V. and he could reproduce it flawlessly. He was damn good, he knew it, and so did everyone else that knew him. When you left his salon and day spa, your hair always looked like you had just stepped out of *Elle, Harper's Bazaar*, or *Vogue* – red carpet ready. He never paid for advertising, not even business cards, yet he could charge 5th Avenue prices. Word of mouth was his advertising. He had done extremely well for himself and had the Manhattan salon and two-story penthouse overlooking Midtown to prove it.

Vanessa was now perched atop her vibrating throne getting a pedicure and manicure simultaneously. She hadn't treated herself to this kind of luxury in a long time. She vowed to start making more time for herself as she gingerly sipped her glass of champagne. She felt light and airy after her confession to Dr. Porter. She felt strong, invincible, and brave enough to confront her mother, but she would wait until after the gala. She wasn't going to let anything spoil her night with her new beau. After the mani and pedi, she had her makeup professionally done and grabbed a cab to head home to get dressed for the evening.

Vanessa instinctively threw her keys on the hall table as she came through the door and headed for her bedroom. As she walked down the hall past her guest room, she stopped and retraced her steps. She leaned against the door jam, folded her arms, and smiled as she looked at her beautiful outfit hanging from the hook on the back of the closet door. The fullness of the skirt and train fanned out over the entire queen-size bed. She was truly going to look like royalty. She checked her watch and realized that she only had one hour to get ready before Dave was expected to arrive.

Vanessa sprinted to her bedroom while disrobing. As usual, her slipper chair caught her

THE SANGRITA CLUB

advertising, not even business cards, yet he could charge 5th Avenue prices. Word of mouth was his advertising. He had done extremely well for himself and had the Manhattan salon and two-story penthouse overlooking Midtown to prove it.

clothes. Since she had already taken care of the primping, all that was left to do was apply a hypnotic scented perfume and lotion, and slip into her lingerie and evening attire. Vanessa had chosen the most beautiful silk, saffron-colored bra and panties to wear under the Carolina Herrera bleached-cotton evening blouse and bronze silk-moiré ball skirt. A tingly sensation came over her as she stood in front of the full-length mirror; she had butterflies in her stomach. She felt like Cinderella getting ready for the ball as she donned accessories to complete her look: gorgeous Dolce & Gabbana bronze and gold pumps, and David Yurman citrine, peridot, and emerald earrings with a coordinating wrist cuff and cocktail ring.

As she touched up her lip-gloss, the doorbell rang. She glanced at the clock; it was two minutes after six. Vanessa sashayed to the door, but stopped just as she got to it. She closed her eyes and made a silent wish, *please let him be the one*. She opened her eyes and peered through the peephole but jerked her head back because all she could see was white.

"Who is it?" she inquired.

"Delivery for Ms. Baldwin."

Vanessa smiled as she opened the door to the familiar baritone voice. She was ready to say, "You're late," but the sight of the huge bouquet of white Casablanca lilies took her breath away.

After the loud gasp from Vanessa and a moment of silence, Dave moved the flowers aside from in front of his face and said, "Well, are you going to tip me or what?" Vanessa took two steps forward, grabbed his chin, and kissed him with a sexy, gentle kiss that took his breath away. She grabbed the train of her skirt and stepped back into her apartment. Meanwhile, Dave continued to stand there with his eyes closed, flowers in hand, and wearing Vanessa's lip-gloss.

"Well, are you coming in or do you need an invitation?" Vanessa offered playfully.

"Mmmm," he said as he opened his eyes. "You taste so good and look like royalty! Who would have ever thought that I would be dating a princess?"

Vanessa blushed and motioned him inside. He entered and set the crystal vase of flowers on the console table in front of a mirror.

"Oh, Dave, they are absolutely gorgeous. How did you know these are my favorite?" Vanessa said as she gently stroked the petals of a bloom.

"I've been paying attention over the past three years. They don't compare to you, darling," he said in a Humphrey Bogart dialect while lifting her hand and kissing it. "Mmmm, you smell delicious too, Sweetheart." They looked at one another in the mirror and laughed.

"Dave, you're wearing my lips."

"I see that. Let's go. The limo is waiting."

"I have to fix my lip-gloss before we go," Vanessa said digging in her VBH evening clutch.

"Wait, don't fix your lips. I'm not through with them yet."

Vanessa handed Dave her keys and giggled like a schoolgirl as she asked, "Would you grab my coat please?" Dave carefully draped a Dennis Basso full-length sable coat over Vanessa's shoulders, guided her over the threshold, and locked the door behind them. They sauntered off blissfully into the night, arm in arm, with their hearts full of promise and passion to come.

Monica arrived via her chauffeur-driven Rolls-Royce at precisely 5:30 p.m. There was no way she was going to miss the cocktail hour. Since she had committed to giving up alcohol, this would be her last hurrah. She also needed a drink to medicate herself from the STD news she had received the day before. She made sure she ate something before leaving home so that the champagne wouldn't go to her head too quickly. Monica kept repeating to herself in the mirror as she got dressed earlier that evening, "It's not the end of the world. This virus is very common." Although the doctor had told her everything would be all right, she was still very frightened at learning that HPV could cause cancer.

She put on her best and brightest corporate smile for the paparazzi as she stepped from her car onto the red carpet. She handed her full-length Lanvin mink coat to an attendant standing nearby while she posed for pictures. Monica looked absolutely stunning in her golden Oscar de la Renta gown, Fred Leighton citrine earrings, and Salvatore Ferragamo sling-back sandals.

Her blonde, shoulder-length hair blew back as she made a beeline for the bar, but she didn't make it. She accosted a server carrying a tray of champagne flutes. She held onto the arm of his waistcoat, while she downed one glass quickly and waved him on his way as she sipped the second. She began her rounds of obligatory corporate networking; in other words, lying to the male executives about how beautiful their wives looked and how they must have robbed the cradle.

Anne pulled up in front of the MET in her black limo at 5:35 p.m. As she stepped onto the red carpet, all the flashes from the throng of paparazzi took her aback. Being new to the Eastern region of the firm, she had no idea how much fanfare there would be around this event, but as usual, she emerged flawless with style and grace in her full-length Giuliana Teso Chinchilla fur coat. She shed it to reveal her five foot seven frame, which stood tall and sleek in her 4-inch Calvin Klein stiletto pumps, midnight-blue Narciso Rodriguez silk crepe gown, and Van Cleef and Arpels cascading diamond star earrings and necklace. Her bone straight hair was pulled back into a chignon with the ends arranged to create a perfect fan; not a hair was out of place. She was a vision of poise and exotic beauty as the paparazzi's flashes washed over her.

No one would have guessed that she had spent forty-five minutes that morning plucking every stray hair around her hairline with a knotted cotton thread in the Chinese tradition to sculpt the perfect hairline before going to the salon. She was not perfect on the inside, but whenever she stepped across the threshold to leave her penthouse, she always had to look perfect on the outside.

When she moved into the grand museum, she looked up as she walked into the crowded gallery. Its ornate beauty took her breath away. Monica spotted Anne from the bar and made her way over toward her.

"Beautiful, isn't it?"

"Oh, yes. Hi!" Anne was a little alarmed to see Monica with a drink in her hand. She would try to watch her closely and report her findings to Vanessa and Maria. "Ms. Kennedy, you look beautiful, like a Greek goddess!"

"Why, thank you, Ms. Wu. You look perfect, as always, with an air of regal elegance."

"Thank you. I usually clean up pretty well," Anne joked. "I guess I was looking like a tourist, walking in with my mouth wide open and looking up." They both laughed. "I've been to New York so many times but I haven't seen the MET since my high school days."

"Anne, let's get you a glass of champagne and I'll introduce you to some of the good old boys you haven't met yet. Oh, but for your career's sake, try not to laugh at what their wives are wearing and don't bother to be humorous because their wives' faces are expressionless from Botox." They laughed and made their way to the nearest floating tray of champagne.

Maria nervously tapped her Manolo Blahnik clad feet on the floor of the limo. She had seen in magazines and newspapers how fabulous these formal events had been in years past. So to make a good impression for the cameras, she had practiced some poses in the mirror before she left home as her daughters watched and giggled. As Maria's limo came to a stop, she closed her eyes and prayed to God not to allow her boobs to pop out of her strapless gown and that the cameras wouldn't make her butt look too big.

Maria stepped onto the red carpet in her flowing full-length black and white fox fur coat. From the neck down, she was a portrait of refined beauty, however from the neck up, she was a deer in headlights. The cameras flashed as she made a dash up the stairs. She had forgotten all of the poses and didn't stop until she was asked for her name at the door by the security guard. Out of breath, she managed to smile and say, "Maria, Maria Vasquez."

Once inside, Maria took a deep breath and stood in amazement as she drank in all of the sights and sounds of the event. The colorful sea of couture gowns, white ties, and tails looked like an amazing Monet painting. The classical music coming from the orchestra filled the entire place with an air of sophistication. Everywhere she looked, there were white-gloved servers weaving in and out through the crowd carrying trays of hors d'oeuvres and champagne. It was a spectacular event.

Maria grabbed a flute of champagne to sip on and calm her nerves. She had made mental notes earlier that day, while sitting under the dryer at the salon, of all the executives she wanted to network with and the ones to avoid. It was time to start her rounds. She had her small talk lines down pat and was ready to perform. She spotted one of the executive VPs on her list and was taking a step in his direction when she heard, "Wow, girl!" She turned and saw Monica and Anne with their mouths open wide. Maria instantly saw the champagne glass in Monica's hand and looked at Anne, but decided not to comment on it. She made a mental note to tell Vanessa.

"I see why you didn't want to give us any information about what you would be wearing tonight," Anne added.

"Maria, is that Carolina Herrera?" Monica inquired.

"As a matter of fact, it is."

"Wow. Who would have ever thought that you could take pinstripe suiting fabric and make a feminine, sophisticated strapless evening gown with it," Monica raved. "Look at how the bodice is cut to form a subtle geometric design."

"And don't forget the hint of tulle at the décolleté," Anne added.

"Maria, it's really magnificent."

"You two sound like commentators at a fashion show," Maria remarked.

"It's definitely not a bridesmaid dress!" Anne cracked.

"Speaking of bridesmaid dresses, Monica, you forgot to mention the bow," Maria said sarcastically.

"Oh, you're right. It has the tiniest little pinstriped bow at the waistline."

"And these are Leslie Greene Diamond earrings and bracelet," Maria proudly added.

"All jokes aside, Maria, you look absolutely stunning," complimented Anne.

"Thanks! You two cleaned up nicely also! Monica, you look like the goddess of love."

"See, I told you that you look like a Greek goddess," Anne said.

"And Anne, you truly look elegant and regal, like Jackie O."

"Regal elegance! That's also what I said to describe her!" added Monica.

"Well ladies, I'd love to stay and chat about our couture selections, however I've got some major brownnosing to accomplish tonight. I'll catch up with you guys later." Maria winked and was on her way with train in tow.

"Oh, here's a tissue to remove my lipstick," Vanessa said to Dave as their limo inched its way up toward the red carpet.

"Thanks, but I want to wipe it off with my handkerchief so that I can save it to remember this special occasion."

"Aw, you're such a romantic sentimentalist."

"I only care to remember things that are absolutely unforgettable. And you, tonight, in this gown – absolutely unforgettable," Dave said as he leaned over to kiss her one more time.

"No, no more kisses. I just reapplied my lips. How do they look? Are they on straight?"

"They're perfect. But, if I have my way, they won't be for long."

"No more kissing until we're back in this limo later on tonight. I need to have my game face on for the good ole boys."

"Okay. And I'll put my best foot forward too. I know the rules. Wait to be introduced, limit speaking to salutations, and try not to touch you above or below your waistline."

"Hmmm, sounds like you've done this before."

"A couple of times."

"Well, I'm sure you'll dazzle them all with your wit and charm. You've already won my vote of confidence with your attire. Mr. Patton, you look very dapper in your tuxedo. I am honored to be on your arm this evening!"

"The honor is all mine," Dave said as he kissed the back of her hand. "Mmmm, you smell so good.

I'm going to have a hard time keeping my hands from traveling south."

The limo door opened as they laughed. Dave emerged first. He took Vanessa's hand and helped her and her long flowing skirt from the limo. She was truly a vision, a reflection of royalty. The paparazzi were jockeying for position to get just the right angle. Dave and Vanessa slowly strolled up the red-carpeted stairs and paused briefly when asked to, as the shutters fluttered and the flashes popped. They made a handsome couple.

As they entered the MET, the sounds of chatter, clinking crystal flutes, and lighthearted laughter filled the air. All of a sudden, Beethoven's Fifth jolted everyone and appeared to announce Vanessa and Dave's arrival. Monica, Anne, and Maria were all engaged in separate conversations with different senior executives in various parts of the room, but they all turned simultaneously to see Vanessa and her escort glide into the room. The three of them said to themselves with an attitude, "I can't believe she brought a date!" They each excused themselves from their respective conversations and practically sprinted toward Vanessa and the man she was wearing. Monica was leading the race with Anne and Maria flanking her heels. When they reached her, they were all out of breath.

"Ms. Baldwin, you are truly a vision this evening," Monica said with a fake smile through clenched teeth.

"Why thank you! Ladies, you are all beyond beautiful tonight," Vanessa said with a wave of her free hand. The other one was wrapped around Dave's arm.

"I'd like you all to meet Mr. David Patton. Dave, this is Ms. Monica Kennedy, Ms. Anne Wu, and Ms. Maria Cabrera."

"It's Vasquez now. Nice to meet you," Maria said as she took her turn shaking his hand. Monica, Anne and Vanessa all looked at Maria with a puzzled look wondering why she had reverted back to her maiden name.

"It's a pleasure to meet all of you this evening," Dave returned. There was a pregnant, awkward pause, so Dave broke the silence. "Vanessa, why don't I get us some champagne? I'll be right back," he said as he lightly patted her hand. He set off to find the bar and check out his surroundings; he knew from the surprised look on their faces that Vanessa had some explaining to do. He would hang back and watch from afar while Vanessa gave her girls an update.

"Who in the hell is that?" Monica said without the slightest bit of diplomacy.

"I thought we were all coming by ourselves," Anne said.

"Hmmm, if I had one of those, I would have brought him too!" Maria said boldly.

Everyone turned and looked at Maria in disbelief given she had just buried her husband.

"What? He is damn fine!" Maria added.

Their eyes got even bigger. Then they laughed it off and figured it was the champagne talking.

"Ladies, I told you I wanted to surprise you all," Vanessa said with a mischievous tone.

"Yeah, but we all thought the surprise was going to be fashion-related, not vaginal-related," Anne said with a sarcastic smile. Laughter erupted from the group.

"I've known him for years, but I was always occupied with Damon. Plus, Dave is married…"

"Married!" Monica, Anne, and Maria practically screamed at once.

"Shhhh, will you keep your voices down," Vanessa implored. "Yes, he's married but soon to be divorced."

From the bar, Dave could tell it was getting serious. They had invaded Vanessa's personal space and were circled around her like a pack of wolves. He ordered another drink and kept his distance.

"He's been legally separated for almost a year. His divorce will be final in a couple of weeks."

"Oh," they all said together with a sigh of relief and took a step back.

"Well, you better take a peek at the divorce decree before you proceed any further, just to make sure he's on the up-and-up. You know men will tell you anything they think you want to hear just to get the tasty treats," Monica added with her head cocked sideways.

"I see your point, but look, I have a vacancy so we're just exploring and enjoying one another."

"Well, when he fills that vacancy, we want details. Blow-by-blow details," exclaimed Anne. They burst out laughing again. They finally remembered where they were and put their corporate postures and demeanors back on.

Just then Dave returned with two flutes of champagne and said, "Shall we begin our rounds?"

"Yes, we shall," Vanessa answered as she took the flute with one hand and his arm with the other. As they walked away, Vanessa looked back and winked.

"Hmmm, I'm scared of her," Monica commented.

"Hmmm, I want to be her," Anne whispered.

They smiled, adjusted their trains, and parted ways to continue the corporate networking dance.

The lights flickered and a hush came over the crowd as they moved towards the stage for the big announcement. With fanfare and lots of handshaking for the photographers, the CEO and the museum's head curator announced the opening of the new exhibit. The orchestra continued their rendering of classical selections as small groups and couples began to make their way through the maze of priceless paintings, sculptures, and relics.

Monica, Anne, and Maria joined up with one another to stroll through the exhibit together while

Vanessa and Dave made their own way, arm in arm. About three-quarters of the way through the exhibit, Dave felt his cell phone vibrating. He checked the caller ID. It was from the restaurant and marked urgent.

"Vanessa, I need to take this call. I'll try to make it quick."

"Okay, I'll be right here waiting for you so we can pick up where we left off."

As Dave stepped into a remote corner to take the call, Vanessa studied a beautiful ancient beaded necklace. He returned a few moments later with a concerned look on his face.

"Dave, what's wrong?"

"Vanessa, I'm sorry, I need to leave."

"Why, what happened?"

"A patron of my restaurant choked on some food."

"Oh my God! Are they going to be all right?"

"One of my servers performed the Heimlich maneuver and saved her life; however, she did lose consciousness for a few minutes. She's being taken to the hospital as a precaution. As the owner, I need to write a report to submit to my insurance company while it's fresh in everyone's minds. I also need to go to the hospital and follow up with my patron to see how she's doing. She's one of my regulars that I've known for years."

"Oh, oh yes, of course.

"I hate to leave you, especially tonight. I was looking forward to the rest of our evening," Dave said as he took Vanessa's hand.

"No, no, go. Don't worry about me. I'll be fine. Best wishes to your patron."

He pressed his lips to the back of her hand and was gone.

As the trio meandered through the exhibit, Anne stopped to admire an ancient, beautifully hand-carved hair comb. From behind her a voice said, "Beautiful women admire beautiful things." The voice was familiar but the comment threw her off. She turned quickly to see Dr. Porter standing there with a brilliant smile.

"Dr. Porter!" Anne exclaimed.

"Please call me Edward."

"Edward," Anne said awkwardly, "what a surprise seeing you here?"

"Yes, my parents are long-time patrons of the museum, so I get invited to all of the openings."

"Oh, well, this feels a bit awkward to see my doctor at a corporate function. Good thing you're not my gynecologist." Anne said with a nervous laugh.

Edward laughed and said, "Anne, you're no longer my patient. I purposefully referred you to one of my colleagues because…" He hesitated momentarily. "Because I wanted to see you socially, however I couldn't mention that during our session. I put my license on the line and took a calculated risk that you would say, *yes*."

Anne stood there looking at him in shock with her mouth wide open and her eyes practically popping out her head. She was so dumfounded that she dropped her Swarovski crystal encrusted evening clutch. Luckily, Edward had good reflexes and caught it in midair, just before it hit the marble floor.

"Whoa, be careful," he said as he straightened up and handed it back to her along with his business card.

"My home and cell numbers are on the back. If you don't call, I'll understand, but I do feel we made a connection. I hope I'm not being too forward."

Before Anne could respond, Monica and Maria walked up and said simultaneously, "Dr. Porter!"

"Wait a minute. You know him too?" Anne said in a confused state.

"Ms. Kennedy, Ms. Cabrera, you are both looking lovely this evening," he said as he noticed the glass of champagne in Monica's hand. Monica realized he was looking at her drink and laughed nervously.

"Dr. Porter, it's Ms. Vasquez now. I decided to go back to my maiden name," Maria said with a smile.

Then from out of nowhere, "Hi, Dr. Porter! I see you've met my friends," Vanessa said with a smile.

"You know him too?" Anne said in sheer disbelief.

"Yes, I've known him for years," Vanessa volunteered.

"Ladies, I wish I could stay and chat, but I must run. I need to quickly make my rounds - I've got an early day tomorrow. Good night!" and Dr. Porter was gone.

"Wait a damn minute. We all know Dr. Porter? I mean from before this evening?" Anne asked. They all nodded their heads in the affirmative.

"Come on ladies, I need another drink, something stronger than this champagne. Let's hit Sangritas," Monica announced. Everyone looked at Monica with shock in their eyes, but didn't know what to say.

"Hold on a minute. One of us is not flying solo tonight," Maria added. "Vanessa, where's that handsome Mr. Patton?"

"Oh, he was called away on an emergency. So, I'm solo. Hey, let's grab my limo. It's just outside."

"Sounds good to me. I've kissed enough ass tonight to get the CEO position!" Maria said. They laughed and made their way through the crowd to the coat check.

After much maneuvering of trains and furs, the foursome settled into the limo.

"Hey, I've got an idea," Vanessa said. "Let's order a pitcher of Sangritas to go, pick it up, and ride around in the limo for a while. That way we can have some privacy and not have to drag these gowns through the restaurant." Everyone nodded their heads in agreement, except Monica.

"Don't you think we need two pitchers?" Monica asked. From the blank stares she received, she knew the answer was no. Vanessa gave the driver their next destination and called ahead on her cell phone to order the drinks. Since she knew the owners, they obliged her request, especially since she mentioned that they would not be driving. As Vanessa hung up, her phone rang.

"Hello?"

"Hey it's me."

"Dave, is everything all right?" Monica, Anne, and Maria were glued to Vanessa's conversation.

"I'm here at the hospital. I decided to come here first. My patron is fine. They'll be releasing her shortly. As it turns out, she choked on a single grain of rice. That's what can happen when you laugh and eat at the same time."

"Wow, I didn't even know you could choke on rice."

"Apparently so. Well, I just wanted to check in with you. I'm on my way to the restaurant to talk with my staff and write my report. I hope you're not too lonely without me."

"Oh, I'm fine, really. I'm in good company," Vanessa said winking at her girls.

"I know what that means. They'll be giving you the third degree about me. Tell them I said to go easy on you."

Vanessa laughed and relayed the message.

"Have fun! I'll be tied up for the next several hours, so why don't you give me a call tomorrow afternoon when you wake up from your hangover. Let me know if you need a remedy and I'll rush to your bedside." Vanessa blushed and smiled.

"I will. Have a good night and thank you for being my escort this evening. I really enjoyed the time we had together."

"Me too. Until tomorrow..." and he was gone.

As soon as she hung up, Monica, Anne, and Maria started teasing her.

"Oh, stop it!" Vanessa said while trying to stifle a big smile.

The drinks were delivered to the limo and they rode around chatting about Dave, his emergency, and about the details of each other's gowns, shoes, jewelry, and hair. They critiqued the executive's wives gowns up one side and down the other, as well as speculated on the status of their marriages based on the body language they observed. All the while, the burning thought in the forefront of each of their minds was the subject of Dr. Porter. Each one silently speculated how the others knew him, how long they had been seeing him, what issues they were addressing, and most importantly, were they ever the topic of conversation in each other's therapy sessions.

After an hour had passed and the pitcher of Sangritas was empty, Monica raided the minibar. Vanessa finally decided to address the big elephant that had been riding around in the limo with them.

"Okay, now that we've gotten all of the pleasantries out of the way, so how is it that we all know Dr. Porter?" You could hear a pin drop. Even Monica stopped in mid-pour of her mini bottle of champagne. "Oh, come on. I know we've all been asking ourselves that question since we met up with him at the MET." There was silence again as everyone suddenly became interested in the manicures that they had spent the early part of the afternoon getting.

"Well, I'll start," Maria volunteered. "I took my girls to see him for grief counseling after my husband committed suicide."

"Suicide!" Vanessa, Monica, and Anne screamed in their *trying to sound shocked* voices.

"Oh, save it! I know it's been all over the office," Maria said half-laughing at their dramatic performance.

"Well, we heard conflicting reports that he may or may not have shot himself accidentally," Vanessa said reaching over to touch Maria's hand.

"Yeah, I know. I didn't confirm or deny the reports when I came back to work. I just wanted to pretend that it didn't happen and go on with my life. Evidently the news media had a different plan."

"Do you know why he did it?" Monica asked delicately.

"Did he leave a note?" Anne followed up.

281

Maria became interested in her manicure again, as she mustered up the courage to tell the story.

"I didn't have a car accident."

"What!" Vanessa, Monica, and Anne screamed in an authentically shocked voice.

"I was trying to avoid the gossip." Maria took a deep breath, grabbed Monica's hand, and fought back the tears.

"Maria, we didn't mean to upset you. You don't have to talk about it," Vanessa offered, knowing full well she was dying to know the truth.

"No, it's okay. The truth needs to be told. José has been beating me for years." The trio gasped. "I finally got up the courage to take my girls and leave him after he came in one night from a drinking binge and raped me." The trio gasped again. "After I left him, I found out from my girls that he had been molesting them." The trio screamed, "What?" in unison. Now they were all holding hands.

"Are they all right?" They asked in unison with tears beginning to sting their eyes.

"They're fine physically. It doesn't appear as though he penetrated them. Thank God! Dr. Porter is seeing them on a regular basis to ensure that they'll be all right otherwise."

"But what about you? Are you all right?" Vanessa inquired.

"I'm okay, really. I don't want any pity. And please don't let tear stains ruin our couture gowns." They all laughed, shared hugs, and searched for tissues.

"I truly feel like I've only just begun to live," Maria said smiling through her soon to be raccoon eyes. They all smiled and held hands again. Monica spoke next.

"Lizzy and I started seeing Dr. Porter for grief counseling about a year ago when Jeff was killed." Monica suddenly found interest in her manicure again also. "I only saw him a couple of times. I really wasn't that broken up over Jeff's death."

"Monica!" Vanessa exclaimed.

Maria grabbed Monica's hand and Anne's eyes grew big as quarters.

"I know that sounds bad," Monica explained.

"No, it doesn't, Monica," Maria reassured her.

"He had been having an affair for a number of years. I was stupid enough to think that after getting pregnant and having Lizzy he would stop. Needless to say, he didn't. I began drinking too much to escape the reality of the situation."

"Speaking of drinking," Vanessa interjected and loudly cleared her throat.

"I know, I know. I started seeing Dr. Porter again, this time about my drinking. I am going to start a twelve-step program." Everyone exhaled with relief.

"We were really getting concerned about you. You were knockin' 'em back tonight like there was no tomorrow," Anne added.

"Yeah, I know. It was stupid. I figured this was my last night to drink, so just go for it. But really, I've learned that drinking causes me to make some really poor choices."

"Well, we're all really proud of you, and we're behind you one hundred percent," Maria said with encouragement.

"So don't let us see you with anymore alcohol in your glass, or else," Vanessa warned.

"Thank you," Monica said with tears in her eyes as they took turns hugging her. They dried their eyes again and Vanessa spoke next.

"Well, I guess I'll go next. I've been seeing Dr. Porter on and off for several years now. I have a recurring dream that was once a reality. It's been haunting me. I started having these dreams in my early twenties about an incident that happened to me when I was six-years-old." Vanessa took a deep breath and closed her eyes. "My brother molested me." Again, gasps and tears came from all. They had run out of tissues, so Monica started handing out cocktail napkins from the minibar. "My mother didn't do anything about it." More gasps were heard. "No doctor, no counseling, no punishment for my brother, no nothing. I've never confronted her about it to tell her how much it affected me all my life. Dr. Porter told me I need to confront her about my feelings in order to help me get over this recurring dream. I guess I should call it a nightmare."

Maria leaned over and squeezed Vanessa's hand and said, "You can do it. I know you can. Do it for all the little girls out there that are going through what you went through. There are so many that can't say a word, or never say a word, because they're afraid. So, they just suffer in silence. Do it for them."

Vanessa said with agony in her voice, "Maria, Monica, keep your girls close to you, always. Trust no boy or man, because no matter who they are, they're all capable of crossing the line at any age." Everyone nodded their heads, wiped their eyes, blew their noses, and looked towards Anne for the next revelation. Anne looked up from folding her tissue and realized they were expecting a confession from her.

"Oh, me? I, I just met Dr. Porter this evening. We were both admiring the same artifact in the exhibit." Anne couldn't bear to tell the truth about something so personal.

"Oh!" was the simultaneous response from Vanessa, Monica, and Maria.

"Well, that's a good thing, because the minibar is out of napkins," Monica said as they all tried to smile through their ruined make up.

"I wonder how you all just happened to choose Dr. Porter?" Anne asked, to try and get the focus off her.

There was a long silent pause then Vanessa, Maria, and Monica said, "EAP," in unison. "That's it! The Employee Assistance Program at work must have recommended the same psychologist to all three of us," Vanessa exclaimed. They all agreed as Anne pretended not to know what they were talking about. She knew exactly what EAP was because that's how she was referred to Dr. Porter as well.

"Well, I'd better be getting home to my daughter," Monica announced.

Everyone nodded their heads in agreement and gave their addresses to the driver.

"Well, I guess this is the last official meeting of The Sangrita Club since I've stopped drinking officially as of this very moment," Monica announced.

"In that case, we need a new name," Vanessa suggested.

"Hey, I know. What about The Corporate Divas' Club?" They all laughed heartily at Maria's suggestion as the limo pulled up to drop Monica off.

"Hey Monica, watch your step when getting off the elevator; the first one's a doozie," Vanessa joked. They laughed and said their good nights.

Monica crunched on some mints on her way up in the elevator. As the door opened to her floor, she gingerly stepped over the threshold and made her way to Mrs. Florence's apartment. She knocked lightly on the door.

"Hi, I thought you were going to pick her up in the morning?" Mrs. Florence whispered as she tied her robe at the waist.

"I was, but I changed my mind."

"Okay, but try not to wake her up. You go get Lizzy and I'll go open your door and turn down the sheets on her bed."

Mrs. Florence took Monica's evening clutch and fur coat, but stopped as she turned to leave. "Monica, I smell the mints. What happened?"

"I've taken my last drink, really! I will fill you in tomorrow morning on my plan and tell you everything. I don't want there to be any secrets between us."

"Okay, but I'm going to hold you to that!"

Monica smiled, "I know you will."

Monica crept into Lizzy's second bedroom and sat down on the bed next to her. She brushed Lizzy's tousled curls from her face and gave her a lingering kiss on her cheek. She thought about Maria's girls and how she would react if someone had molested Lizzy. She said a quick silent prayer that she would never, ever have to face that situation. She pulled back the covers and lifted Lizzy into her arms. As she walked out of the apartment and down the hall, her golden gown flowed behind her as tears began to flow from her eyes. In her arms was the reason that she would never, ever take another drink again. Monica didn't just want to be in Lizzy's life; she wanted to be available to Lizzy physically and emotionally, as well as truly know her in every way. Monica was determined not to repeat history and follow in her mother's footsteps. She and Lizzy would create their own lovely history, together.

As the limo pulled up to drop Maria off, Vanessa grabbed her hand. "Maria, thank you so much for sharing your story with us. I'm encouraged and even more determined now. I know what I need to do." They all exchanged hugs and good nights.

Maria walked into her apartment expecting to be alone, since her girls were spending the night with their grandmother. But what she got was a Kodak moment. She walked into her living room and found her two girls curled up together on the chaise lounge fast asleep and her mother rubbing the sleep from her eyes as she got up from the couch. Maria pulled out her cell phone and took a quick pic of Elizabeth and Christina.

"How was it?" Maria's mother whispered.

"Oh the evening was wonderful! I met so many influential people. The gowns were exquisite and the exhibit was very interesting. It felt so good to be among them."

"Them. You are one of them. You always have been. Now you've just made it official. José held you back for so long, but now the sky is the limit. You can reach for the highest rung on that ladder." They smiled and hugged one another.

"What are you all doing here and why aren't they in bed?"

"They wanted to be here when you got home. They didn't want you to be alone. They tried to wait up for you and refused to go to bed, so I put on a movie and they eventually fell asleep."

"Thanks for taking such good care of my girls, Mami. You just don't know how much I appreciate you being involved with them every day now. It is so comforting to know they are in a safe place and in safe hands while I work. There is nothing in this world like a mother's love and protection, and that includes grandmothers, too." They smiled and hugged again.

"Well, what an emotional roller coaster ride that was," Anne said nervously.

"Yes it was, but it was very cathartic," Vanessa agreed. "I'm really glad we shared our stories. I think it helped us all realize that there are a lot of similarities underneath our differences. We can encourage each other by listening and leaning on one another. It makes the burdens we all carry seem a little bit lighter," Vanessa said in reflection. The limo pulled up in front of Anne's building. Anne said good night as she stepped out onto the sidewalk. Vanessa saw a business card on the seat where Anne had been seated. She picked it up and saw the letter, "H" written on the back next to a telephone number. She flipped the card over and saw that it was Dr. Porter's card. Vanessa suspected that Anne had lied about just meeting Dr. Porter, because she had observed them talking just before she joined them at the exhibit. The business card confirmed her suspicions.

"Just a minute driver," Vanessa said as she rolled down the tinted window of the limousine. "Anne," she called. Anne turned and walked back toward the car with a puzzled look on her face. "You must have dropped this," Vanessa said in an expressionless voice. Anne's face instantly flushed with embarrassment as she reached to take the card from Vanessa's hand. But Vanessa held on to it and said, "When you're ready to ride the roller coaster with the rest of us, let me know." With that, she released the card and rolled up the window. The limo pulled off leaving Anne standing at the curb, speechless.

At that moment, Anne realized that Vanessa knew that she had lied about meeting Dr. Porter for the first time at the gala. Anne stood there and watched the limousine roll away while a single tear rolled down her cheek. Her integrity was now in question; she knew what she needed to do next.

Anne always wore a façade that didn't allow for a very large range of emotions. She swung between indifference and extreme anger, but tried not to allow hurt, disappointment, or fear show on her face. She was always afraid of showing any sign of weakness, even to herself; however, this night would change everything.

Anne made her way past the doorman, into the elevator, and up to her penthouse apartment. As her keys hit the inside of the crystal bowl that sat on a marble pedestal next to her front door, she finally broke down and began sobbing uncontrollably. She made her way to the bedroom undressing along the way, leaving a trail of designer shoes, French lingerie, and her fine couture gown like bread crumbs through the forest of packed boxes. She sat, weeping in her steam-shower as it melted away the remainder of her makeup and hairspray from the evening's festivities.

She sat there replaying over and over in her mind what she needed to say to him. She needed to free herself from all of the pent up anger that had burdened her from the years of alienation she suffered at the hands of her father. She needed to tell him how inadequate he had made her feel, how his treatment caused her to never want to date a man from her own culture, and how his behavior had made her mother's heart ache. She wanted him to know that she knew he had stayed with her mother because of her money, and that if he had divorced her, she would still be rich and he would have been just another struggling attorney. She wanted him to know that she had left China and come to the U.S. just to get away from him, which broke her mother's heart. Although her mother had never said a negative or unkind word to Anne about her father, she could hear the hurt, disappointment, and fear every time she listened to her mother's voice. Somehow, some way, she wanted him to pay.

After spending half an hour in the shower, Anne emerged emotionally spent. She threw on a white terry cloth robe and made her way to the kitchen to make a cup of green tea. As she set the teakettle onto the flame, the phone rang, startling her. She wondered who could be calling her at such a late hour.

She checked the caller ID and saw that it was her mother's phone number. She picked up the phone and answered immediately.

"Mother, is everything all right?"

"Anne, I've been trying to reach you for the past six hours," her mother answered in Chinese with desperation in her voice.

"I'm sorry. I was at a formal event this evening and had my cell phone turned off. What's going on?"

"It's your father!"

"What about him? Did he tell you he eavesdropped on our last conversation?" Anne said cynically.

"No. Anne, your father... well, there's just no other way to say it. He's left us."

"What? What do you mean, left us? Are you telling me he walked out on you after all that he has put us through, all these years?"

"No, Anne, your father is dead."

There was a long pause. Anne stood frozen in disbelief as she leaned against the marble kitchen countertop. After a few moments, she stood up straight.

"Mother, what are you talking about?"

"Oh Anne, he committed assisted suicide," her mother said with anguish in her voice.

"Assisted? You mean someone helped him?" Anne bellowed.

"Apparently, his doctor prescribed some pills for him to take. He was terminally ill and wanted to end his life with dignity."

"Apparently? You didn't know he was ill?"

"No. He didn't tell me."

"Figures," Anne mumbled under her breath. "Did he say anything to you before he, he killed himself?"

"No, but he left me a letter. One of his law partners delivered it to me right after he died."

"Delivered? Wait, how did he know when to deliver the letter?"

"Your father took his life at the office. He confided in one of his law partners about his illness and had him draw up all of the necessary legal papers. He then chose the day and time to end his life. He told his partner to check on him in an hour. When he did, he was gone."

"I can't believe his partner didn't say anything to you!"

"You know your father felt that attorney client privilege was stronger than moral obligation."

"Yeah, you're right about that," Anne retorted.

"He wanted to end his life, his way."

"Mother, I am so sorry I didn't have my phone on when you called! Are you all right?"

"I'll be better when you get here."

"I'm on my way. I'll take the next flight out. Mother, I love you."

"I love you too!"

Anne hung up and dialed the concierge, ordered a limousine to the airport and a plane ticket to Hong Kong. She pulled her Ralph Lauren Cooper bag from the top shelf of her closet and threw in a toiletry bag that she always kept packed. She grabbed a few changes of lingerie and a pair of ivory silk pajamas with matching slippers from a drawer. Anne stood back and looked at her expansive wardrobe hanging before her. Suddenly, she felt weary and overwhelmed by the thought of having to choose several outfits to take with her. She let out a heavy sigh. "I'll just buy some clothes when I get there," she said out loud. She dressed quickly in her usual travel outfit, a pair of black slacks, a white cotton blouse, a camel colored cashmere V-neck sweater, and a pair of Cole Hahn driving shoes. She took her cell phone and charger and threw them into her Ricky bag then pulled a black, Burberry trench coat from the hall closet. As she locked the door to her apartment, she remembered Dr. Porter's business card. She went back inside and searched through the trail of evening attire for her clutch and retrieved the card.

Once inside the limousine, Anne began to lose her composure for the second time that day. She rolled up the privacy window between her and the chauffeur and dialed a phone number on her cell phone. A sleepy voice on the other end answered,

"Hello?"

"Hi, it's Anne."

"Anne? It's so late. What's going on? Is everything all right?"

"Vanessa, I'm sorry I lied to you all about knowing Dr. Porter."

"Oh, it's okay, Anne. Don't lose any sleep over it. I respect you for wanting to keep your personal life private. Besides, we all tried to keep our personal struggles under wraps too. But I think we all learned that there's no need for us to hide our pain and lie to one another. We can all be there for each other and help each other overcome anything. Just know that I'm here for you when you need me."

"Thank you, Vanessa," Anne said wiping tears from her eyes, again with napkins from the minibar.

"Vanessa, I need you to do something for me."

"Sure, name it!"

"I have to leave town tonight. I'm going home to Hong Kong."

"Hong Kong? Tonight? Why?"

"My father died." Anne completely broke down.

"Oh, Anne! Oh, my God! What happened?"

"He was terminally ill and wanted to die with dignity, so he committed assisted suicide."

"Oh, Anne. I am so sorry."

"Would you please let the senior team know that my father died unexpectedly and tell Connie that I will contact her as soon as I can."

"Okay, no problem."

"I'm not sure how long I'll be away."

"Anne, don't worry about a thing here. You just concentrate on taking care of yourself and your mother."

"Thanks Vanessa, for everything," Anne said smiling through her tears.

"That's what friends are for! Keep your chin up and safe travels. You are in my prayers."

Anne hung up and dabbed her eyes once again with cocktail napkins. She felt so strange and conflicted for crying over a man she had developed such a deep hatred for, but also an unquenchable longing. She dialed another phone number. A sleepy baritone voice answered,

"Hello, this is Dr. Porter."

"Edward, this is Anne."

"Anne!" Suddenly he sounded wide-awake.

"I didn't expect to hear from you so soon."

"Edward, I just wanted you to know that I'm leaving for Hong Kong in a few hours. I'm on my way to JFK right now."

"Are you traveling for business or pleasure?"

"You were right about a catalyst changing my father's behavior. My father just committed assisted suicide. He was terminally ill."

"Oh Anne, I'm so sorry to hear that!"

"Please don't say anymore. I'm trying not to fall apart again tonight. I don't know when I'll be returning, but when I do, I'd like to see you on a," she paused, "a personal basis."

"Anne, I'm really glad to hear you say that. But in the meantime, please call me if you need to. I'm available to you anytime, day or night."

"I'll be fine, really," Anne said sniffing and attempting to sound cheery. "You have my cell number on your caller ID, so we can keep in touch while I'm away. Okay?"

"Oh, absolutely. Anne, are you sure you're going to be all right?"

"Edward, I'll be fine," she said again, trying to smile through her tears. "I'd better go. I'll call you when I get there and get settled in."

"Okay. Please take care of yourself."

"I will. I promise."

Anne hung up, threw her cell phone in her Ricky bag and dug through it in search of a pair of sunglasses. Although it was night, she wore them to cover her puffy red eyes. She didn't want anyone to see that she had been crying. As always, she was concerned about her image.

Just as Anne was about to go through security, a hand grabbed her elbow from behind. She was startled and spun around to meet Edward's eyes. Without saying a word, he removed her sunglasses, wrapped his arms around her and kissed her on the mouth, not with a kiss of passion, but with a kiss of concern and empathy, for he too had recently lost his

father in a long battle with cancer. She held onto him
tight and wept in his arms.

15

Vanessa awoke early despite being out late the night before. Her mind found it difficult to relax because of the previous night's revelations and Anne's news about her father's death. She also kept thinking about what she was going to say to her mother when she confronted her. She decided it was time to get it over with, so she leaned over and reached for the phone. As usual, it wasn't on the base. She hit the page button and somewhere deep underneath her covers she heard the beeping sound. She searched until she found it, took a deep cleansing breath, dialed the number, and pulled her grandmother's quilt over her head to provide a safe haven.

"Hello?" her mother answered cheerfully.

"Hi Mom."

"Vanessa! You never call me this early. Is everything okay?"

"I'm fine. Everything is fine."

"Oh good! Girl, don't scare me like that!"

"Mom, I need to talk to you about something. Are you busy right now?"

"Not too busy for my baby! What's on your mind?"

"Well, for about the last four years, on and off, I've been getting professional counseling."

"You have. Pray tell, what for?"

"About ten years ago, I started having a recurring dream. It stopped about three years ago, but it started up again recently. My therapist suggested that I talk to you about it. He's hoping that our conversation will give me some answers to the questions I've had on my mind and help me gain some closure and peace of mind."

"Well honey, what is your dream about?"

Vanessa took a deep breath.

"Mom, do you remember when I was six years old, and I didn't go back to school after lunch one day?"

"Hmmm... not off hand."

"You came home and found me on your bed crying because Kenny had hurt me." There was a long pause in the conversation. Finally, whimpers came through the phone from Vanessa's mother.

"Yes, yes, baby, I remember, I remember, I remember," Vanessa's mother said with anguish in her voice.

"Mama, why didn't you comfort me? Why didn't you take me to a doctor?" she said gradually raising her voice. "Why didn't you do something to him, like punish him, get him counseling, or send him away to live with our father!" Vanessa was now shouting at the top of her lungs through her sobs.

"You're my mother! You were supposed to protect me!"

Vanessa's mother began wailing through the phone. Vanessa burst out from under the quilt gasping for air, her chest heaving up and down so heavily that she thought she was having a heart attack. She had never, in her whole life, raised her voice to her mother. After a few moments of crying and nose blowing, they collected themselves enough to continue the conversation.

"Vanessa, I am so, so, sorry he did that to you. I know you two never really got along growing up, but it never, ever crossed my mind that he would do something like that to you. He was only twelve years old. I didn't think something like that would even be on his mind."

"Why didn't you take me to a doctor? Didn't you care about the physical and mental scars that it would leave on me? Look at me! I'm a 36 years old woman, no husband, no kids, and no self-esteem. All the relationships I've had were with men who just wanted to use me. I've had the words 'desperately seeking love' written across my forehead ever since the day Kenny took my innocence."

"Baby, I'm so sorry! Back in that day, it wasn't something you talked about. Taking you to the doctor and telling him what had happened was out of the question. I didn't know what to do or where to turn. We didn't have Oprah back then! I was afraid and ashamed. I felt ashamed because I couldn't afford to pay someone to look after you two during lunchtime

301

and after school while I was taking classes and working at the University. I was afraid that if I took you to a doctor that Child Protective Services might take you both away from me."

"You could have comforted me instead of just telling me it was nothing. You could have at the very least punished him!"

"Baby, I was afraid if I let you think it was serious that you might tell someone, like your teacher or the school nurse. But I assure you that I did punish your brother."

"What! You punished Kenny? When? Where? How?"

"Vanessa, I took you in the bathroom and bathed you down there and checked you out. There was some blood and you were in pain, but it didn't seem to be too bad. I gave you some aspirin, and told you to stay in your room and lay down. Then I waited. When Kenny got home from school he was surprised to see me there, but I didn't let on that you had said something to me about what he'd done. I sent him to the basement to play while I started dinner. Then I went upstairs to check on you and you had fallen asleep across your bed. I covered you up, closed your door, grabbed my belt and went down into the basement. I made Kenny strip down to his underwear and I whipped him like I had never whipped him before. I whipped him so bad that he peed all over himself. He had welts all up and down his back and legs so bad that I had to keep him home from school the next day. I didn't want one of his teachers to discover that I had whipped him or why. I told Kenny if he ever touched you again, I would send him away to a home for bad boys."

"Oh, Mama, why didn't you tell me you punished him? All these years I thought that you didn't do anything. I thought that you didn't care about me. I was so glad when God took him because I felt like he was finally getting his punishment for what he'd done to me and that you were getting punished too for not protecting and comforting me."

"Oh, Baby, forgive me, please forgive me," she begged. "When your father left I had no one to turn to. I didn't know what to do. I was scared and all alone. I did what I thought was best."

They both sobbed for a long time while continuing to unleash their burdens. They professed their love for one another and that day started a new relationship based on truth, forgiveness, and understanding.

CHAPTER

16

It was a hot, humid, overcast day in Hong Kong. In keeping with the Chinese tradition, the wake and funeral for Anne's father was held in a beautiful roof top garden instead of his home, because he had died outside of his home. Afterward, Anne and her mother made their way, arm-in-arm, up the elevator to their forty-fourth floor penthouse. When they entered, all the servants met them in the foyer with bowed heads showing their respect and regret. The butler took their coats as Anne's mother asked the upstairs maid to draw her a bath. Meanwhile, the chef humbly presented them with tea in Anne's father's study. Anne's mother dismissed the other servants so that she and Anne could be alone.

"Mother, I will serve the tea," Anne volunteered.

"No dear, I will serve. I need to keep my hands busy."

The tea was served and they drank it in complete silence out of respect for tradition and the history of their husband and father surrounding them in that room.

"Anne, I have something for you from your father."

"What?" Anne asked in shock as she carefully placed her cup on the tea cart.

Anne's mother pulled a sealed legal-sized envelope from the top drawer of her husband's desk and placed it in Anne's shaking hands. Anne was surprised at the sight of her name written in her father's handwriting across the front of the envelope.

"Mother, what is this?"

"I don't know. You'll have to open it to see what it contains. I only know that your father requested it be given to you after his funeral."

"Do you mind if I ask what he said in his letter to you?"

"No, not at all. He explained why he had chosen to keep the news of his illness from me. He didn't want me to carry the burden and responsibility of caring for him while his health declined. And that he chose assisted suicide in order to die with dignity."

"Mother, we haven't discussed what his illness was."

"It was an inoperable brain tumor. He had been having headaches on and off for a few months. I finally convinced him to go to the doctor. Afterwards, he never complained again. I assumed it was stress-related and that the doctor had given him pain medication and, perhaps, instructions to cut back on his work hours. He was home more often and we were spending a great deal of time together. It was like a second honeymoon! I guess in some way he was trying to make up for lost time. Apparently, on the morning of his death, he woke up quite early and discovered that the right side of his face was completely paralyzed. He left the house before the servants awoke. Later that morning, I received a call from his partner; it was 7:49 a.m. I'll never forget the time. He was gone."

"Oh Mother, I can't imagine what you must have gone through here all alone after receiving the news."

"Daughter, I'm a lot stronger than you think," she smiled. "He also apologized to me for the years of anguish he put me through in regards to you. He told me to tell you that he truly loved you."

Anne's mouth dropped open. She was speechless.

"Now, I'm going to leave you alone with your father's last words to you." She arose, kissed her daughter on the forehead, and left the room. As she closed the door behind her, a tear fell from her eye and came to rest on the back of her hand, for she knew all too well the story the envelope contained.

Anne stood and pressed the envelope to her nose. It smelled like her father's cologne. She made her way over to a wall of windows that gave a panoramic view of the city. "What could possibly be in this envelope?" she said to herself. "It's probably some legal papers or his will that he wants me to handle for my mother. It most certainly couldn't be anything personal."

Anne went over to her father's desk and placed the envelope on it as she sat down reluctantly in his big leather chair, the chair she had never been allowed to sit in. She opened the top drawer and pulled out a letter opener with a hand carved jade handle. She sat there studying its ornate beauty. She had seen her father use it many times, but she had never been allowed to touch it. She turned on the desk lamp and carefully opened the envelope, being careful not to crack the large, black wax seal. Inside she found a seven-page handwritten letter on legal size paper. Anne was stunned that her father had taken so much time to write a letter to her in his own hand. If anything, she would have expected it to be typed in legal brief format. She took a deep breath and began the journey.

> *Dearest Anne, I come to you in the humblest way I know how, begging for your forgiveness.*

"Forgiveness! Who the hell is he to beg for my forgiveness," she fumed as she slammed her fist down on the desk, jumped to her feet and started pacing. "Why do I have to read your words of regret? Why couldn't you have been man enough to say them to my face?" At that point she realized the servants were probably lined up outside the study door listening to her screaming at the top of her lungs. She took a deep breath and sat down as the anger continued to boil up inside her. She clenched her fists and continued.

I know I haven't been the kind of father you wanted or needed.

"Yeah, you've got that right!" Anne commented under her breath.

I know that I don't deserve your forgiveness either.

"Forgive you? This is just crazy!" She said as she angrily pushed the letter across the desk. She sat back in her father's chair, trying to decide if she should continue reading. After a few moments of silence, she reached for the letter again.

> *If you choose not to forgive me, I understand. I know I took the easy way out by way of this letter after my death rather than facing you. I've taken the coward's way out because I am ashamed of how I behaved towards you all of these years.*

"Well, you should be you son-of-a . . .!" she remembered the servants again while the angry fire continued to build in her heart as she read on.

> *What I'm about to tell you doesn't justify my behavior and I am not making excuses. I just want you to know why I never tried to develop a father/daughter relationship with you.*

As you know, I grew up on a rice farm in the rural countryside. But what you don't know is that I had two younger sisters. Unfortunately, I don't know if they are still alive. Several years ago I attempted to find them, but was unsuccessful.

"What! I can't believe I have two aunts that no one told me about!" Anne read on stunned by the revelation.

We were too poor to get medical care, so my mother died when I was thirteen after a very long illness. I think it may have been pneumonia. My sisters were eleven and twelve years old at the time. We were left to be raised by our father; we had no relatives or neighbors nearby. We had to work the farm ourselves, so there was no schooling for me after age ten, and at that time, it was not customary for girls to be educated.

After my mother had been dead for some months, my father began to spy on my sisters while they bathed and dressed. I caught him standing in the dark outside of my sisters' bedroom one night, as they got ready for bed. He was peeking through a crack in the wood panel of their bedroom door. When he saw me, he got down on his hands and knees and pretended he had dropped something and was looking for it, but I knew what he was doing. I was ashamed to tell my sisters what I had seen, so I told them that their room would be warmer if they stuffed some rags in the cracks of their door to keep the drafts out. They did as I said, but when my father discovered that his view was blocked, he became outraged. He beat me for telling them to put rags in the cracks of their door and ordered my sisters to remove them.

Soon, he began creeping into my sisters' bedroom at night while they slept. The first time I heard the screams, I ran to see what was the matter. My father met me at their door and told me to go back to bed and never to return, no matter what I heard. He threatened to beat me if I did not comply. He closed the door and I peeked through the same crack he had looked through to see what was happening. The sight was unspeakable. I ran back to my room and cried because I felt so powerless.

I could do nothing to help my poor, dear sisters.

Anne stopped reading, closed her eyes, and took a deep breath. "I can't believe my grandfather was a pedophile," Anne whispered in horror.

Soon, both of my sisters were heavy with child, yet my father made them continue to work in the fields and they were forbidden to go to town. Their babies were born, one right after the other, just one week apart. They had no one to help them, so they delivered each other's babies. Late one night, I was sitting in the outhouse when I heard the sound of digging. I followed the sound and saw my father digging a hole. I walked up to him and said, "Father, what are you. . ." but before I could finish my sentence, his hands were around my throat. Then I saw them. Two lifeless baby girls were lying on the ground next to his feet.

"That murdering bastard! He killed his own flesh and blood!" Anne whispered covering her mouth in shock.

He told me girls were of no value except to breed boys. He also told me I was going to grow up to be just like him. I was his spitting image and I was horrified at the thought of following in his footsteps. He made me finish digging the shallow grave, place the infants in it, and cover them up. All the while, I kept throwing up to the point where I had dry heaves.

"Oh, my God, my poor father," Anne began to sob uncontrollably. She got up to get some tissues from her purse to wipe the tears from her face and from her father's letter. Although the story was gruesome, she could not stop reading about her father's history.

When I finally made it back to the house, I went into my sisters' room where they sat in their bed huddled and crying hysterically, asking when our father was going to bring their babies back. All I could do was shake my head no. I never told my sisters what I had seen or what he made me do that night. I let them assume our father had sold their babies. When I lay down in my bed that night, I cried and vowed to myself that I would do everything in my power to never, ever be like my father.

The molestation continued. When my father would finish with my sisters at night, I would wait until I heard him snoring then slip into their bedroom to console them. They were sick with grief at the loss of their babies and deathly afraid of getting pregnant again, only to repeat the horrible tragedy. They would talk of running away, but they knew if they left me there, I would be killed for helping them. So we devised a plan for all three of us to escape.

Harvest time was approaching and our father always hired extra help. He provided the laborers with a place to sleep and three meals a day in exchange for their work in the fields. I was to meet them when they arrived to give them a tour of the farm and fields while my sisters cooked and my father readied their sleeping quarters in the barn. The night before the hired hands were to arrive, each of us packed a small bag and I hid them in the bushes by the side of the road. When the time came for the workers to arrive, my sisters slipped away from the kitchen and we all went down to the road. My sisters hid in the bushes as the men arrived and I asked the driver to wait. I pulled out a map of the property I had drawn on the back of a rice sack and explained to the field hands that they would be going on a self-guided tour ending at the barn. This would give us at least thirty minutes before my father realized we were missing. I sent the men on their way and my sisters and I got in the back of the wagon to ride into town. On the way, my sisters admitted that they had left the food they were cooking on the fire. We all hoped that the house burned to the ground.

When we arrived in town, we hopped on a freight train to Hong Kong. It was the first time any of us had ever ridden on a train. We were scared and penniless, but we were so relieved to be away from our father. We were free. We thought it would be best if we split up and went our separate ways. It would be easier for us to be found if we stayed together. So, I said a tearful goodbye to my sisters. I went my way and they went theirs. I never saw or heard from them ever again.

The tears continued to flow heavily as Anne read on.

I lied about my age and joined the People's Liberation Army. I excelled in my training, so after completing my required service time, they arranged for me to attend the Chinese University of Hong Kong and Harvard Law School. I returned to Hong Kong after graduating to work for a prestigious law firm where I met your mother as a young practicing attorney while taking care of some minor legal matters for her family. We fell in love and, although I was from a lower class, she agreed to marry me even against her family's wishes. I had finally found someone to love, and to be loved by, to fill the void that had been left in my heart by my mother's early death and the separation from my beloved sisters.

All was well with our marriage, however, I was mortified when your mother gave birth to a girl. I admit I wanted a boy because we were allowed to have only one child. In addition, I was petrified at the thought of raising a girl. I was sick with anxiety because I didn't want to be like my father. In my anguish, I decided the only way to keep from following in his footsteps was to distance myself from you and not allow a relationship to develop between us. I hated myself for ignoring you and for pushing you away, but I was too afraid of what I might become if I didn't. Although I appeared distant and cold, I always knew what was going on in your life. From violin, to law school, to your latest promotion, your mother kept me abreast of it all. I wanted to show my love for you, but I didn't know how and I was afraid to learn. By the time I got up the courage to try, you were leaving for Julliard and didn't want anything to do with me.

I want you to know I am so proud of the beautiful young woman you've become. I know this won't make amends, but my law firm is yours, along with all of my personal holdings. You may do with them as you wish. Anne, I love you and I regret that I never had the courage to demonstrate it.

Sincerely,
Your Father

Anne was stunned. She could not believe what she had just read. She rose from her father's chair and went to her parents' bed where she lay curled-up, crying and conflicted while she waited for her mother to finish bathing. Fifteen minutes later, Anne's mother emerged from her dressing room, refreshed, yet weary from the painful day. She wore a beautiful deep purple silk floor-length robe. As she moved across the room to where Anne lay, it appeared as if she were floating on air like an angel. She sat down on the bed and Anne put her head in her mother's lap.

"Now you know why I stayed with him all these years," she said as she stroked Anne's hair.

"You knew about his sisters?" Anne asked raising her head to connect with her mother's eyes.

"Yes. We tried to find them, but were never able to."

"What a horrible ordeal he had to endure."

"Yes, it was.

"I can see why he acted the way he did towards me. He was so afraid."

"Yes, he acted so strange when we brought you home from the hospital; he wouldn't hold you or look at you. I was so hurt by his behavior, but having just given birth and being married a little more than a year, I just focused on you. I told myself that he would eventually come around, but he didn't. I made up my mind to leave him when you were a year old. I had our things packed and ready to go. It was only then that he told me what transpired when he was a boy. It was then that I understood. Sweetheart, he did love you very much. He was just too afraid to show it."

Anne burst into tears once again as she held onto her mother, "Oh Father, I forgive you. I really tried to love you, but you wouldn't let me. I've always loved you!" She tearfully confessed. Finally, she could begin healing.

CHAPTER

17

"Hi Edward, I'm back!

"Anne, it's so good to hear your voice. Are you home?"

"Yes, and I'm weeding through a mountain of mail and airing the place out. It smells pretty stale in here after being closed up for a month."

"I bet. Hey, have you eaten yet? I'd love to take you out to dinner. I know you haven't had time to have groceries delivered."

Anne laughed and thought to herself, *I won't tell him just yet that I not only don't cook, but I can't cook.* "You know, as a matter of fact I haven't eaten and my cupboards are bare. Having dinner with you would be lovely."

"Great! I will be finishing up some reports over the next couple of hours. I should be free around six. Do you have a place in mind?"

"As a matter of fact I do. How about Sangritas?"

"Hummm, I've heard of the place, but I've never been there; I'm game. May I collect you around six-thirty?"

"How about I arrange for a car and meet you in front of your office building around six-o-five?"

"Sounds like a plan to me!"

"Great! See you then."

After Anne called Sangritas to make reservations, she had a couple of hours to kill before picking up Edward, so she decided to do something that she hadn't done since moving to New York. She took a long, hot, luxurious bath to soothe her fatigued muscles from the long flight. As she watched the tub fill with bubbles, she poured in various bath salts and oils. She was physically and mentally drained from the month she had spent in Hong Kong. There was not only the funeral and the big revelation she dealt with, but also her father's personal financial affairs and his law firm. Since she inherited the firm, she had to meet with all the partners and associates, review the firm's client list and financials, and, most importantly, try to figure out how she was going to run the firm from New York. She put the most senior partner, the one who had assisted her father at the time of his death, in charge.

Anne took her clothes off and let them drop to the floor, then slid down into her six-foot soaker tub for two and turned on the jets. The bubbles turned into foam as they gently caressed her hips, thighs, shoulders, and feet. She began to daydream about what it would be like to share this experience with Edward. The thought made her giggle like a high school girl with a crush. She felt like she was floating in a heavenly cloud and made a mental note to take time out for baths more often. She laid her head back on the bath pillow, closed her eyes and relaxed. Then all of a sudden she sat up abruptly and screamed.

"That's it! That's the solution!" she said with excitement in her voice. Then she dropped her shoulders in bewilderment. "But, can I really do it? I've never done anything close to this before." She leaned back once again and exhaled loudly in resignation. But a smile slowly appeared on her face as her shoulders lifted. "I think I can do it. No, I know I can do it, and I will. Yes!" she said with confidence as she raised a bubble coated fist pump.

18

The doorbell rang as Vanessa was spreading out the last of her grandmother's quilts, covering the entire floor of her sunken living room. She transformed the room into a comfortable haven with fluffy throw pillows, flickering candles, and fragrant flowers, a crackling fire, and soft jazz music in the background. When she opened the door, they all screeched with excitement as they entered and kicked off their shoes. This was somewhat of a reunion; it was the first time they had gotten together since the night of the gala. Vanessa sent a car to pick them up and bring them all to her home for a slumber celebration. As they shed their overcoats, pajamas of silk and satin in rich jewel tones were revealed. Vanessa wore ruby red, Anne, emerald green, Monica, citrine gold, and Maria, sapphire blue. They took turns hugging their hostess, while exchanging salutations. Vanessa escorted them in from the foyer and they all gasped and stood frozen in shock as they admired the beautiful sanctuary she had created for them.

There was a decadent dessert station to the right of the French doors that led to the terrace with a beautiful panoramic view of Central Park and the city surrounding it. Gracing the table was a New York style cheesecake with a variety of delicious fresh fruit toppings, double fudge brownies, tiramisu, and a beautiful selection of petit fours. To the left of the French doors was a libations station with bottles of Aquafina and Pepsi, and an icy pitcher of Sangritas. Everyone eagerly picked an array of confections and took a seat on the sea of quilts. They reclined on the fluffy down-filled pillows and moaned in unison, as they enjoyed the delicious desserts.

"Mmmm, if I had a man that tasted like this, I wouldn't be here right now," Monica volunteered as she licked her fork.

"Oh, thanks a lot! I guess the only reason you showed up tonight was because your vibrator batteries were dead," Vanessa added. Anne and Maria snickered.

"Ha, ha. Come on now; that was just wishful thinking. I was kidding. Besides, you all know that there's not a man on the face of this earth that tastes as good as New York style cheesecake with dark chocolate and salted caramel syrup drizzled all over it."

"Mmmm, hmmm!" Everyone nodded in agreement as they finished their tasty treats. Vanessa collected the hand painted porcelain dessert plates and headed for the kitchen. She returned with a silver tray on which Sangritas sparkled like red jewels in crystal, Margarita glasses. Vanessa sensed Maria and Anne's uneasiness because Monica had given up drinking.

"Ladies, not to worry," Vanessa said as she handed each one a glass. "These beauties are virgins. I made them with cranberry and pomegranate juices instead of sangria and rum. I thought it was high-time we started celebrating ourselves and our successes instead of drowning our sorrows."

"Amen!" Maria added. They all smiled and nodded in agreement. Monica winked and mouthed, *Thank you* to Vanessa.

"Let's raise our glasses," Vanessa said. "Let this meeting of The Sangrita Club officially begin." Everyone echoed, "Here, here." They all took a sip from their drinks.

"Well, what do you think?" Vanessa asked.

"Mmmm, is this a great faux Sangrita or what?" Anne exclaimed.

"It's really good!" Maria commented.

"Hmmm, I would say that this is definitely top shelf," Monica added with a sarcastic smirk.

"I'm glad you all like them. I really didn't want to give up our club name, so I came up with an alternative to the alcohol," Vanessa said cheerfully.

"Now, our first order of business," Monica announced, "is to welcome back our newest club member. We are so sorry about your father. And we are so glad to have you back with us."

"Thank you. I really missed you guys. All the concern and support that you've shown me in the past month has been phenomenal. And to properly show my appreciation to you all, I have a little something for each of you." Anne reached for her

Ricky bag and pulled out three rectangular black velvet boxes.

"Anne, you shouldn't have!" Vanessa exclaimed.

"Speak for yourself," Monica added as she took her box.

"I know that's right! Nothing bad ever comes in a black velvet box," Maria added.

They chuckled and opened the boxes. In each box was a letter opener with a beautiful hand carved jade handle, just like the one Anne had inherited from her father.

"Jade is for good fortune, and I am fortunate enough to have three wonderful new friends in my life." They all took turns hugging Anne and thanking her for the thoughtful gift. She recounted her father's story to them and explained the significance of the gift. The tears flowed heavily as the tissue box was passed around. They hugged Anne again, and again and wiped each other's tears.

"I also need to apologize," Anne added.

"For what?" Monica questioned.

"Remember the night of the gala when everyone opened up about why they were seeing Dr. Porter? Well, I lied about just meeting him that evening."

"Oh, Honey, don't worry about that. We knew you were lying through your teeth," Maria said with attitude and a smile.

"How? How did you know?" Anne asked with a puzzled look on her face.

"Well, Monica and I saw how intently he was talking to you. And your face had a look of shock on it, not the kind of look that a person has when just saying hello for the first time. Then we saw you drop your evening clutch and Dr. Porter caught it in mid-air. That's when we walked over. We thought you might need rescuing or something. Well, okay, honestly, we were just being nosey," Maria confessed with a smirk.

"Well, why didn't you all confront me about lying?" Anne asked.

"Oh, we knew you'd come to your senses and come clean eventually," Monica answered. They all laughed as Anne hid her face in her hands in embarrassment.

"We knew you were lying when we saw him slip you his business card when he handed your clutch back to you," Vanessa said.

"You saw that?" Anne exclaimed.

"Of course we did. And I also saw the home phone number written on the back of the card that you accidentally dropped in the limo." Monica and Maria gasped, "What! We didn't know about that."

"Oh, yeah. He's was a smooth operator that night. Anne, I've known Dr. Porter for years and I know he wasn't trying to drum up business for his practice at the gala," Vanessa announced. They all laughed again.

"Well, I guess I can't pull anything over on you guys."

Vanessa, Monica, and Maria replied in concert, "I know that's right!"

"Well, since you all seem to know my business, I might as well come all the way clean. I've been in communication with Edward. . ."

"Oh, you're on first name basis. Communication! That's a good word for it." Monica added.

"But anyway, as I was saying, I started seeing him professionally because of the way my father had treated me. In fact, I've been in counseling pretty much all of my life. However, Edward was the first doctor that I truly came clean with. I don't know. It was just something about him that made me feel comfortable enough to bare my soul. Then, he referred me to one of his colleagues, so that we could see each other socially. So, we haven't broken any doctor/patient conduct rules."

"Soooooocially? Oh, yeah, I bet! This sounds like a case of the doctor falling head-over your heels," Monica added.

"No, he didn't just fall for me; I think it was mutual," Anne retorted with a smile.

"Girl, I don't blame you. He's hot!" agreed Maria.

"Okay, okay, it's time to cool off a bit. Who wants ice cream?" Vanessa announced. They all laughed and made their way to the kitchen. Vanessa placed a half-gallon of Rocky Road in the middle of the island and they all filled their bowls to capacity and returned to their quilt haven.

"You know, Anne, there's a burning question that has gone unasked and unanswered!" Vanessa said with a prying tone.

"Yes, I went out with him after I returned from Hong Kong," Anne admitted. They all screamed with their spoons in their mouths. "And that's all I'm going to say for now."

"Hmmm," Vanessa snorted, "Anne, I might have to change therapists now, because I don't want my business in the street and all over the company.

"Mmmm, hmmm," Monica and Maria said as Anne looked at Vanessa sideways.

"Not to worry, Vanessa. I'm not interested in Edward for what he can tell me about any of you. I'm interested in him for what he can do to me."

"Mmmm, go for it girl!" Maria exclaimed. They all screamed with laughter, finished their ice cream, and refilled their Sangrita glasses.

"So Vanessa how's Mr. Patton?" Maria asked.

"Oh, we're fine, thank you. And before you ask, no, we have not had sex."

"What?" everyone exclaimed in unison.

"He's not having any trouble in the men's department is he?" Monica probed. Anne and Maria almost spit out their drinks laughing.

"Cute! No, not at all," Vanessa blushed. "I've made up my mind to concentrate on the intellectual, social, and emotional sides of our relationship. I want to be certain that, number one, he likes me just the way I am and is not going to try and change me, number two, that he always treats me with dignity and respect in every situation, and number three, that he thinks I am worth the wait and worth my weight in diamonds." They all cackled and clinked their glasses.

"Well, since we are in the prying mode, what's up with you two?" Anne instigated. Monica and Maria looked at each other.

"Oh, I'll go first," Maria, volunteered. "My girls and I are having the time of our lives in our new bachelorette pad. We're doing all kinds of things and going all kinds of places together. And for the first time, I feel comfortable at home, relaxed, and at peace. I lived for so long on pins-and-needles that I didn't realize how stressed out I was. My blood pressure has even dropped considerably, so I'm a new woman with a new purpose."

"Maria, that's wonderful! We're so happy for you and the girls," Monica offered.

"Thank you. Oh, also, I'm in the process of interviewing for the Chief Technology Officer position at the firm. I'm determined to land it!"

"Well, with that attitude, and our recommendations, you certainly will!" Vanessa added.

"I want you all to know that I really appreciate the flowers that you sent me when I was recovering from . . ." Maria paused and bowed her head as her voice failed her. Monica put her arm around Maria's shoulder, Vanessa reached out and held her hand, and Anne handed her a tissue.

"Maria, it's okay. We're here for you," Monica assured her.

Maria lifted her face as she wiped the tears from her eyes. "You know, José was the only person I have ever received flowers from, but he always sent them the day after beating me; it was his way of apologizing. When your flowers arrived, I almost threw them out because I thought they were from him, but something told me to read the card. I'm so glad I did because it gave me the encouragement that I needed to leave him. I knew you all cared about me and would be there for me and my girls if we needed you." A group hug ensued followed by lots of tissue passing and nose blowing.

"Okay, I believe another round of Sangritas is called for," Vanessa announced. She refilled their glasses as the conversation continued. "Okay, Ms. Monica, what's up with you?"

"Well, all is well on the home front. As you know, I'm on the wagon. I've also taken a hiatus from men for now to concentrate on Lizzy."

"Hiatus? We didn't know you were seeing someone," Vanessa pried.

"Well, I wasn't exactly seeing someone. I was kind of involved in this thing with a guy that was sort of purely sexual."

"What?" Anne and Maria screamed.

"Oh, this ought to be good," Vanessa said as she raised her glass to her lips.

"I know it sounds completely removed from who I am. I know, I know, it was stupid," Monica tried to explain. "There was no real emotional attachment between us, but we shared similar feelings

330

of deep regret in our lives. My acquaintance, if you want to call him that, regretted never making-up with his wife after they had an argument the night before September 11th; she died that day in one of the twin towers. My regret is that I didn't confront Jeff before he died about his ongoing affair and it practically consumed me. I had so much pent up anger from not being able to have closure it caused me to not only develop alcohol and sexual additions, but also to neglect my relationship with Lizzy. I found myself mimicking Jeff's sexual behaviors and my alcoholic mother's neglectful actions."

Monica recounted the story of her childhood and her mother's alcohol addiction, illness, and subsequent death. The tears were rolling and the tissues flowing once again.

"But, for now I've given up both of them, alcohol permanently and sex temporarily. I've been sober for thirty-three days!" Everyone clapped, sincerely smiling through their tears. "I couldn't have done it without your support. Thank you so very much." Another group hug formed.

"That, my dear, deserves a toast," Vanessa said as they clinked their glasses again and sipped.

"Ladies, you know what?" Vanessa asked.

"What?" they said simultaneously.

"Cute!" Vanessa said with a wink. "Although we are different culturally and socioeconomically, and we have differing professions, religions, and skin colors, we have a common bond. We're all women searching for the same things in life. We all want to be

331

loved. We all want to love ourselves. And we all want *a way*."

"You're definitely right about the love part. It took me too long to realize that I didn't love myself and that I deserved to be loved. But what do you mean by *a way*?" Maria inquired.

"By *a way* I mean, we are all trying to find *a way* out, *a way* up, *a way* in, *a way* around, or *a way* through something in our lives."

"God knows, I am trying to find *a way* to make it through each and every day without a drink," Monica confessed.

"We share a gift. We have the unique ability to see through the external symptoms of our struggles, to the illuminating value that lies within our sisterhood," Vanessa continued. "Our sole purpose as a group is to help one another find *a way* to understand and confront why we have become who we are, learn from that discovery experience, and use it to become who we truly desire to be."

"Vanessa, you are so right," said Anne. "For so long I just concentrated on gaining my father's approval that I never received. My bitterness towards him became so all-encompassing that I built up walls around myself and prevented anyone from getting close to me. But you Vanessa, you are the only person that took the time to see through my façade and willingly sought *a way* to gain entry to the real person that I am inside. For that I am truly thankful to you."

"You're welcome, Anne," Vanessa replied as they hugged. The tissue box made its way around again.

Vanessa continued. "You know, for so long I thought love and sex were synonymous. I guess I never really had a true understanding of how male/female relationships work, because my father wasn't around and my brother was sexually, physically and emotionally abusive toward me." Vanessa told them the details of how her father abandoned her family when she was born and how her brother had molested her. She expressed her frustration because of her inability to confront her brother, because she feared he would molest her again. She also told them of her recent confrontation with her mother and her side of the story.

"I wanted so much to gain the approval and love of a man, so much so, that I lowered myself to knowingly share Damon with other women. I used up so many precious years chasing a fantasy that would never come to fruition. I'm so glad that I had your support as I sought *a way* to free myself from that caustic situation that was gradually chipping away all of my self-esteem. It feels so good not to have to paint on a happy façade as I exit my front door anymore. Now my smile is genuine because I'm truly happy from within, even when I'm all alone. Now, when my feet are cold, I don't long for the warmth of a man's body. I just get up, put on a pair of wool socks, crawl back into my bed, pull my grandmother's quilt up around my shoulders and sleep peacefully."

"Vanessa, we love you," said Monica. Anne and Maria agreed as they all took turns hugging Vanessa.

Vanessa continued, "Let the truth be told, there is nothing better in this entire world than having honest-to-goodness girlfriends that you can count on and confide in. Because, you know why?" Vanessa asked as a tear fell from her eye, "boyfriends, lovers, and husbands come and go, but your girlfriends, they are forever. To The Sangrita Club!"

They all raised their glasses and sang out together, "To The Sangrita Club!"

Recipe

Amanda's Sangritas with Drunken Fruit

Ingredients:

6 oz Tequila
4 oz Lime Juice
2 oz Triple Sec
1 Bottle Fruity Red Wine
8 oz Cranberry Juice
5 oz Grenadine
4 oz Sweet Vermouth

10 Maraschino Cherries
2 Apples – cored and sliced into wedges
2 Seedless Oranges – sliced into thin circles
2 Limes – sliced into thin circles

2 Cups Crushed Ice
1 Lime cut into wedges
1/8 Cup of salt
1/8 Cup of red sugar

Yield 8 - 10 servings

Recipe

Amanda's Sangritas with Drunken Fruit

Directions:

Mix all liquid ingredients together and stir well. Add cherries, apples, oranges and lime circles. Let the mixture sit overnight in the fridge. When ready to serve, mix salt and red sugar in a saucer and set aside. Remove fruit from mixture and set aside. Add 2 cups of ice to a blender along with mixture. Blend well on high. Pour into chilled Margarita glasses rimmed with a lime wedge and dipped in the sugar and red salt. Garnish with Drunken Fruit.

Virgin Version: omit tequila, triple sec, sweet vermouth, and fruity red wine. Add 2 ounces of orange juice, 24 ounces of pomegranate juice, and 10 ounces of pineapple juice to the remaining ingredients. Blend with ice, pour, and enjoy!

Cheers!

Amanda Adams

Author's Note

Initially, I set out to write a book about diversity, however I ended up writing a novel about diverse women in Corporate America who look beyond their differences, celebrate their similarities, and develop a sisterhood. My goal for this series is that it may become a catalyst for women of all ages, races, religions, cultures, orientations and socioeconomic backgrounds to create a way to escape negative circumstances that inhibit their abilities to become who they are truly meant to be.

•

About the Author

Amanda Adams

Michigan and New York native Amanda Adams began her quest to become an author through journaling and writing poetry as a method of catharsis during her college years. Amanda earned degrees in Information Systems and Management Science, as well as an MBA and worked as an Information Technology Executive and Management Consultant for multiple Fortune 100 companies.

Amanda spent two decades crafting a back story for her debut, The Sangrita Club, the first in a series of stories about compelling corporate women. Currently, Amanda is an entrepreneur and lives in the Chicago suburbs with her husband and daughter where she's active in community activities and continues to write.

CPSIA information can be obtained
at www.ICGtesting.com
Printed in the USA
LVHW01s0106110518
576787LV00001B/1/P